PENGUIN

TRAINING AN ACTOR

Sonia Moore was born in Russia. She attended the universities of Kiev and Moscow, the Studio of the Kiev Solovstov Theatre, and the Third Studio of the Moscow Art Theatre and has degrees from conservatories in Rome. She now lives in New York City, where she teaches at the Sonia Moore Studio of the Theatre and is Artistic Director of AST, the repertory company of the American Center for Stanislavski Theatre Art, which she founded. Mrs. Moore is the author of *The Stanislavski System: The Professional Training of an Actor* (available from Penguin), and she has translated and edited *Stanislavski Today* and *The Logic of Speech on Stage*.

Konstantin S. Stanislavski

Training an Actor

The Stanislavski System in Class

Revised Edition

Sonia Moore

PENGUIN BOOKS

Penguin Books Ltd, Harmondsworth,
Middlesex, England
Penguin Books, 625 Madison Avenue,
New York, New York 10022, U.S.A.
Penguin Books Australia Ltd, Ringwood,
Victoria, Australia
Penguin Books Canada Limited, 2801 John Street,
Markham, Ontario, Canada L3R 1B4
Penguin Books (N.Z.) Ltd, 182-190 Wairau Road,
Auckland 10, New Zealand

First published in the United States of America in
simultaneous hardcover and paperback editions by
The Viking Press and Compass Books 1968
First published in Canada by The Macmillan
Company of Canada 1968
Revised edition published in Penguin Books 1979

LIBRARY OF CONGRESS CATALOGING IN PUBLICATION DATA
Moore, Sonia.
Training an actor.
(A Penguin handbook)
Includes index.
1. Acting—Study and teaching.   2. Stanislavski
method.   I. Title.
PN2062.M62   1979   792'.028'07   78-26024
ISBN 0 14 046.380 1

Printed in the United States of America by
Offset Paperback Mfrs., Inc., Dallas, Pennsylvania
Set in Baskerville

Dedicated to the memory of
Konstantin S. Stanislavski,
to actors,
and to all who are concerned with
theatre in America

contents

acknowledgments

I am grateful to Vladimir Nemirovich-Danchenko, Vsevolod Meyerhold, and Eugene Vakhtangov—the masters whose genius has influenced theatre throughout the world—and to today's Russian theatre experts, actors, directors, writers, critics, and scientists who study Stanislavski's teachings and give me the nourishment that has made this book possible: Arkadi N. Anastasiev, Vladimir B. Block, Anatoly V. Effros, Oleg N. Efremov, Peter Ershov, N. K. Gey, Nikolai M. Gorchakhov (deceased), Lubov Y. Gurevich (deceased), Yuri S. Kalashnikov, Mikhail N. Kedrov, Maria O. Knebel, Grigori M. Kozintzev, G.G. Krijitski, Grigori V. Kristi, Andrei M. Lobanov (deceased), Boris A. Lvov-Anokhin, Pavel A. Markov, Valentin N. Plucek, B. A. Pokrovski, Alexei D. Popov (deceased), Vladimir N. Prokofiev, Joseph M. Rayevski (deceased), Konstantin I. Rudnitski, L. Shikhamatov, P. V. Simonov, Ruben N. Simonov (deceased), Y. Smirnov-Nesvitski, Inna N. Solovieva, M. N. Stroeva, Vassili O. Toporkov (deceased), Georgi A. Tovstonogov, I. Vinogradskaya, Victor

Zakhava (deceased), Victor F. Zalesski, Yuri A. Zavadski (deceased), S. Zimball, A. Ziss. I also wish to thank the writers of articles in *Theatre* magazine (Moscow) and of other recent illuminating works.

Great artistic work requires the ability to look into the hearts of today's spectators, into the soul of a role, and into the heart of the actor who will play it. This requires technique and stamina.

First educate a group of actors, and then you will have a play and a theatre.

—Stanislavski

It is possible to construct a magnificent building, to light and heat it magnificently, to assemble an orchestra and set designers, and to engage a wonderful administrator and director—and yet there will be no theatre. There will be only a well-kept building. But when three actors come to a square, spread a small rug on the ground, and begin to perform—there is theatre.

—Vladimir Nemirovich-Danchenko

It has long been recognized that without a permanent company few actors can thrive indefinitely.

However, it must also be faced that even a permanent company is doomed to deadliness in the long run if it is without aim, and thus without a method, and thus without a school. And by a school, naturally, I don't mean a gymnasium where the actor exercises his limbs in limbo. Flexing muscles alone cannot develop an art; scales don't make a pianist nor does fingerwork help a painter's brush: yet a great pianist practices finger exercises for many hours a day, and Japanese painters spend their lives practicing to draw a perfect circle. The art of acting is in some ways the most exacting one of all, and without constant schooling, the actor will stop halfway.

—Peter Brook

foreword

This book has been prepared to demonstrate how an actor is trained in a class. Four years of study are required for assimilation of the Stanislavski System, but since in their third and fourth years the actor-students work on full-length plays to put into practice the techniques they have learned and to acquire experience, these twenty-four chapters concentrate mainly on the first and second years of the training. As the work of the actor-students proceeds through these typical sessions, I hope the reader will see why the System should be the required training for all actors. It is also my hope that the book will dispel the distortions which sometimes undermine the very basis of the System.

Some say that the System cannot be discussed, just as musicians play their instruments rather than discuss their techniques; but music teachers and students do talk about their techniques, and we should be able to talk about those of acting.

Those who say, "Oh, I know Stanislavski backward and forward. But why should we use only the Stanislavski System? We want to broaden our horizons and use all the methods," and those who quote Stanislavski out of context, should know that they are speaking about only certain stages of his work. In order to be absolutely up to date, I have been engaged for years in research on Stanislavski's writings and the works of Russian theatre experts and scientists who study his teachings. Stanislavski's writings have been collected, thoroughly studied, and commented upon by Russian specialists. The publication of his writings was completed in Russia only in 1961. Few of these and practically none of the works of those who research his teachings have been translated into English. And the fact is that there is no other method of acting but Stanislavski's.

Work on speech, diction, voice, Shakespeare, historical ceremonies, and the wearing of costumes is obligatory for actors—as are classes in body movement, such as dance, fencing, and acrobatics. But the psychological technique—the Stanislavski System—is also obligatory. It is as important for actors and directors as the theory and technique of music are to musicians. Many great men of letters—Diderot (*Paradox of Acting*), Lessing (*Hamburg Dramaturgy*), Goethe (*Rules for Actors*)—and such actors as Irving, Talma, Riccoboni, Iffland, Rossi, Salvini, and Coquelin tried to formulate laws for dramatic creativity. But only Stanislavski succeeded in reconciling the contradictions between the actor as creator and the actor as character, and he alone developed the concrete technique by which an actor consciously transforms his psychological and physical behavior into those of the character and creates the unique life of a man in every role. Stanislavski alone discovered and systematized the laws that lead an actor to his ultimate goal: "reincarnation"—the state in which he creates subconsciously.*

The Stanislavski System is neither a religious cult nor an aesthetic dissertation; it is the technique of an art. Every creative process demands great concentration of the artist's spiritual forces; the fact that an actor creates before his audience makes an especially difficult demand on his willpower. The peculiarities of dramatic art, the exceptional conditions in which the actor's creative process takes place, were determined with astonishing precision by Stanislavski. Through his System actors can consciously control their imagination and emotions— their whole psychic and physical nature. Like musicians and dancers, actors must learn their art step by step. Stanislavski said that the most dangerous dilettante is the one who denies the need for technique and insists that it interferes with inspiration. As Tyrone Guthrie has said, "The greatest drama is absolutely and elaborately prescribed, and the greatest acting contains a minimum of spontaneous invention and a maximum of carefully calculated effect repeated with only minute variations at every performance of the same part. Dramatic performance therefore is concerned with repeating a series of intelligibly prescribed actions in order to form an intelligibly prescribed design."†

*The contemporary Polish director Jerzy Grotowski, who has stirred a great deal of interest in America, experiments with the expression of the inner life; readers of this book will recognize in his work Stanislavski's teachings on physical and verbal actions. The American director William Ball seems to be concerned with the same problem.
† The New York Times, August 28, 1966.

One of the gravest distortions of Stanislavski in the American theatre has occurred in regard to the actor's physical training. An actor's control over his body should be as complete as that of a dancer. And Stanislavski was relentless in his demand for control in speech. "Love the comma," he said. "It will make others listen to you. It serves as a warning, like a raised hand." Bad speech, he said, is often responsible for overacting, tension, banal gestures, and artificial intonations. He insisted that actors be rhythmical, musical, plastic. The actor must learn to shape his speech into contrasts in order to disclose its meaning; the phrasing must be worked out in a completely conscious manner. American actors know very little about working on speech from the point of view of rhythm and music. In England, where no "method" cult has been created, and where physical training has always been given great importance, the level of theatre is much higher than here. The physical excellence that Stanislavski demands is intimately related to the psychological side of the technique.

In giving actors the most important place in theatre, Stanislavski imposes a heavy responsibility on them. He does not believe that even good education and professional skill are sufficient, but subordinates these creative requirements to ethical demands. The most important of his views is his demand for harmony between the actor's personality and his professional work. The actor must also have a sense of responsibility toward his fellow actors. A theatre where an individual "star" is the center of attention is not art, Stanislavski felt, but a deviation from it. Theatre cannot depend on one person: it is an ensemble, and it is disrupted when actors have different habits or techniques and no common training. Such actors interfere with instead of helping each other. No single actor—not even a great one—can be responsible for the situation on stage if he is surrounded by a void. Theatre, in order to present an image of man in his many aspects, must have actors who are properly trained, and who realize that they are dependent on one another. Ethics is the foundation of Stanislavski's aesthetics: "The life of a human spirit, infused with poetry, deeply felt, impregnated with truth, will reveal not only a unique person but a universal phenomenon. Thus it takes on not only personal but social significance." Stanislavski firmly believed that theatre ought to contribute to the moral and aesthetic education of the people.

When the Moscow Art Theatre, founded by Stanislavski and Nemirovich-Danchenko, opened in 1898 with actors of gigantic talent, it was criticized as a group of poor actors. It was Stanislavski who realized that theatre of social significance cannot depend on talent alone. The art of directing and acting has reached its high level in Russia because of Stanislavski's discoveries and his aesthetic and ethical principles. His reform embraced all facets of the theatre.

Stanislavski himself was a brilliant actor, and his portrayals of Astrov in *Uncle Vanya*, Vershinin in *The Three Sisters*, and Gaev in *The Cherry Orchard* are considered the best in Russian theatre. Vsevolod Meyerhold said, "Those who knew Stanislavski only when he was old do not have the slightest idea about him as an actor.... Stanislavski was an outstanding actor with an astonishing technique.... If I am anyone at all, it is only because I spent years next to him.... Stanislavski is an actor with hands which handle the rapier masterfully, with a healthy and agile body, with a voice of enormous range, with a face of overwhelming expressiveness even without make-up...with love for rich theatrical costume, with a penchant for Shakespeare, Molière, Pushkin, and Schiller.'' Meyerhold believed that Stanislavski's vocation was to incarnate on stage what Pushkin called ''the truth of passions'' as well as the masks of exaggeration.

This was true also of Stanislavski's directing. In such productions as *The Inspector General, The Days of Turbiny* (Bulgakov), *The Marriage of Figaro, The Passionate Heart* (Ostrovsky), *Othello, Armored Train 14-69* (Vsevolod Ivanov), he demonstrated his superior ability in bold and vivid portrayals, profound subtlety, and superb grace. These productions of the ''director-composer,'' as the Russian director Yuri Zavadski calls him, became milestones in Russian theatre.

It is wrong to consider Stanislavski an exclusively naturalistic director. Superficial knowledge of Stanislavski's technique has created another point in confusion about what he called ''truth.'' Life's truth is often confused with theatre's; Stanislavski insisted on theatre's truth. Photographic truth on stage, he recognized, often distorts reality. He laughed at actors who were satisfied to eat, drink, smoke, or speak ''naturally.'' Yes, the audience must believe that this is the way the man eats, drinks, smokes, and speaks, but every character is natural in a different way. Every character must have a different *timbre* in his voice, and a different way of moving his body. Since every play presents a different world, each will have its own organic dramatic truth. The System is a means for finding it.

In *The Inspector General* (1921) Stanislavski put great emphasis on external form. Khlestakov, played by Michael Chekhov, was in a notably grotesque style; Stanislavski wanted Chekhov to play the quintessence of the role. He called grotesque "the boldest and most vivid justification for intense exaggeration of the inner content." Although he said that only Salvini, Givokkini, and Varlamov had achieved this art, he himself created unforgettable grotesque portrayals. Later, a number of Russian actors, with the help of his technique, became masters of this form.

Stanislavski, however, rejected all external form that failed to express internal reality. He was skeptical about many forced innovations in scenic creativity; he believed that if one had something to say, one would find the right form to make the content live. He disliked any originality used only for its own sake.

Stanislavski wanted audiences to comprehend all the inner essence of a play, and demanded that productions be given all possible color, tone, vivid speech, vivid movement. He wanted the actor to live the experiences of the character and "incarnate" him, to express inner truth in vivid form. Not to understand this is to neglect Stanislavski's teachings on the union of content and form.

A frequent question from the audience at my lectures on Stanislavski is "Can Shakespeare be staged in accordance with the System?" Actors trained in the Stanislavski System build live characters on stage. The multifaceted characters who inhabit Shakespeare's plays must be alive if the great thoughts of Shakespeare are to be projected on stage. The proper style will not be achieved in a purely external way. Only with a knowledge of the environment and of the character's inner behavior can the actor achieve an external style that is authentically human. If actors think only of external manner their behavior will be false. But, as Stanislavski said, "Shakespeare has great thoughts, and you cannot speak about something great as you speak about sausage at breakfast."

Another question is "Can the Stanislavski System be used in staging Brecht?" According to the opinion of some people in our theatre Stanislavski's teachings are irreconcilable with Brecht. One answer is that Brecht is now widely produced in Russia, where all actors are thoroughly trained in the System. Brecht wanted to shock the audience, and he realized that in order to surprise people theatre must present the "ordinary in an unordinary way." This is also true in life; we become aware of the customary when we see it in an unexpected light. To create the sense of "alienation," Brecht prevented the fusion of the spectators with the action on stage. He demanded that the actor step out of the character and criticize him, and he used this as a means of propaganda. Vakhtangov in some of his unconventional productions also required this, although in these cases the actor criticized the character only from his own point of view. Many artist-innovators of the twentieth century have presented "the ordinary in an unordi-

nary way": Pirandello—who probably influenced
Brecht's demand that actors step out of their roles—
Leonid Andreyev, Evreinov, Meyerhold, Vakhtangov, Kafka, Samuel Beckett.... And Stanislavski
himself, shortly before his death, wrote: "Theatre
needs the shaking and the deafening of inspired
unexpectedness." He foresaw a theatre that would
"tear the ground from under the feet of the spectators
and put them on new ground where they had never
stood before." Stanislavski dreamed of acting that
"would be beautiful in its bold neglect of traditional
beauty, beautiful in its bold illogicality, rhythmical
in its irrythmicality, psychological in its rejection of
the ordinarily accepted psychology, in violation of
customary rules." And though Brecht's *theory* says
that actors should not live the life of the character but
only demonstrate, his practice was different. Yuri
Zavadski wrote, "The best actress in Brecht's theatre,
Elena Weigel, merges with the character of Mother
Courage in such a way that we are not only stirred
but truly involved." Brecht's demand that actors
perform "dispassionately, without involvement,"
stemmed, I believe, from his realization that actors
cannot command their emotions, and can achieve
better results without forcing them.

The "duplicity" of which Salvini spoke—
"An actor cries and laughs, but he watches his tears
and his laughter"—and which Coquelin called "the
characteristic trait or an actor" can be seen in many
forms in the theatre. It is Stanislavski who established the double nature of scenic action and spoke
of the distance between an actor's "I" and "not I."
"The actor-role" was Stanislavski's term.

The actor must be able to live his role

organically, "today, here, now." The performance staged by the director and played by the actors has a firmly fixed score, but, just as the playing of a symphony will vary at every concert, so every night will the score of a director and the actor sound different. And today's actor must be able to step out of the character, into other given circumstances. Only those who have mastered the technique of building a character are able to achieve this.

Stanislavski's System does not contradict any dramatic literature, and that is its strength. "There will always be phases of the realistic and of the unconventional in the theatre," Stanislavski said. "Every such evolution will leave its mark....Too bad for those who do not understand this natural flow of life and the natural development of our art." Any means used by a director is valid if it helps to express the essence of the play. Our current preoccupation with empty "theatricality" is a reaction against the American "method" and its "naturalness." It will soon exhaust itself when both the "natural" and the "unconventional" are replaced by the synthesis that will subordinate everything to the revelation of human personality. The fashionable should not be mistaken for the everlasting. It passes quickly. The "new" will be brought into the theatre through profound understanding of life by authors and directors and actors who are masters of the inner technique. They can make even the old look new. An actor's art will be contemporary if he is capable of concentrated thought on stage. Thanks to Stanislavski, this need not be a quality possessed only by genius.

Life moves forward constantly, and life's

problems must be the object of theatre's creativity. Only through closely observing life will theatre discover what is new and contemporary. It is important that theatre, like other arts, reflect life in all its variety, giving nourishment to people, always revealing something new. When the author and the director build sharp dramatic conflicts, they must study whether an unconventional style can express them best. But whatever theatrical means the director uses, his actors must be able to live true emotions.

An unconventional production must be even more subtly truthful psychologically than a conventional one. The most picturesque or even the boldest form must have complete inner justification. Vsevolod Meyerhold, *the* revolutionary director, who was known for bold contrasts between tragedy and satire, who was the archenemy of all that was old in the theatre and said that he was trying to build the antithesis of naturalism—Meyerhold became convinced of the need of truthful living on stage and demanded it from his actors in the most bizarre situations. Meyerhold, who had no equal in his ability to create sharp psychological situations with plastic means alone, said in a speech (published in Russia) that he and Stanislavski were moving through the same tunnel, but from opposite ends. He said that they would inevitably meet near its center, where there is only one united internal and external form. "Live powerful emotions, and have an expressive, plastic body," he said. The director can use symbols and other expressive means, but these have to be realized by actors who are in a lifelike state. Only actors who are able to live organically on stage will bring contemporary values to the theatre. The problem of dramatic art is *man* and his relationship with the world that surrounds him. It is the actor-man who is supremely important in the theatre.

Every author presents a different world, and it is of paramount importance that the director and the actors, in preparing a play, understand the author's style and grasp the meaning as soon as possible. The technique of analysis that Stanislavski developed makes this possible. It brings the essence of the play to the surface; it often suggests an unexpected blocking (*mise en scène*). It helps to bring all the nuances of life to the stage.

The director's special problem springs from the fact that theatre is a collective art. Ensemble is extraordinarily difficult because it requires that the director achieve harmony among people who often have strikingly different and difficult personalities. Ensemble is possible only when the actors have the same training. The director will be most creative if he has assimilated the System and knows the actor's problems. But even his most interesting ideas will remain dead if the actors are not able to realize them.

Theatre's progress depends on acting and directing as well as on good plays. In the twenties, when a wave of massive theatre construction swept across Russia, Stanislavski warned that disappointment was inevitable if there was nothing to present in those theatres other than sets and theatrical effects. Stanislavski warned that if the purpose of theatre— to build the life of a human spirit and to incarnate it in an artistic form—were neglected, theatre would die. There is no theatre if it is dull, even if it is intellectual. But neither is it theatre if there is nothing but empty amusement. Theatre must be beautiful entertainment and it must embody serious ideas. Stanislavski calls for a theatre that is artistic and educational, for "enlightenment through spectacle." Sometimes what we see on stage only tends to confuse and corrupt us and spoil our taste. During the Twelfth Congress of the International Theatre Institute in New York in June, 1967, Arthur Miller deplored the state of the American theatre. His words echoed those of Leo Tolstoy, who, at the beginning of this century, condemning *his* contemporary arts, said, "Art became the empty amusement of empty people and lost the importance for which it is destined." Only at its highest level does art enrich man's spiritual world.

The actor's ability to reveal the inner world of a man can be a profound spiritual experience for the people in the audience. The art of living on stage leads to the multifaceted revelation of a human being. Stanislavski gives the theatre the opportunity for endless discovery, unlimited possibilities.

It is easy to detect lack of professionalism in other arts. Few will say that they know or understand music, but everyone has an "expert" opinion in the theatre. Introduction of the Stanislavski System will provide one professional language and the one criterion. Critics who are educated in the System and who know all the elements and the means of building a performance can be of great constructive value in the theatre. Such critics know that it is easy enough for an actor, by means of clichés, to represent a businessman, or a man who is timid, or one who is eccentric. They know that to act organically, following the logic of a character, is a different problem.

We have a great many talented young people in America who want to make theatre their profession. They will have to learn from Stanislavski. Without actors trained in the Stanislavski technique the repertory theatres being organized throughout the United States are doomed. All the five hundred professional theatres in Russia use the Stanislavski System, and among the more than thirty repertories in Moscow alone there are even better companies than the celebrated Moscow Art Theatre. The System is studied in Russia by opera and ballet students simultaneously with their own disciplines. If we are seriously concerned about good theatre, the Stanislavski System must be taught in all drama schools, colleges, and universities. We must have a network of theatrical institutions teaching the Stanislavski System.

"As a seeker for gold," Stanislavski said, "I can transmit to future generations not my searching and my privations, my joys and disappointments, but the precious 'mine' that I found. This 'mine' in my artistic field is the result of my whole life's work. It is my so-called 'System,' the technique which permits the actor to create a character, to reveal the life of a human spirit and to incarnate it naturally on stage in an artistic form. This method is based on laws of the organic nature of an actor, which I studied in practice. Its strength is in the fact that there is nothing in it which I 'invented' and nothing which I did not verify by applying it to my students and myself. It developed naturally out of my long experience." That is why he said, "There is no Stanislavski System, only the system of nature herself."

The Stanislavski System creates life by following the laws of nature through which the human being functions in life; *therefore it can never become dated*. Stanislavski gives us a precise, highly expressive theatrical language to achieve the most important objective in the theatre: the revelation of the complex inner world of a man.

Gogol said: "Theatre is not a trifle. It can make a mass of five or six thousand people who have nothing to do with one another feel shaken by the same event, sob with the same tears, laugh with the same laughter. It is a tribune from which great good can come."

S.M.

publisher's note

This book was prepared from tape-recordings made during Sonia Moore's classes at her Studio in New York City. The twenty-four chapters represent typical classes but are not necessarily consecutive. In these pages all students' names are fictitious, and each illustrates several cases.

The Classes

Inspiration is a guest who does not like to visit lazy people.

—*Tchaikowski*

class 1

SONIA MOORE: Welcome to the Studio. Our first objective here is to train actors in the Stanislavski System, which is the only concrete professional acting technique.

It may come as a surprise to you that there is a concrete technique for actors. People with talent who play or dance without professional skill might do so for their families, but they would never dare to audition for a professional orchestra or a ballet company. It is time that we faced the fact that neither can the theatre tolerate unskilled actors. An actor is not simply someone who has decided that he is an actor. He is a talented person who has learned how to build and reveal the inner world of the character he portrays on stage. It is through the characters that a playwright projects the meaning of his play. Only actors able to create what Stanislavski calls the "life of the human spirit" in every new personality they meet in a play will be able to perform in a repertory theatre, where sometimes they must portray a different character every night. A good play brought to life by good actors—this is what people come to the theatre for.

An audience will enjoy a serious play and a classic, when it is performed by good actors. Orchestras are still playing serious music, even though many people do not like it. Theatre, too, can lead audiences to an appreciation of good plays, instead of adjusting to their superficial preferences.

I must warn you that work on the Stanislavski System is not all fun. Acting is a profession. Stanislavski believed that actors were the heart of the theatre, and he imposed tremendous demands on them. But if you want to become professional actors who will contribute to our theatre, this is the only way. The System is as important to you as the technique and theory of music are to musicians. And since the System is based on natural laws of human behavior, it is the same for old and young actors, for classic and contemporary plays, for conventional and unconventional productions, for all nationalities and in all times. We cannot make any of you into another Laurence Olivier or Eleonora Duse, but we can teach you laws which, when they are assimilated, can help talented actors to be as good. How much you succeed will depend on your talent and on your diligence.

I want to warn you also that here your attitude toward your work is just as important as your talent. You must start out with enthusiasm, and learn to cooperate, to work for a common objective. One person cannot make a play into a work of art; it is the group that can. An actor who is interested only in his personal success is destructive of theatre. The theatre must have actors with a code of ethics and a sense of discipline, just as it must have actors with talent who have mastered their professional technique. Stanislavski said, "Every interference with collective work and every attempt to strive for personal profit or success hurts the whole; it is a violation of the personal and artistic ethic of an artist.... Creativity is possible only in the right atmosphere." He even went so far as to say that those who violate that atmosphere commit a crime against art. You must respect each other and each other's interests.

Some of our mumbling actors believe that the stage exists only for them. Some even like to be surrounded by inferior actors so that they can display themselves to advantage. Such an attitude is impossible in the discipline and artistry of the Stanislavski theatre. Some actors are concerned mainly with "being naturally themselves." Some of these actors are using an antiquated means for stirring their *emotional memory*, bringing the actor to a state of contagious hysteria that is confused with inspiration. It comes not from a profound inner experience but from irritated nerves. We do not achieve art when we are demonstrating the poor state of our nerves.

Human emotions have countless nuances, and a good actor can stir precisely the right one for a particular moment in the life of a character. When you receive tragic news, one kind of sad emotion arises; when you lose money, there is a different kind of sad emotion. To transform an actor's emotions into those of the character, according to scientists, is as complex as, for example, transforming the energy of Niagara Falls into the lights on Broadway or in this studio. It is the responsibility of technology to transform elemental forces of nature into useful work. And Stanislavski gives us a technology with the help of which an actor transforms his own emotions into those of the character he portrays. It will take time to learn control over your emotions and all your organic resources, but you will learn it if you have the will to learn and to overcome the difficulties. You will become actors when you control your physical and psychological nature to build characters in a play.

Because the System teaches you this control, it cannot be learned through discussions. It must be understood organically, not only mentally. Through constant training and practicing you will understand and assimilate it. I believe in concrete work, and therefore I shall tell you only briefly that Stanislavski believed that theatre must influence the audience, and only when actors are in the lifelike state can they achieve this. Please always remember that Stanislavski sought means to stir an actor's emotions with the sole purpose of stirring the audience's reciprocal emotions.

Having studied the laws that govern human nervous activity, Stanislavski gradually developed a System that permits an actor consciously to control his entire apparatus of experiencing and of incarnating. The System progressed as Stanislavski learned more about the human being, and his greatest discovery, made at the end of his career, was the fact that we behave in life in a psychophysical way. This discovery became the basis of what he called "the method of physical actions" and considered to be the result of his whole life's work and the heart of his System. It is the summary of all his teachings and is the means for stirring emotions, thoughts, imagination—all the psychic forces. "I thought before that for a moment of creativity an actor needed this technique and that," he said. "Now I insist that only one inwardly justified physical action is necessary. The method of physical action is the greatest achievement of the System." When you learn to control psychophysical behavior, you achieve the concentration of your senses, thoughts, feelings, memory, and body. Your whole spiritual and physical nature is involved then, and you are in a lifelike state on stage.

Psychophysical behavior, or, as we call it, psychophysical action, is the means of an actor's expression. The character is built with typical psychological and physical behavior. To become actors you must master the choice and fulfillment of typical, expressive actions for your character. If you have the need, the determination to master your profession, you will learn your means of expression. You will learn to be part of an ensemble because you will understand and use the logical mutual behavior of characters who strive together for the projection of the same superobjective of the play.

I know the difficulties you have earning your living while studying, but it is my duty to warn you that the training of your psychological instrument alone is not sufficient. I hope that you will also take body movement, speech, and Shakespeare classes in addition to acting technique. I want to emphazise that there are two inseparable parts in the training and formation of an actor. The first is the preparation of an actor's apparatus: his body, voice, speech, his powers of observation and imagination, his constant control over the "feeling of truth," his spiritual involvement. This is where an actor's training begins, and I'd better tell you right away that it never stops. You must continue to practice through your entire life. The second part of the training is the actor's education—the education of the future artist who must create. It is important to develop yourself personally—your culture, your needs, your will to learn, your artistic point of view....

Now we turn to the exercises, which will be simple at the beginning and gradually, as you progress, become more difficult. Will you all come on stage, please?... Stand in a circle. Check your posture: heels together, toes a little apart, knees stretched, diaphragm and stomach pulled in. Stretched knees and pulled-in diaphragm are very important for your voice. Buttocks in, shoulders down and back, chest out. Look straight forward and relax your neck. Check tension in your fingers. During the following exercise, try to observe these rules.

Wait for four beats of the metronome. On the fifth beat, move your right foot to the right, then move the left foot to the right so that you are standing now one behind another. Repeat this again in four counts of the metronome. On the next seven counts walk forward starting with your right foot, and on the eighth count move the left foot to the right foot and begin walking backward for seven counts, starting with your right foot. On the eighth count bring the feet together. Let us do it all again, but before starting, justify what you are doing. Why are you walking, where you are.... Think.... Go on. ... Let your body express what you have in your mind.... Let us do it again but skipping one count, i.e., each step is done on every second count. First, check your posture and justify why you are walking so slowly. Have a definite image of what you are doing in your mind. Try to see people and places you know in life.*

Now we shall do an exercise which we call "disobeying hands." Your right arm goes forward. Evoke an image in your mind of what you are doing with your arm stretched like that. Adjust your body so that it expresses what you do. Raise your arm. Evoke another image of what you are doing, and express it with your body. Use your spine; this will make your body expressive. Anyone entering this room should understand what you are doing without hearing any words. Now move your arm to the side and evoke another image in your mind, and express it with your body. Your arm, another image, think of your body....

Good. Now you do the same thing, but then your left arm follows one movement later. When your right arm goes up, the left goes forward; when the right goes to the side, the left goes up; right goes down, left to the side, and so on....

After each movement, stop, evoke an image of what you are doing and make sure that your body expresses it.... Again, please ... only after your right arm moves do you move the left. Go on.... You see that it is a question of concentration and of overcoming the resistance of your body. (The

---

*Such exercises are performed at the beginning of every class. They become gradually more complicated, as for instance, walking on toes, squatting, jumping, sliding, or on a count indicated by the teacher, students may multiply or say a line of a poem, etc.

exercise continues for some time.) That is enough. Later we shall do a more complicated version of it. Don't sit down. We are going to do a vocal exercise. Your posture is the same as in the walking exercise. When you pull your diaphragm in, you must feel an uplift. If you have one leg in front, you may bend its knee, but the weight of your body should be on the left behind with a straight knee.

Inhale, don't let your diaphragm out, it must be in always or the air you took in loses support. When inhaling, the ribs dilate. As soon as you inhale start the sound "mi." Begin the sound on your teeth and start it at once or you lose your breath. . . . Now begin the sound "mi" and turn into a "la." (Students continue to vocalize.) Now divide into two groups and face one another. One group accuses the other and the other group defends itself. Have a definite image of why you are accusing the others or why you are defending yourselves. Do it with the sound "mi." All right. But what about your body? Involve your body in the action of accusing or defending yourself. Move your body before you begin the sound and after you have finished the sound. The body must begin the action and it must finish it.*

Let us proceed with a simple improvisation. I would like one of you to please open this door. . . .

(*Evan opens the door.*)

Why did you open it?

EVAN: Because you asked me to.

s.m.: Right. You see, you opened this door in a certain situation. Here you are in the Studio, where you have come to study the Stanislavski System, and

---

*Vocal exercises are done in every acting class.

all of a sudden Sonia Moore asks you to open the
door! In life, whatever you do always takes place in
certain *given circumstances*. When you open the
door you know where it happens and why you do it.
With this first improvisation you learn to become
aware of what you do in life. On stage the given
circumstances are those which the author provides—
the other characters and the play's whole world—but
here in class you must build the circumstances
yourself. Now I want you all to imagine some other
situation in which you open a door. Unless you build
the circumstances, your action will be a mechanical
cliché. Therefore will you all please concentrate and
build in your mind the imaginary circumstances in
which you may be opening the door? Think.
. . . Build the imaginary circumstances.

Peter, put your hand down. I don't believe
that you could possibly have built the circumstances
so quickly. It is the situation that will determine your
actions and give them color. Do not attempt to be
anyone but yourself in improvisations. However,
you yourself may be in different circumstances: a
student, a doctor, a teacher. Know where and why it
happens. Opening a door is different in a hospital, in
an office, or on a train. Know when it happens, too,
because it is different during the day and at night.
While building the circumstances in your mind you
are developing your imagination, and you are also
training your concentration on inner objects. You
will see how your imagination will gradually
develop, and the circumstances you build will
become richer and richer. Then your action will be
more colorful. Ready?

(Several students attempt the improvisation.)

That was quite good for the beginning. But I shall insist from the start that whatever you do on stage must be crystal clear to your audience. When you speak on stage you must be heard and understood; when you open the door on stage the audience must understand why, where, and when it is happening. . . . Yes, I know it is difficult, but you have chosen a difficult profession. And the only reason you are on stage is to make everything that happens there clear to those who come to the theatre.

LIZ: It is difficult in an improvisation because there are no sets and not enough props.

S.M.: Yes, but when you do have sets and props in a play, it is often even more difficult to project what you want to project in your role. . . . Every improvisation must have a beginning, a development, and an end. Whenever you begin doing something in life you always change what you were doing before. For instance, before you open the door you might have been reading or eating. Therefore, whenever you fulfill an action, you are overcoming an "obstacle." If you were reading or eating and heard a knock at the door, you would probably take a little time to evaluate what was happening and put aside your book or your food before opening it. What all of you did in this improvisation was quite good for the first try. However, if you want your action to be lifelike, in addition to using the circumstances, you must fulfill the action with the amount of *concentration* you would need in life, in the right *tempo-rhythm*, and with the necessary *relaxation*. You will find the right actions if you ask yourself, "What would I do in life *if* I had to open the door in the circumstances that I have built here?" This "if," which Stanislavski called the "magic if," is truly miraculous. Do not hurry, but honestly answer the question, "What would I do *if?* . . . " Do not try to do anything to impress me or the others in the class. Search for an honest answer and behave the way you would in life.

(Liz attempts the improvisation.)
Did you know where this happened, Liz?

LIZ: Yes.

S.M.: This is good, but the audience must know it too. Your behavior must project where you are. Now let us "close the door." Concentrate and build in your mind the circumstances: why you close the door, where you close it, and so on. Please do not think *how* you will do it until you know the circumstances. Otherwise you will limit your imagination. You will do it in different ways in different circumstances; therefore build them first and the situation will suggest to you how to do it. . . . Ready?

(Each student performs the improvisation. Jeff pantomines a conversation.)
These should be improvisations without any need for speaking. While you pretended to speak to someone who does not exist, your action was mechanical, and we did not believe you.

JEFF: Couldn't there have been someone who has just left, and I was talking to him before I closed the door?

S.M: Yes, but you are not ready to do that. To be able to do it as we do in life, you must know who the person was, what he was doing in your room, whether you were glad that he was leaving. You could not possibly have thought of all that in the short time you used to build your circumstances. What you did was mechanical also because there could not have been a reaction from someone who was not there. Therefore, at this early stage of your study do not talk to a nonexistent person. When you have no words to hide behind, you are forced to think. Is anyone else ready to close the door?

(The students perform the improvisation.)
Thank you. Peter and Liz did especially well. When Peter closed the door and put some of his photographs back in his album, he made it clear by his self-assured action that he had just had a successful interview with an agent or a producer. Liz was obviously leaving a doctor's office, taking a pill, and looking at herself in a mirror. Do you see the difference between the actions that went with closing the doors in two different situations?

Some of you tried to make faces to indicate something. Please do not do this. Indicating is wrong. Only think, think and make your body project what is in your mind. The most important thing for you now is to learn to think on stage, to see images in your mind, and to express these inner processes with your body. Know your objective and overcome at least one obstacle on your way toward it.

Michael, why did you close the door? I did not understand it.

MICHAEL: Because I didn't want to let the dog out.

S.M.: Is this the outside door?

MICHAEL: Yes, and there is a storm going on.

S.M.: There is something I must explain. You see, *you* know what is going on outside, and you are satisfied with this. You do not care that the people who have come to see you and paid good money for their seats have no idea of what you were doing on stage.

MICHAEL: I thought you did not want us to indicate.

S.M.: And you are right. An indication is only the physical side of an action. When Liz took her pill, this could have been an obvious way to indicate that she was leaving a doctor's office, but she convinced us that she had to take it. I think you were afraid of doing something that might look artificial, and so you did nothing at all. You did not fulfill both a psychological and a physical action. If you do know the situation and use it fully, you perform a lifelike action that has motivation and is directed toward a definite purpose. Therefore, it will never be an indication. If you fulfill a simple, truthful action, you live on stage.

You thought up the story about the dog, Michael, but we in the audience did not know either that there was a dog or that there was a storm outside. Of course, in a production there would probably be a real dog, and that part of it would be easier. But when you work on a play there will be other things to project that will be more difficult than the presence of a dog. Please do not be upset. These are only the first steps in learning to achieve the greatest expressiveness on stage. Remember also that if you cannot project something it does not belong on stage. It is as simple as that. There is no art if it does not reach the audience.

We shall proceed to the next improvisation. Here is an antique. Yes, a very precious object. Looking at this dirty bottle, you do not have to try to believe that it is valuable. All you have to do is treat it *as if* it were. If you find and perform truthful actions in treating it as an antique and succeed in convincing us, you will begin to believe it yourself because you are doing it as you would in life. Before thinking of how to do it, please build the imaginary circumstances: why you handle it, where, when, and so on. These will all give color to what you are doing....

(Improvisation by Jeff)

Please, Jeff, do not stop an improvisation until I stop you. It was not clear to me what kind of object it was, and I was hoping that you would improve and find more expressive actions. What you did, you could do with a bottle of Scotch.

JEFF: It was probably because I put it in the closet. I am trying to project that I am always afraid to leave my antiques lying around on tables, and this one is especially valuable to me.

S.M.: That is an interesting story. But how on earth do you think we could have known all that?

JEFF: I knew very well what I was doing.

S.M.: But it is not enough that you knew it. No matter how interesting your ideas are, they have no value if you do not find the form which expresses them. Go on. Yes, you, Mary.

(Improvisation by Mary)

You did too many things—combed your hair, tied your shoe, put on lipstick. What did all this have to do with handling an antique? Any action that has nothing to do with the main action, anything that does not help to project what you must project, is harmful. It distracts those who watch you from what is essential. What we saw you doing seemed to come out of the blue, and you could have been doing it in many different circumstances.

MARY: I agree with you. Did you at least know that I was in an antique shop?

S.M.: Yes, the way you moved and looked around made that clear. It is quite natural that you do not know all of what you are expected to do. My criticism is intended to be constructive.

(Jean performs the improvisation.*)

Well, Jean, you treated the bottle very carefully—I think too carefully. It looked as if you were handling a baby. Don't you think it was a bit overdone? In such cases Stanislavski used to say, "Cut ninety-five per cent." You should always watch what he called "the measure of truth."

Do you all have the paperback copy of *The Three Sisters* that I asked you to buy? All right, you can share the books. Next time I shall explain why I chose scenes from this very difficult play for your first taste of work on a role. Did you read the play? How many times? Once is not enough. You will have to read it many times in order to understand what Chekhov wanted to say. We will discuss the play later, after you have read it again. Now open your books at the very start, and let us read the beginning of Olga's speech. Liz, you read it. [See excerpt on page 311.]

(Liz reads.)

Thank you. I want to explain one of the first steps in building a character—the creating of *images*

---

*Each improvisation and exercise is performed by all the students, but these are not always noted here.

in your own mind corresponding to those of the character. When you say, "Father died...," you must have an image of a man who means to you what Olga's father means to her. He does not have to be your own father, but I would like you to have a real person in mind. Please dig deep into your memory and bring out people, events, and places that you really know. They must be the right ones for the given situation and the given role. You must have images for everybody and everything you mention in your role, and you must know your attitudes toward them. If the images *are* your own, you have an attitude or feeling toward them. The work on images should be done at home, with paper and pencil.

Let us go on. When you, as Olga, say, "On the fifth of May—your saint's day, Irina," you must have your own real images of a party and people that are right for Olga. Further, when you say, "It was snowing then"—is that what you were saying?

LIZ: "It was very cold and snowing."

S.M.: Yes. You must see New York or any other place that means to you what this town means to Olga. Do not try to see Moscow or this town, for that does not mean a thing to you. You must see images in your mind, and your body must express your attitude to them before you speak. Otherwise your words will be only dead sounds. An actor must see vivid images and make his partners see them; then the audience will see them too.

But before you work on images, you must read the play many times, and then write a biography of the character you will start building. You must know a great deal about him or her to project his essence. While you read the play, mark all the hints about your character, whether in your own words or in the words of other characters, and from these write down what you think of him. When you know him well, you will know what to choose to build his spiritual life. Selecting and building images is one of the steps.

As I have told you, the Stanislavski technique is based on what happens to us spontaneously in real life. One of these laws is that we see a continuous film of images, as I will demonstrate in our next class. Often you will realize that the images you have chosen for a role are wrong, and then you will have to change them. This is a normal process in our work. You may have to change them many times until you find the best ones.

At this stage of your work, the teachers will tell you what the play is about and what the event on which you will be working is about. We will also suggest your actions. We want you to concentrate on "subtext," images, continuous thinking on stage, and your body expressing these inner processes. We want you to start assimilating these steps, which are essential in building a character.

class 2

SONIA MOORE: I do not think that everyone has arrived, but we will start the class and will not wait. Stanislavski never allowed anyone to come to a rehearsal or a class after it had started, but I will give those who are late a chance to attend the class. I am sure that when you are late you have a serious reason for it.

Please come on stage, and we will perform again the posture and walking exercises.

Now let us do "the disobeying hands." It will warm you up. Right hand forward, up, to the side, down. Do it without me. . . . Again. . . . And now your left arm goes one movement later. . . .

Now let us do an exercise that will help to develop your will and memory. You say a word, the next person repeats the word and adds his own, the third person repeats the two words and adds another, and so on. Use only nouns; they are easier to remember. See in your mind what you hear and what you will say. The word you add should be suggested by the image of the word you heard, so that a continuous logical story may develop. This is your objective.

ALBERT: Cigarette.

EVAN: Molasses—oh, I mean cigarette, molasses.

NINA: Cigarette, molasses, necklace.

ALBERT: Cigarette, molasses, necklace, chair.

ANNE: Cigarette, molasses, necklace, chair, dog.

(The exercise continues. It is stopped when there are too many words to remember, and is repeated several times with new words.)

EVAN: This is very hard.

S.M.: Well, it is nothing in comparison with what you will have to do in your mind when you work on a role. The work you have undertaken is very difficult, and is based on willpower. What you need is the will, the desire to learn your profession. This means a great deal of work at home and in class.

Next we will perform an improvisation— "reading at home." Know your objective, for instance reading in preparation for an exam or for an audition. Think of the people involved in this, such as your teacher or a casting director. After you have thought of all the possible details, think which emotion should be stirred and remember an analogous emotion you experienced in your real life. Then go on stage and think of your physical behavior to express your imaginary circumstances. If you find the right physical behavior in the given circumstances, you will achieve psychophysical involvement; the logical physical action will involve the psychological side of the action that dictated your physical behavior.

Think of the circumstances: what you are reading, why you are reading, when, and so on.

Reading at night or during the day may make a difference. Furnish your own room with these chairs and tables—and please use other props. We have a closet full of them—hats, coats, books—even a dummy head. It is only in sense-memory exercises that we do not use any props; then you do everything "with air," and you must do the exercises with such concreteness that we believe you are handling real objects. In all the other exercises you will destroy the concreteness we are trying to learn if you do not use props. Are you ready, Peter? Go on.

(*Peter sits in a chair and reads.*)

Now, how were we to know that you were in your own room, and not in the lobby of a hotel? The main action of this improvisation is "reading at home," and you must select a chain of logical actions that are necessary to project gradually the circumstances that you have built. Everything you do on stage must be clear to the audience. This rule applies to both actors and directors. A play lasts about two and a half hours usually, and in that time you must express the life of the character and the meaning of the whole play. To do it in that time, you must find the most expressive actions and discard those that do not help. We here have no idea that you are at home, whether you are reading for pleasure or because you have to, and so on. *You must know your objective.*

PETER: Something is distracting me, and I don't feel like reading. Anyway, the book is too long.

s.m.: Well, that is interesting, but you are the only one who knows it. You are speaking of obstacles. You must have an important objective for your reading and project overcoming the obstacles to it. Please understand that no matter how interesting your ideas are, they have no value if they are not projected. Every action must help to reveal "reading at home."

Now, Jean....

(Jean performs the improvisation.)

That was good. You can all see how simple, expressive actions can project what you want to project. Jean was so engrossed in her book that she carried it with her to the refrigerator when she went for something to eat. Her objective not to waste a minute was clear. What you are doing now is the fulfillment of the psychophysical action that always includes an objective. This is your first step in learning to behave on stage as a living human being....

(All the students perform the improvisation.)

And now we are going to "read in a library." Do not go on stage until you have built the circumstances.

(Peter performs the improvisation.)

What disturbed me is that you moved the table. Would you move it in a library?

PETER: No, I wouldn't.

s.m.: Otherwise it was good, and I am satisfied. When you come to a more advanced stage of actual work on a role, you will realize how difficult it is to select the right actions. That is why you are learning it in these improvisations.

(Meg does the improvisation.)

What were you writing?

MEG: Some lines from a poem, but I was distracted by people in the library.

s.m.: Yes, you made it clear that there were people around you. But looking around at people like that can also be done in a café. Also, you held the book in your lap, and it seems to me that people in a library keep their books on the table. . . .

All right. Now let us "search your roommate's bureau." Obviously you must have an important reason to do such an unattractive thing. You do not have to be roommates. You may be husband and wife, brother and sister, anybody, but you must know what the other person is to you! Think of an analogous emotion in your own life. In life have you ever gone through an experience of doing something so unethical as searching someone's bureau? It does not have to have been searching, but something you should not have done. Think of people you know who were involved in the experience.

(Improvisation)

I did not understand what you were searching for, Anne.

ANNE: I had one idea, and then, I don't know why, but I just couldn't develop it, and then I got all mixed up.

s.M.: If you yourself did not know what you were doing, then it is no wonder that we did not. First of all, you seemed too comfortable about doing this unethical thing. Project your physical state. Why didn't you at least close the door?

ANNE: There is no door, only a doorway.

s.M.: Well, it seems to me that if there were no door, you would have behaved differently because you might have been seen.

ANNE: My roommate is not there at certain hours.

s.M.: This is fine, but only you know this—your audience does not. . . .

Now let us turn to *The Three Sisters*. Did you all have a chance to read the play again? ... (*Not everyone did.*) I do appreciate that you do not have much time, but we cannot afford to waste time, so I shall tell you a little about it, so that we can begin working on a few scenes. In *The Three Sisters* Chekhov is writing about the longing for a better life. His characters are subtle, well-mannered people who love each other but also have isolated inner worlds of their own. Their tragedy is that they submit to evil without fighting it. Uncompromisingly, Chekhov tells us that one must not live this way. They are tortured by boredom, anguish, monotony, but they are unable to do anything. Moscow is the symbol of their faraway ideals, which will never be realized, and Natasha and Protopopov are symbols of vulgarity. Triviality invades people's lives; it is a dangerous force, and Chekhov is warning against it. The first act, which we began to read last time, takes place on Irina's saint's day. In old Russia, as in many parts of Europe, one's saint's day was as important as a birthday. In this scene it is spring, with singing birds, flowers, gaiety.

Since you are not ready to begin the analysis of the play, I'll tell you that we give a noun name to every event or episode. Let us call this episode which begins the play "celebration." This means that all the performers in this episode must project "celebration." The actions will be different for everyone. For instance, Olga insists that everything is wonderful, Irina is building happy plans for the future, and Masha is trying to block out her troubles so as not to spoil Irina's saint's day. Now that you know what the episode is about and your actions have an objective, you can begin to select your images and your thoughts.

In our first class, I explained how you should work on the images that flow through a character's mind. Now I will demonstrate what happens in your minds in real life. Will you all think of someone you met today who impressed you in some way?...All right, Peter. Come on stage. Sit down. Who was it—a man? A woman?

PETER: It was a taxi driver.

s.m.: Describe his clothes.

PETER: His jacket was brown and pretty dirty, and he also wore dark glasses.

s.m.: How old was he?

PETER: Oh, about fifty-five.

s.m.: Do you think he is married?

PETER: ...Yes.

s.m.: Is he a good husband?

PETER: I think so...and I think he is a good father.

s.m.: Are you aware that as you spoke you saw in your mind the man and everything you said about him? And, all of you, do you realize that you each had your own image of what Peter was talking about? Peter, do you think he is a good-natured man?

PETER: I think he is, but he wasn't today because he told me that he had worked twelve hours, and this would not put anyone in a good humor. He said he loves to drive and would like to have a day off and drive out to Long Island. So I figured he loves his work.

s.m.: Do you all realize that you had mental images for what Peter said?...Now, Sally, tell us about someone you met today.

SALLY: I don't remember anyone.

S.M.: Make an effort and you will.

SALLY: Oh, I remember a woman I saw in a restaurant with a red hat and a green dress. She looked like Christmas. That's all I can remember.

S.M.: Are you aware that when you describe it, you see it? When poor actors read their lines, they rush over them, seeing nothing. In life our images are spontaneous, and we take them for granted, but on stage you must form them consciously. It is like hard labor in the beginning. But you must learn to see images on stage, and to describe them so well to your fellow actors that they see them too, and so that you also stir the images and associations of the audience.

And now we come to another step in building a character: *inner monologue*. At the beginning of *The Three Sisters*, Irina does not have any lines during Olga's speech, but she must be thinking continuously. At this particular moment, Irina does not listen to Olga, because she is entirely engrossed in her dreams. This continuous thinking while another character speaks, or during pauses in your own lines, is called inner monologue. Jean, Sally, and Nina, you will work on the role of Irina. In this scene Irina is building dream castles in her mind. Your thoughts and images must be your own, which would be right for Irina. They must mean to you what Irina's thoughts and images mean to her. Remember that at this point Irina is still hopeful and thinks that life can be wonderful.

I would like Meg and Liz to work on Olga. Anne and Mary, you will work on Masha, and if you read the play you will know that Masha does not say a word at the beginning. Therefore, you, too, must have continuous thoughts during the scene. You will learn that those actors who do not say a word occupy as important a place on the stage as those who speak—sometimes even more important. Life does not stop when we are silent. Thoughts flash through our mind all the time. We know now that thinking on stage need not be a special achievement of genius alone. Stanislavski has given us the technique by which every actor can master it.

Images and inner monologue are essential steps toward building the character. They are part of the *second plan*—this was Nemirovich-Danchenko's term. The existence of a character on stage is only a small part of his whole life; the second plan includes the parts of his life before what happens in the play and after it. Like Stanislavski, Nemirovich-Danchenko believed that the audience must be made aware of the whole inner life of the character, his entire destiny, while he is on stage.

If you do not use images and inner monologue, you will only be another prop. Actors who do not use them on stage, Stanislavski said, look like prematurely born people. But to be able to do this, you must know and understand the play. You must understand the meaning Chekhov wants to project.

When you work at home, write down every thought that must go through your mind on stage; they must be right for you as Masha, or you as Irina. Later in the first act, Irina says, "Masha is in a bad mood today." *You* must know why you as Masha are in a bad mood. Masha is refined, talented, and bored. She is a happy person; she loves life; she may be the only one here who faces life, who knows that life is difficult and still loves it. She has more courage than her sisters, but today she wants to leave her sister's party. Why? You must find concrete thoughts that go through your mind as Masha.

I think that Jeff and Ken should start with the role of Andrei. Maybe you, too, Jack. Evan and Albert work on Baron Tusenbach, and Peter and Michael, I would like to see you begin with Ferapont.

We shall work on the beginning of the first act. The scene starts with Olga's speech and ends with Baron Tusenbach's entrance. We will also work on the scene with Andrei and Ferapont in Act Two. I expect you to read the play again, even those of you who have already read it twice. The play must be read many times, and I hope you will give it more thought. Then, write biographies of your characters and put down the thoughts that you think should be in your mind when you are not speaking. And search for analogous emotions, images of people, places, and events in your own life that would be right for the given moment when you say your character's lines. Put down whatever you think is right. Don't be afraid of making mistakes. It is impossible to find the perfect thoughts and images at once. But they do have to be written down, or there will be nothing concrete to correct or change.

I hope I have not given you the impression that we are preparing a production of *The Three Sisters*. I chose parts of this play because Chekhov's characters answer each other's thoughts, not only each other's text. In his plays there are many pauses and silences that provide a perfect opportunity for working on inner monologue.

class 3

SONIA MOORE: Good afternoon. Will you all please put your chairs in a circle and sit down? What are you doing sitting in the circle? Evoke an image of it and express this with your body.... Without looking at each other, stand up together. All together, turn toward your chairs. Take hold of them. Raise them. Put them down again. Turn around. And sit down. Now, do not look at each other but "sense" each other. You are rarely alone on stage; there are other people around you, and it is good to become aware of this at the very beginning of your training. Repeat this again, and now after every change of movement, evoke an image in your mind of what you are doing and express it with your body....

And now you are on a beach at night, by yourself. But all of you are to go on stage together.... Build the circumstances in your mind: Who are you and why are you alone at night on a beach? Though you do not see anyone, because it is very dark, you hear sounds all around you, and you know there is someone nearby. Remember an analogous experience in your life. See images of real people you know. . . . Spread out, so that you aren't close to each other. React to sounds as you would in life. You must learn to do consciously what we do in life spontaneously, without knowing it.

The "magic if" is of great help if you use it honestly. You ask yourself, "What would I do if I heard footsteps in the darkness? Would I run away, or would I go toward the sound?" It would depend on the situation that you have built in your mind. Now concentrate on building the circumstances. Everyone go on stage, please. . . . (*After a while*): Start walking fast; justify why you have suddenly begun to walk fast. Faster, faster—justify. . . . When I give the signal, stop and assume any pose. . . . Stop. . . . All right, Jack, can you justify why you took that pose?

JACK (*after thinking for a moment*): Because I thought someone was near me.

S.M.: All right, drop the pose. . . . Now, assume it again with that justification. . . . Good. You see, you look alive now. And you, Liz—why did you stop?

LIZ: Because I got some sand in my eyes.

S.M.: Relax, and take the pose again with your justification in mind. . . . Good. Ken, why did you stop?

KEN: There is water under my feet.

S.M.: Start walking again, and stop for that reason. . . . All right.

(*All the students transform the movement into a purposeful action.*)

S.M.: Now, another improvisation. The girls have discovered that they have lost a piece of jewelry, and the men have lost their wallets. Remember an emotion in your life when you lost something important. Build the circumstances. Know when you discovered the loss; where; what kind of jewelry it was, who gave it to you, whether it was insured; or how much money was in the wallet—and so on. It may be a family heirloom or a present from your fiancé. The circumstances will determine your actions. I want this to be an important loss for you. Make an effort and remember an analogous emotion. The circumstances do not have to be the same as they were in life. The emotion that you went through must be analogous; think what you did or would do in such a case if it happened in real life. Make decisions. Do not try to "act" or to amuse us.

(Ken performs the improvisation.)

I told you that this should be important to you, but you do not seem to be interested. You seem to be imitating someone with your "I don't care" style. I am afraid that if you follow that style you will not be interested in building characters either, and will always play your own impassive self—and this is not even yourself, but your mannerisms, your own image of yourself.

(Improvisation by Michael)

That was pretty good, but your tempo-rhythm—the speed and pattern of your actions—did not change when you realized that you had lost your wallet. In life, any little change of circumstance stirs a different tempo-rhythm. Watch for this in life, and you will see how often it changes. All your actions were in the same tempo, and that is why they weren't truthful. Stanislavski said, "If you learn to think and to fulfill actions, and in addition you have control of your rhythms, you're in the driver's seat." Rhythm expresses inner experience, and control over it is one of the conditions for mastering the inner technique.

Overcoming obstacles on the way to your objective should be of tremendous help in changing the tempo-rhythm.

I do not mean that after discovering the loss you must become frantic. You might even stop entirely in order to evaluate what has happened. In life we do not have to think about the change of tempo; it takes care of itself. But when you work on your roles, you must be aware of it as an essential element of truthful action. Tempo-rhythm is essential for uniting the psychological and the physical in an action. It discloses the depth of human experience. It may vary while you are talking—be aware of this too. I would like all of you to think up at home some theme on the change of tempo-rhythm. Create obstacles and think of ways to overcome them.

LIZ: Would the tempo-rhythm change depending on the value of the object that was lost?

S.M.: Of course. Can you imagine what would happen if you lost a thousand dollars that might not even belong to you? Or suppose you lost a family heirloom? Or let us say you lost an earring that you bought at the five-and-ten. These are all different circumstances. Also, each of you will behave differently because you are different people who react in various ways. You know that after you have built the imaginary circumstances you do what you would do in life; however, your actions on stage must not only be lifelike, they must also be interesting. So you have to find interesting ways to express your situation.

ALBERT: What did you mean when you told us to make decisions about it?

S.M.: I am certain that in life you would look

in your pocket, in the bureau; you might call your insurance broker, and so on. In life you constantly make decisions to do something or refrain from doing it. Decisions will also make your inner monologue in a role more active, more interesting.

Your instrument is still totally unprepared for this work. But now you know what is ahead of you. You are training your instrument and taking control over it in order to be able to build what Stanislavski called "the life of the human spirit," or the inner spiritual world of another human being, with your own resources. You will build a new person who has different thoughts, different images, different emotions—a completely different inner world from your own. To be able to do this, you must stir your own inner life, because an actor creates his work of art with himself. He is his own instrument. A pianist has his piano, and a painter his paint, but the actor has only his own organic nature and his body. Unlike artists in other fields, he is the creator and the material and the instrument all in one—himself. I have to keep repeating that unless you master the psychological and the physical techniques you will not become actors—not even if you study for twenty years. To build another living human being, you must have physical and psychological training.

ALBERT: I wish we could do more exercises by ourselves.

S.M.: I wish you would. And now that you have begun to realize how we function in life, do not waste any opportunity to observe.

SALLY: Since I've been studying here I can't cross my office without analyzing what and why.

S.M.: That is wonderful. That is what you

must do. Someday you will be able to use what you have observed, and you must also know why you are doing these exercises and improvisations, because you will use in your roles what you learn from them. Artists in all fields must learn to observe, to digest their observations, and to express them in their work.

LIZ: I don't know how to use what I observe. Other teachers told me to observe, observe, and I never knew how to use it.

S.M.: I am glad you brought up this point because it is important. The main purpose of our exercises and improvisations is to become aware of what is happening inside us and around us; to become aware of other people, of our own reactions to all kinds of people and events. You will gradually learn to understand what the process of human psychophysical behavior is. Listening to music, observing nature, and admiring works of art enrich your impressions and help you learn more about yourself. You will be able to see what the artist who created a work of art wanted to express. You will learn to register what others do not notice, and express it for them on stage. You will have in your memory a reserve of images which you will be able to use as an artist uses sketches. There is life around us everywhere, and it provides a limitless treasury for observation. Do not limit your observations to yourself. "Store" what you see, and someday you may use it for building a character.

Every time that I have asked you to try to remember an analogous emotion in your life, you have been learning to use your *emotional memory*. It is time now to tell you about this most important attribute in the actor's art. Past emotions, and every adult person has gone through a great deal of emotions, leave a trace on our central nervous system and make the nerves which participate in the given emotion more sensitive. According to scientific data, emotional memory is the only source for an authentic emotion on stage. The actor will create a true emotion only through stirring in his emotional memory the imprint of an analogous emotion which he experienced in his life. Actors must be capable of bringing out the imprint of a past emotion and making it respond to the conditioned stimulus on stage, when the need for it arises.

The quality of an actor's performance depends upon the sincerity of his emotion. The actor must live true emotions, but true *stage* emotions. The stage emotion is a "repeated" emotion, not a "primary" one, as Stanislavski said. Actors who have achieved such true *stage* emotion know that they are not the same as life emotions. No actor could survive long if he had to go through a true tragic shock every time he performs. And if an actor is honest, he will admit that an authentic emotion of suffering while performing gave him true joy.

We have all experienced different feelings of love, hate, suffering, rejoicing, etc., though these feelings may have been for different reasons. For instance we may have suffered a headache or because a close person passed away. But there is something common in these cases, and that is why they are all called "suffering." Scientific data tells us that emotional memory, in addition to retaining the imprints of an emotion, also synthesizes feelings of a different nature. For instance if we have experienced "suffering" many times, though for different reasons, the common element in all the cases will have left a deep imprint on our memory.

Through rehearsals, the actor develops a conditioned reflex in which his emotion is stirred through the stage stimulus. Such a "repeated" emotion, though absolutely sincere, does not absorb the actor completely and he never forgets that he is performing on stage.

As you know, in the early stages of the System actors were forcing their emotions. Stanislavski realized that forcing emotions brought actors to inner hysteria, and this was detrimental to the actor's health and to art. With the *Method of Physical Actions* Stanislavski revolutionized the use of means to achieve the creative state. You have been studying this means. To relive the emotion stored in the actor's emotional memory, he must be capable of selecting indispensable logical purposeful physical actions in the given circumstances. And I have stressed to you the importance of an objective in every action. You must remember that an action without an objective is only a mechanical movement. If you are capable of such selection and of executing these purposeful actions honestly, with the adequate concentration and relaxation and in the correct tempo-rhythm, you will stir different nuances of emotions. There are as many different nuances of emotions as there are different physical actions.

To enrich the reservoir of your emotional memory, you must observe the outside world—an inexhaustible source. You must visit museums, see paintings, study sculpture, listen to music, and watch people. Remember: The well-developed emotional memory is an important requirement, and it is an essential requirement for an actor of the School of Living Experience, because it is the *only* source for emotions on stage.

And now to *The Three Sisters*.

Did you read the play again? Good. What do you think Chekhov wanted to say with this play? Keep in mind that whatever you do in your roles must help to disclose the *superobjective* of the play. Every detail must contribute to the atmosphere on stage. When you choose your images and thoughts, you must be certain that they help to project that these lovely, noble people cannot fight the triviality they are caught in. To build a character means to establish his relationship with the surrounding world, his attitude toward every fact and event.

LIZ: Mrs. Moore, I cannot understand these people. They seem so weak and ineffective.

S.M.: Yes, they are weak. Through them Chekhov discloses what was in the hearts of all the Russian intelligentsia: their dream of a better future. Chekhov tells about a life without purpose: the dull, uneventful days of people whose minds, as time passes, are gradually invaded by the dangerous force of triviality. He shows how this threatening force penetrates people, kills their dreams and sometimes their serious ambitions. Anguish and boredom torture Chekhov's characters. He wanted to stir people to search for a better future, which could be achieved only through hard work. He demonstrates two antagonistic forces—on one hand the subtle feelings of good people, their beautiful souls, their inner search for a road to happiness, and on the other hand the degrading force of vulgarity: Chekhov clearly says that we must not live this way.

In the first act it is springtime; there are singing birds, flowers, sunshine. In a Leningrad production of the play, directed by Georgi Tovstonogov, the cake that Protopopov sends to Irina for her saint's day is enormous, it has vulgar decorations, and according to one critic you feel that another character is coming into the Prosorovs' house with a threat of destruction.... The arrival of Vershinin puts everyone into a wonderful mood. Masha, who had been bored, suffering from the lack of real people around her, revives. Vershinin, the dreamer who savors his philosophizing, is unable to stop it even when it embarrasses him. Though his life is distorted, Vershinin still wants to dream of what it could be. He is accepted with joy at this house, and he frequents it as if it were his own. Tusenbach, the passionate dreamer, is overwhelmed with his strong love for Irina. This wonderful man spreads goodness around him. He is liked by everybody and likes everyone. Even in Soliony, the gloomy officer, he does not find any great faults.

Act One is happy. It is the end of a year of mourning for the dead father. Irina decides to go to work, and dreams about it. Tusenbach now can speak of love to Irina. Masha and Vershinin meet; Andrei proposes to Natasha. And Olga does not have her usual headache.

With Act Two we sense a gradual change in the atmosphere. It starts to become more difficult to breathe. As time stagnates, people's destinies are gradually broken, their dreams and hopes killed.

Only Natasha, Andrei's wife, steadily improves her situation. There are still some of those tea evenings and some remnants of the charming atmosphere which will eventually be ended. Natasha takes firm steps to take over the household. This cruel woman, vulgar in her self-confidence, occupies a significant place in the play. Chekhov wants her revealed gradually but without mercy. Natasha represents the humiliating and degrading force. She is the quintessence of life's hard prose, and a contrast to the spiritual life of Prosorov's sisters. Every episode involving Natasha is full of a petit-bourgeois aggressiveness which increases steadily. She leads an entirely different existence from the others, never to be reconciled.

In Act Three there is a real clash of opposing forces. The general mood is tense and nervous, and the fire siren outside intensifies it. That is why Irina and Andrei both explode and Masha confesses to her sisters that she loves Vershinin. The more these people become troubled, the more Natasha, the condensed energy of vulgarity, attacks. Irina, this tender, uninhibited girl of the first act, is fading away. She has lost her hopes. In contrast to Tusenbach, who really dreams of work, Irina hates it. The sunny young Irina of the first act, full of hopes and dreams, is now a woman with her dreams killed by time. She obviously goes down as Tchebutikin already has—he keeps repeating, "It is all the same." Andrei meets his downfall in the same manner: Andrei, the good-natured, happy young man of the first act, when he was full of projects, is the first victim of what Protopopov and Natasha represent. He knows what is happening, but he submits to his wife Natasha without a word. In Act Two he was still defending himself indecisively. In Act Three he is neurotic, and almost screams his monologue, which is really a scream about the wasted life.

Neither Andrei nor anyone else pays attention to Soliony. Masha, for instance, who understands Soliony better than the others, does not do a thing that could ultimately save Tusenbach from being killed in a duel with Soliony. She and the others are too occupied with themselves. Soliony, full of the pain of realizing his inferiority, is an annihilating force. Soliony is the symbol of the oppressive force. He is dangerous because people with inferiority complexes are sometimes destructive. Soliony is not funny at all; no one is laughing at him. Soliony suffers especially because he is anxious to have a spiritual closeness with others but is unable to achieve it. It is painful for him because he loves the atmosphere of the house of the Prosorovs. He is not intelligent, and that is why he does not understand that he will never be close to them. Trying hard to be an equal, he constantly says stupid things. His actions are always directed by his sense of rejection. This finally brings him to the duel and makes him a killer. Even such a man as Soliony needs spiritual closeness with others.

Masha is still happy in Act Three, although her love is doomed. She carries happiness throughout the play. It is her theme. She is courageous and is capable of living with the present reality. In this she differs from her sisters. She is the strongest among them. In Tovstonogov's Leningrad production, they say, Masha sparkled, full of unused energy that is expressed in her eccentric ways and her overwhelming love for Vershinin. Masha should not be portrayed with a demonic quality about her, as is sometimes done. She cannot stand boredom and apathy. She needs real people around her. Masha has married Kulygin, who is accepted in the house only because he is her husband. This well-groomed, self-satisfied man is content with just the form of relations. He can, however, be inwardly humiliated. In this third act, Tusenbach, the dreamer, is the only one who does not worry. Everybody is at the edge of his nerves at the fire, but Tusenbach falls asleep.

In Act Four, Tusenbach, the best man among them all, is killed in the duel. Andrei's destiny comes to an end, and there is tragedy in the parting of Masha and Vershinin. These two were born for each other. They both knew that their encounter was brief, and this knowledge has made it even sharper. Though Masha feels the tragedy strongly, she survives it. Olga, the symbol of moral force, is still the wall on which everyone leans. She is always modestly heroic through the whole play.

I hope that I have given you a general idea of the play. Though we will work on only a few scenes, you must always keep in mind what Chekhov wanted to say. Even more, just the "message" or the "moral" is not enough. I want you to think of all the conflicts in the play. Bringing out the conflicts gradually reveals the theme of the play. This will also help to make it "new," contemporary—clear and understandable to today's spectators.

Let's all go on stage and perform an improvisation in which the characters could find themselves, but which is not in the play. You will all prepare for Irina's party. Such improvisations help us to learn about the character's inner and physical behavior.

(All students perform the improvisation.)

All right. Now all sit down and only Liz, Sally, and Anne stay on stage. This is the living room of the Prosorov family. As the play begins, it is around noon on a cheerful spring day. Irina is full of hope; Olga does not permit herself to be sad; only Masha is in a bad mood. All think of your physical state. Masha is trying to concentrate on the book, but she cannot. She is haunted by a line from a poem. You know the objective and the action. Did you write down your inner monologue, Anne?

ANNE: I didn't have time.

S.M.: That is too bad. If you do not write it down, it will always be accidental and primitive, and your work will always be accidental and primitive. At first you must put down whatever you think is logical for Masha to be thinking. You will keep changing it as you know the play better and better and come to the best possible thoughts for your character. Irina is immersed in happy thoughts, and she does not hear Olga. Our stage is very small, and it is difficult not to hear, but you will have to build in your mind such a strong and exciting inner monologue that it will seem natural that you do not hear anything. I hope you chose images of people you know who would be right for you as Irina. Let us begin. Concentrate on the images and thoughts which you have prepared at home. I do not want you to smile, Irina; only think, build castles in the air, so that your eyes will radiate such thoughts.... Olga has been correcting her school papers. Liz, what would you do *if* you were correcting papers as Olga? The "magic if" helps to find something personal which is right for the character.

LIZ: I would be sitting. . . .

S.M.: All right, you think you would be sitting, and Irina is standing there at the window. Liz, please start Olga's speech.

(Liz begins reading Olga's speech.)

Stop. You are rushing, and you evidently do not see anything. Words without images are dead. But most important is to move your body before you begin speaking. An action begins with the body expressing your thoughts and images before you speak. The verbal action depends on the physical action. Only when you find the right movement of your body before speaking will your intonations be right, fresh, and always new. And your pauses! If you pause, there must be a thought. Dead pauses interrupt the character's life. Images, thoughts, the body expressing these inner processes, and words should be one uninterrupted process on stage, but I do not expect you to be ready for that now. Make an effort of will, and do not speak before you see your images and your body expresses them. Your work will be judged by your ability to concentrate on inner objects.

(Liz reads the speech.)

And did you have your inner monologue, Irina?

SALLY: I didn't have time to read the play again.

S.M.: Of course, if you have read it only once you cannot know very much about what is going through Irina's mind. I thought you had worked at home, but you were trying to improvise here. Your inner monologue and your images must be studied thoroughly; they also must be carefully selected to fit the play and the character. Just as not all words make poetry, not all actions make theatre.

class 4

SONIA MOORE: Please stand up. Check your posture.... Begin walking, skipping a count of the metronome. On the eighth step multiply by two. On the eighth step, walking backward, jump.... Now walk squatting and continue your table of multiplication.... Make sure that all you do is justified....

Let us perform the "disobeying hands" exercise again [see page 37], but in a more complicated version.... The left arm goes one movement later.... Very good. Now do not stop moving your arms, but start walking around. The walking version is for those who have already mastered the arm movements.

(There is some confusion.)

It is a question of concentration. And now those who are walking, do not stop, but start to recite lines from some poem.... See images and use your body in pauses to express what is in your mind.

(The exercise proceeds for some time.)

That is enough. Sit down....

Now, Ken, please go on stage. Raise your right arm, squat down, and then put your hand over your eyes. Justify and connect these three movements. . . .

KEN: I am hailing a cab; I am squatting in a dance. . . .

S.M.: What does a cab have to do with the dance? I told you to justify and connect; the three movements must make sense together.

KEN: Oh, I hail a taxicab; I squat down to pick up a nickel I dropped; and something went into my eye.

S.M.: Very good. Next, Liz, please come on stage. Put your hands on your hips, look up, and then bend down. . . .

LIZ: I am thinking. . . . I can't think of anything.

S.M.: Yes you can, Make an effort.

LIZ: I have to clean this room; and I don't like doing it; I put my hands on my hips, look up at the dirt everywhere, and then down at the dirt on the floor.

S.M.: Good. Who is next? All right, Mary. Touch your hair, bend down, and cross your arms. Justify and connect.

(Mary pantomimes.)
What was that?

MARY: It has to do with a song. It was a feeling. . . .

S.M.: You should justify the movements I gave you and make them psychophysical actions. Every movement becomes an action when it has a purpose. In the Stanislavski System, what is called an *action* is human behavior, not just a muscular movement. When you fulfill an act of human behavior you will stir feelings.

MARY: I lost a bobby pin. I bent down to pick it up and I don't see it.

(Mary repeats the exercise.)

S.M.: Good. This exercise certainly helps to develop your imagination, which must be quick and rich because you will have to be able to find actions that are interesting in addition to being truthful and logical.

PETER: Did Stanislavski use all these exercises?

S.M.: Some of them are his, some were invented by other Russian teachers, and some are my own.... Next we are going to hide.

EVAN: Everyone together?

S.M.: No, each in turn. Do not think of *how* you will perform it before you have a clear picture of the circumstances in your mind. Different circumstances will make you hide in very different ways. It must be obvious to you that hiding from children in a game is different than hiding from a gangster who is following you. If you think of how to hide before you build the circumstances, you limit your imagination, and your action of hiding will be a cliché. But after you know when, where, why, and so on, you must think of *how*—the adaptations or the means to perform it in an expressive way. With some actors the word *how* is offensive, and I want to make it clear that, on the contrary, it is obligatory. An action is composed of three elements: *what* you do, *why* you do it, and *how* you do it. It is with the *how* that you make your action clear to the spectators. The more imaginative *how* you are able to find, the more interesting your work will be, and therefore, the better actor you will be. The most important thing is to fulfill the action truthfully. This means to fulfill it in the right tempo-rhythm, with the necessary concentration, with the necessary relaxation of muscles. Now concentrate and build the circumstances. Try to remember an analogous emotion in your life. Perhaps you were afraid of somebody. You may adapt it to the situation you will build here. Think of people who were involved when you experienced fear. Is anyone ready? All right, Evan. Go on.

(Improvisation)

After all I just said, I did not understand why you were hiding, or where or when.

EVAN: I had not done my homework, and I saw the teacher in the hallway, and I wanted to avoid him, so I hid behind the door.

S.M.: I did not believe you at all. You did not even hide; you just went over there. Your story sounds interesting, but don't you think that we should have known while you were performing the improvisation what you are telling us now? Please do it again. What did you say you were doing?

EVAN: I was supposed to write a composition on European civilization for homework.

S.M.: That would be interesting, if you made it clear—which is not easy to do! But if you cannot project what is going on, there is no place for it on stage. Evan, first of all, you must project that you are not doing what you are supposed to be doing, and suddenly you see the teacher coming. For example, couldn't you have been writing and then started playing card tricks instead or just playing around and this is why you have to hide when the teacher comes along?

(The improvisation is repeated.)

That was much better. Now we know why you went behind that door. Who is next?

(Mary performs the improvisation.)

Mary, did you know the room you were hiding in?

MARY: No, I really didn't know it.

S.M.: But you went behind the screen as if you already knew it was there. This is why we do the improvisations. In life you would have had to look around before you knew that there was a screen. Whatever you do on stage must be as if you were doing it for the first time. And oh, how many little things you did that did not help to project why or where you were hiding. These are harmful because they clutter up what has to be projected. Only actions that help to project the situation should be used. Your objective must be clear, and so must the obstacles on the way to it.

(The students perform the improvisation.)

S.M.: I feel that I must tell you at once that you will have to stop all improvisations that have a definite sexual quality. I shall not tolerate this kind of distortion, which has taken place in the name of Stanislavski. One of the most outrageous misrepresentations has occurred in regard to Stanislavski's "public solitude." Here is what Stanislavski said: "Public solitude is achieved when an actor is concentrated on his action...and does not try to amuse his audience. When an actor is in public solitude he communes with his partner, and this creates communion with the audience." This term of Stanislavski's has been transformed into a sinister "private moment."

I find this distortion offensive to the name of Stanislavski, and also to human privacy. Sex is not taught or exploited in this studio. It is sick behavior; it will not teach you to become actors.

I hear about actresses who, while rehearsing a scene, become so "involved" that they tear off their blouses and perform "topless." I suggest to such actresses that they start learning the Stanislavski technique, which teaches control of an actor's behavior on stage.

I would also appreciate it if you would dispense with improvisations that take place in toilet rooms. Artists must develop their artistic taste, and such themes are in poor taste....

Let us now perform an improvisation in the characters' circumstances in *The Three Sisters*. You are all in your rooms occupied with a characteristic for your character activity. For instance, do you know that Andrei likes to carve wood?

(Improvisation)

Now let us see the scene between Andrei and Ferapont from the second act of *The Three Sisters*—Jeff as Andrei. Peter, will you please read for Ferapont.

(Scene)

s.m. *(interrupting)*: Please, Jeff, do not *pretend* to be Andrei. It is not that easy to build the character. We will learn to do that step by step, and we have only started to work on assimilating images and inner monologue. And you had better eliminate that artificial laugh. Let us start again.

(Scene)

You seem to be only trying to impress us with how well you read. But I want you to know why you say what you say and see the images, if you have worked on them at home. And move your body logically to express your inner monologue and your images before you speak. The movement of your body must lead into words. Concentrate on this. Only when there is a need to say the words can you expect your intonations to be right. Let us repeat it. Peter, do not come in until Jeff is concentrated on his inner monologue. Do you know what has happened just before this moment? Do you know what is on Andrei's mind? Believe me, I do not expect much—I am only trying to put you on the right road. Natasha has left the room, and Andrei is thinking about what has happened to him and his family. Protopopov and Natasha, as we have seen, are trivial and vulgar, and Andrei is beginning to submit to Natasha without protest.

(The scene begins again.)

Your objective is to shut out your troubles. Peter, do not *pretend* to be Ferapont. Let us do it again with Jack as Andrei. . . . Concentrate on your inner monologue before Ferapont enters. Peter, enter when you see that Jack is immersed in his thoughts. By the way, Peter, you should have a file or a folder to keep the letter or document in that Andrei has to sign. . . . No, take out only one sheet and give it to Andrei. Ferapont is illiterate, and he treats every paper with great respect. Both of you, Jeff and Jack, must decide what kind of book Protopopov has sent you. Are you interested in it? Is it a book Protopopov promised you, or did you leave it behind in the office, or what? Chekhov is a good playwright, you know, and there must be a reason for the book. When you look at it and put it aside, we in the audience must know your attitude toward it. Then you take the paper Ferapont gives you, and after Ferapont says,

"The master, they say, is busy," step into your den for the moment to sign it.

JACK: Why can't I sign it here?

S.M.: This is the living room, and there is no inkstand here—and remember, they didn't have ballpoint pens!

(Scene)

I must interrupt. What is your inner monologue?

JACK: I think, "This is how Natasha has changed our house."

S.M.: Right. Good. Please say it aloud as you do the scene. You must be thinking as the character every second you are on stage. We stop thinking in life only when we are unconscious or dead; and the character is dead when you stop thinking as the character. Now, concentrate on what you think when Ferapont says, "They wouldn't let me in. The master, they say, is busy." And your body must express it.

(Scene)

S.M.: Jack, when you say, "Tomorrow is Friday. I don't have to attend, but I'll go anyway, just to occupy myself," you say it in reaction to what Ferapont has said about your being busy. All you are doing is taking care of the children, because that is what Natasha wants. Your words must be a logical continuation of what you are thinking. Did you write the biography, Jack?

JACK: Not yet.

S.M.: I can see that the character is vague in your mind. That is why I asked you. If you do not know that Andrei is a good but weak man, how will you build his behavior? You will not know what he thinks or what images he sees. Writing a biography of Andrei will make you go back to the play and study it more closely.

Let us see the beginning of the scene in Act One with Olga, Masha, and Irina.

(Scene)

s.m.: Liz, you are trying to see the images, but they are very pale; nobody else will see them. You must transmit them to your partners on stage. If you succeed in that, the audience will see them too. When you work at home, go through your lines in your mind and see your partner in your mind. But never speak to an empty chair, because that will make you accustomed to receiving no reaction, and will eventually cause trouble when you do the scene with someone. In life we have a certain attitude or feeling for everyone and everything. We all have feelings about one another. We may be largely unaware of this, but I have a feeling about each of you, and you have one about me. And you must know your feeling or attitude toward your images. When you energetically transmit your images, and your attitude toward them, to your partner, you create *communion* on stage. Liz, when you have chosen the image for your father from among people you know, you must have the same attitude about him that Olga has about her father. However, your father—Olga's father—died a year ago. Today you are having a party for your sister Irina. It is not a funeral. Though Olga is not in the best of moods today, she is not mourning. Olga is strict with herself; she is dissolved in others; she has inner strength. She compares the situation today with the situation last year on the same day. Today marks the end of mourning and an attempt to start a new life.

LIZ: But how can I speak without sadness when I am talking about such sad things?

s.m.: You are not sad. What you consider "sadness" is your own sympathy with Olga. Sadness is an emotion, and you cannot command it and be sad because the father of the character you are portraying is dead. It is a scientific fact that our emotions are stirred only when what happens concerns our personal interests. Do not confuse your own sympathy, or the sympathy of an actress for the character, with the emotion of the character. We are in the process of learning how to stir our own emotions and transform them into those of the character, but you do not know how to do this yet. You must learn to fulfill psychophysical actions. The first act of *The Three Sisters* starts with life vibrating, with high hopes, especially for Irina. Olga would never spoil Irina's mood.

SALLY: Does Irina react to what Olga is saying?

s.m.: No, Irina is immersed in her happy dreams. In this scene we must project the fact that, though the sisters are close, they live entirely separate lives. Irina decides to go to work. She is like a little girl who has discovered that life is wonderful. Sally, you must find the right images and inner monologue for Irina, so that your face will be radiant without smiling.

LIZ: Mrs. Moore, it bothers me to have to hold the book and look at the lines all the time.

s.m.: But I do not want you to memorize the lines yet. I have said to you that first you must know the subtext—why you say the words—have your inner monologue during pauses, and have your images. If you memorize the lines at this stage, your intonations may be entirely wrong. When you have done all the necessary work, you will see that then you will know the lines, too.

LIZ: It bothers me to have the book in my hands.

S.M.: You will be even more bothered if you memorize the lines before you have studied all that has to be studied. However, you do not have to hold the book, since you are saying your own words. And now, back to Irina. Sally, why did you laugh?

SALLY: Because yesterday I told Olga something funny, and remembering it makes me laugh.

S.M.: I do not believe you. It looks to me as if you decided that this would be a good time to laugh.

SALLY: Why shouldn't I laugh if I am happy?

S.M.: Happiness is also an emotion, and you cannot be happy only because you decide to be happy. But if you really remember something funny that would be right for Irina, and should this make you laugh, it would be perfectly all right. I do not expect you to do this correctly right now. What are your lines here?

SALLY: "The weather is good today. I don't know why my soul is so bright."

S.M.: You see, you think that you must be happy, and you try to pretend to be. But instead of doing that, you must dig in your memory and find the right images and thoughts which would make your eyes shine. It must be done at home, not here. In class or during a rehearsal, you must see that you use what you have prepared at home, and we check whether what you have chosen is right. What you did just now looked empty. I am sure there are days when you wake up feeling especially good. Think of what you do then. We do not want just words. You must be able to think on stage. And your body must express it.

And now, Masha. I would give a penny for your thoughts, Meg! When Olga said, "Don't whistle, Masha," you looked totally blank. If you have the right thoughts and are able to think, believe me, you can "steal the show" even though you are silent. Let us do this moment again, and Meg, I want you to say your inner monologue in a low voice.

(Scene)

MEG: I did skip a lot of the inner monologue, and I am blank, especially at the point you mentioned.

S.M.: Well, please work on it carefully. Make an effort to use it.

Let us see Baron Tusenbach's entrance.

(Scene)

Evan, do not sit down before Irina does. A Russian officer would not sit down before the ladies were all seated. Tusenbach is very much in love with Irina, and this should be clear when you enter the room. Tusenbach's speech is full of images. Did you work on images of Vershinin, his wife, and his two children, the mother-in-law? With this speech Vershinin is established for the first time. You must give a truly vivid description of the man. When you say, "not stupid, certainly," you must have specific words in mind that you heard Vershinin say which impressed you. Tusenbach is an intelligent man, and he has a sense of humor.... And Olga, Masha, and Irina, I do not want to see any mechanical movements of your heads looking at each other or at Tusenbach. This is what most actors do. While Tusenbach is speaking you must have your own images of what he describes and your inner monologue in reaction to it. Your body must express these inner processes. You are learning to react psychophysically, as in life. Let us see it once more, this time with Albert as Tusenbach.

(Scene)

That was quite good. Did you really see the images? You know I am not omniscient. . . . Don't laugh—I will not be fooled often! Tusenbach is in good spirits most of the time. He is somewhat naïve and enthusiastic. . . . Thank you. That is all for today.

class 5

SONIA MOORE: Good afternoon. Please turn your chairs so that you can see each other. You are on a bus. You do not know each other, but each of you observes the others without being noticed. Build the circumstances. Make sure also that you know why you are watching the other person. In life, if we observe someone, we know the reason—maybe the face seems familiar, and you are trying to remember where you could have met him, or you may recognize a thief, and so on. Be aware of the obstacles to your objective and find ways to overcome them.

(The students perform the improvisation together.)

All right. That is enough. Now turn your backs to each other. Nina, can you describe Liz's clothes?

NINA: She is wearing... a brown pullover.

S.M.: Do you all agree that Liz's pullover is brown? Is it brown, Liz?

LIZ: No, it's green.

S.M.: Albert, please describe Michael's clothes.

ALBERT: He has on a white shirt and a black tie.

MICHAEL: I have no tie at all.

s.m.: What color are his socks?

ALBERT: I don't know....

s.m.: Jack, can you help?

JACK: They are gray. I think he is wearing a ring and a pair of corduroy pants, sort of blue.

s.m.: Liz, can you describe Mary's clothes? (*Liz says nothing.*) I asked you to observe each other, though I did not tell you why, and you do not remember a thing. Do you remember Peter's clothes?

LIZ: Well, he has on a long-sleeved shirt.

(*All the students answer similar questions.*)

s.m.: You remember a great deal, after all.

And now, everyone, please come up to the table, all together.... Put one hand on the table. ...Push up your sleeve, Jeff. Put down the other hand, Liz, the one without any rings or bracelets. Now examine all the hands closely. Then you will turn around, close your eyes, and try to guess by the touch whom they belong to. I shall count to twenty.... All right. Everyone come upstage. Come here, Meg. Stand at the table with your back to it. Come here (*pointing to another student*). Put your hand on the table. Meg, you touch it, and tell us whose hand it is. Touch it.

(*Meg guesses right.*)

Good. You, Anne. Whose hand is this?

(*Anne guesses right.*)

But you should not walk so heavily because Anne recognized your footsteps (*laughter*). Don't help them to identify you.

(*All the students in turn identify each other's hands.*)

s.m.: Now you come to a friend to tell him some exciting news, and he is not at home. Do not rush on stage. . . . You must know what the news is, who your friend is. Think why you want your friend to know about it. Remember an analogous emotion in your life. The situation does not have to be the same, but an analogous emotion is important. See in your mind all the people involved. They must be real people. Concentrate and build the situation. . . .

(*Albert performs the improvisation.*)

It was all external. I did not see you thinking even for a second. And that is why it was all continuous *indicating*. The external means that you use to express what is inside must be economical; what is inside must be full. I do not believe that you were trying to concentrate on real people you know in life. Think of the real person who gave you the exciting news. You must learn to think on stage. You did too many things. You must learn to make decisions—to make up your mind—right there on stage. If this happened in life, you would have to make a decision because you would not have known in advance that your friend was not home. You have encountered an obstacle on the way to your objective, and you must think of ways to overcome it.

(*Nina performs the improvisation.*)

Why aren't you leaving after you find that your friend is not home?

NINA: I could leave but I want to wait and tell him the news.

S.M.: But he may not return for hours. Aren't there others whom you would like to tell? Wouldn't you try to reach your friend on the telephone or write a note.

NINA: I just wanted to wait.

S.M.: If you were thinking logically . and

moving your body logically while waiting, that would be all right, but you just sit and sit.

NINA: I have a justification, but I guess it did not come through.

S.M.: No, it did not.

Let us work on *The Three Sisters*. Great effort is needed to change your own psychological and physical behavior into the behavior of the character in a play. You must promise that you will write down your images and your inner monologue, otherwise there will be nothing concrete to correct. If you do not write this down, you will try to improvise every time you rehearse, and it will always be accidental and primitive. When you work on your character, you must also study your partner's lines. Most of the time you think in response to what you hear. This is how you learn the first step of *ensemble* work.

In the scene at the beginning of the first act the three sisters are separate. Each is immersed in her own world. But they love each other, and this should come through without hugging or kissing. From time to time Masha may hear Olga, and then her thoughts should be in reaction to what the other person says. This is ensemble work. What you are learning is all conscious work, but it prepares the best conditions for subconscious creativity. This is what we hope for. But we cannot order this state, and therefore we must learn the technique that will bring you to it.

Let us do the scene with Sally as Irina and Liz as Olga. We will start with the clock striking, which brings back the memories of last year. This is how the

Russian director Tovstonogov begins the first act in his Leningrad production, I hear, and I like it.

(*Scene*)

Listen to a sound, Liz. It does not have to be the sound of a clock. Listen, really listen to a sound. Treat the sound you hear, even if it is a car outside, as if it were the clock, and then say your words. And each time you stop, Liz, I mean when you pause, please say your inner monologue aloud and express it with your body before you speak your lines. You had quite a few pauses that were unjustified and empty. This is a customary thing with some actors. As Stanislavski says, those are pauses for the actor's sake, not for the character's. Actors believe that such pauses are impressive, but they only create a void on stage because they kill the character's life.

(*Scene*)

Well, that was better. Thank you. But Sally, you are standing there as if you were being punished, as if someone ordered you to stand there. Your physical expression does not correspond to what goes through your mind. In life, your body expresses the inner experience spontaneously, without any effort. But on stage you must think consciously about the physical side and find the form that would be most expressive of what is inside you. You are supposed to be building dream castles, and there you stand like a schoolgirl being punished. Think of what pose would be right while standing there at the window or at the door to the terrace. Birds are singing and flowers are in bloom. . . . Good, yes, lean on the screen. Nobody has ordered you to stand there—you want to, and that must come across. Move up stage more. It is difficult for us to believe that you do not hear Olga. Your concentration must be so strong that we believe you.

SALLY: I don't hear her even when she speaks of the funeral?

S.M.: You may come down to earth for a second and then go back to your dreams again. Masha is not listening either. Anne and Mary, while working on Masha, you must study Olga's lines and decide when you hear her, and what your thoughts are at those moments. I do not remember whether we did the exercise of making a decision without moving a muscle on your face. That is how Irina and Masha should be concentrated. Your concentration must be deep. To be able to do this, your thoughts must be concrete. Do not force a smile; your eyes must radiate the thoughts.

Let us go on to Tusenbach's entrance.

(Scene)

That was not bad, Jack, but try to describe your images more vividly. It is a physiological fact that in life our bodies move before we speak and before the thoughts and images in our minds materialize completely. Before you begin the description, move your body to evaluate what you are going to say. As you do it, you will become aware that your thoughts and your images become more concrete. Your words then will be those that are needed and your intonations always fresh. Do not forget that you must know how you feel about all these people, how much you like Vershinin. You must understand the author's text so well that you could express it with your own words. Only then can you use the author's words. When you transmit your images to your partner, you must transmit your attitude toward them also. Olga, you must know your attitude toward your father's death, but this is not a funeral. You speak of home. Your images must be the subtext.

MEG: That's very difficult for me.

S.M.: Of course, it is difficult for anyone. Somehow this scene puts everyone into a melancholy mood. But the first act of *The Three Sisters* is not sad at all. It is a day full of hopes and dreams, for Irina especially, and no one knows yet that these hopes and dreams will never be realized. Jack, you are doing the speech much better, though.

JACK: I think I know now what you want me to do.

S.M.: Good. . . . Do you have an uncle?

JACK: Yes.

S.M.: How old is he?

JACK: About fifty.

S.M.: How tall is he?

JACK: Oh, about five feet eleven.

S.M.: Do you think you see Vershinin and his family in your mind the way you are seeing your uncle now? This is what must happen when you say "No, at most forty or forty-five," about Vershinin.

JACK: Yes, I understand, but it's not easy.

S.M.: No, it is not. While you are talking about him, never lose your image. I do not see Vershinin's wife when you describe her, neither do I see his mother-in-law.

(Jack repeats Tusenbach's speech.)

Do not rush. It looks as if you want to be through with it, instead of working and unrolling your film of images for these three women.

ANNE (Masha): Mrs. Moore, I have a question

about inner monologue. When he describes the person, am I supposed to have other thoughts that may not be related to the person he describes?

s.m.: If you think that would be logical for the moment on stage, it is all right. If you are listening to him, then you should have thoughts and images related to what he says and what you hear. However, when you are trying to concentrate on the book, you may be thinking of what is disturbing you. Talk to all the sisters, Jack. Make sure your partners understand you and believe you.

Blocking depends very much on the relationships between people. For instance, Tusenbach is in love with Irina and wants to be near her. Please, Jack, continue to work. I like what you are doing.

Let us do the scene between Andrei and Ferapont. Jeff, I hope you wrote the biography of Andrei.

jeff: Yes, I did.*

s.m.: You must study the character's psychophysical behavior. If Andrei were a nasty man, you would have to build him differently. His behavior toward his sisters or his wife would not be the same. Let us see the scene.

(Scene)

Oh, Jeff, why do you interrupt all the time? I was so happy to see that you were able to concentrate for a moment, and here you are interrupting again.

jeff: Because I don't feel anything.

s.m.: What do you want to feel?

jeff: I don't become emotional.

s.m.: Haven't I said that you can only begin

* See Appendix 3.

now to learn how to stir your emotions? And Jeff, stop gesticulating continuously. Do not move your hands until you feel the current of energy flow from your spine into the tips of your fingers. You must study and choose your poses and gestures in the same way you choose your thoughts and images. Nothing can be accidental on stage except when the accidental action happens under inspiration. But inspiration will not come until you have done a great deal of conscious work. Please go on and do not interrupt. And you do not have to scream at Ferapont.

JEFF: But he's hard of hearing.

S.M.: That is true, but you give the impression that you are angry at him, and that is wrong. We are going to do this scene again, and Jeff, please, before Ferapont enters and also in every pause, say your inner monologue aloud. You see, we are trying to do what Chekhov did before he wrote the words for his characters. In novels we often encounter descriptions of people's thoughts. A playwright studies all about the character: his thoughts, his images, his whole inner world—but usually writes down only what the character says. We are trying to complete what the playwright left out. Please say your inner monologue aloud.

JEFF: You mean say what I am thinking?

(The scene proceeds.)

S.M.: You should go on thinking while you are looking at Ferapont, but instead you are sitting there dead. What do you think while you are looking at him, Jeff?

JEFF: I have my inner monologue.

S.M.: You know, not every inner monologue may be right. You may have to change it quite often, not only because I may suggest it, but because you yourself will be able to realize that something is wrong. Perhaps your objective must change, or the behavior of your partner is different from what you expected. And, of course, your body must be expressive of what is in your mind.

JEFF: A lot of times you get so tense, you cannot begin to think, and then the best thing to do is to sit back and relax your muscles.

s.M.: That is fine, but it also works the other way; if you are able to concentrate on an image or a thought, you will relax. What you were trying to do now, this shaking of your arms and hands, you can do only backstage. Then you go on stage and you are tense all over again. I do not mean to say that what you do is bad. I only want to say that you must learn to control your tension all the time during your work on stage, and relax the part of your body which is tense. Gradually, you will develop a "controller" to watch over this. When you work on Andrei and feel that your neck is stiff, relax it, right there on stage. And do not be afraid that this conscious control may interfere with your inspiration.

Some actors are unhappy when I say that they must do everything consciously on stage. They like to imagine themselves working subconsciously all the time. This is a great mistake, and one of the worst distortions of acting. On our bulletin board you can see what Salvini said about the double existence of an actor on stage. He said, "An actor cries and laughs, and at the same time watches his crying and laughing." An actor who does not know what he is doing is not acceptable on stage. Otherwise, there might be real murders on stage. Conscious control does not hurt an actor's performance. On the contrary, it is obligatory. That is why I want you to learn to control your behavior from the very beginning; it should gradually become habitual. The scientist Pavlov said, "Isn't it quite natural that while we are busy with something, especially a thought, we can at the same time do something else that is a habit with us?" Constantly watch whether you are using the work you have prepared at home. Do not let the images and inner monologue escape you. And another thing—do not listen to those who tell you that you must forget the audience. It is useless even to try. Moreover, Stanislavski calls the audience the "co-creator" of a performance. You depend on its reactions. That does not mean that you must "amuse" the spectators. And you must also have them in mind when you analyze and study your role at home. You must carefully select the behavior that will be most expressive of what you want the audience to understand. You are working for the audience, remember this.

JEFF: Mrs. Moore, in a performance, for instance, if I am making too many pauses and this is slowing down the action of the play, or if I am not establishing a strong enough relationship with Peter—should you think of these things consciously when you are on stage?

S.M.: Don't you think that is the only way to correct what is wrong?

JEFF: And what would he think? Would he think that I am slowing down, pausing between lines, and that I am not establishing a strong enough relationship with him, or would he continue to have his inner monologue for the character? Should this be done in rehearsal, and is it wrong to do it during a performance?

S.M.: Everything should be worked out at home and at rehearsal, and, you must endeavor to prevent such errors on stage. However, control over your behavior is obligatory, so that if such errors do happen you will be able to correct them quickly. If your partner is really an actor of the Stanislavski school, he may be able to help you while continuing his own inner monologue and without stepping out of character.

LIZ: I saw a professional actress come off stage and say, "That was a good show," and I had seen it and knew it was terrible. Did she think it was good because she was totally unaware of what was going on around her?

S.M.: Did she say she was good?

LIZ: She meant it, because she was so involved in herself that she did not know what was happening with the show and how the audience was reacting. Maybe she thought that she looked pretty.

S.M.: Sometimes it happens that even if you control your performance, you still do not know whether it was good or bad. I hope you understand that our final objective is to achieve on stage a state of subconscious creativity, which is inspiration. *This* is our goal, rather than the conscious work. But conscious work is the means which prepares the most favorable ground for possible inspiration. It was while watching geniuses that Stanislavski realized it was possible to stir the subconscious mechanism of emotions intentionally, though this inner mechanism is not under our control. And he made it his objective to disclose the secret of those geniuses. But not even they can always depend on inspiration. And that is why no serious worker of the theatre can bypass the Stanislavski System. Stanislavski gives capable actors the possibility of being in the state which only some geniuses achieve, and he gives geniuses control over their talent. Even the greatest talent will gradually fade without technique to control it. Let us go on with the scene.

(Scene)

Jeff, every time you do this scene, it is always an accident. Your thoughts are different every time. I would not mind if they improved, but at best they are primitive, and mostly they are wrong. When you said you wanted to be a professor at Moscow University, I did not believe you because this professorship did not seem to mean anything to you. You are having difficulty because you are not writing down your inner monologue as I asked you to. There is nothing concrete for you to correct and improve. You must work at home and find what is as important to you as this professorship is to Andrei. All I can do is point the way. You must do the work.

class 6

SONIA MOORE: Let us perform a group exercise—something we have not done yet. Sally, come here behind everyone.... All of you sit as you are; don't turn around. You will have to guess by the sound what Sally is doing. All right, let us begin....

LIZ: She is erasing something.

S.M.: No. Do it again, Sally. What is she doing? Your effort to understand the sound is important.

ALBERT: She is dusting the table—with a cloth—

S.M.: That is right. Come here, Jack, and take Sally's place. I want you all to guess what he is doing....

MEG: Isn't he taking a Kleenex out of a box?

S.M.: Yes, very good.

(The exercise continues.)

Now we shall perform the will and memory exercises again. The first person says a word; the next repeats that word and adds his own, and so on. Only nouns, please, because they are easier to remember. [See page 48.]

(The exercise is repeated several times, always with new words.)

EVAN: It's very hard.

S.M.: This is preparation of your instrument. Musicians have their instruments—pianos, violins, and so on—but you have only yourself. It is your voice, your emotions, your memory, your feelings, your body that you must learn to control.

And now a "sense-memory" exercise. You will "thread a needle." You must "see" what you are doing; concentrate on it; feel the objects you imagine; know their weight. This is an especially useful exercise because it teaches you to be concrete in your actions. All right, Jean.

(Exercise)

Your actions must be so truthful that we in the audience really believe that you are threading a needle. I want you all to criticize each other. You know, when I thread a needle, first I have to take out the box, find the needle and thread. But when you do it, everything seems to be right under your hand! The sense-memory exercises teach you to be concrete and train your imagination, concentration, measure of truth, relaxation, tempo-rhythm—all the elements of a truthful action. Since you know that every action will be different in different circumstances, I want you to build the circumstances in these exercises, too. For instance, if you are a tailor and sew all day long, your action of threading the needle will be different from doing it as if you were dressing for a party and a button fell off your shirt. The important thing is to fulfill a *simple purposeful action in the given circumstances*, and you had better learn to do it from the beginning. . . .

(Exercise)

Now, an improvisation—you are "preparing to go to a reception." It is important for you to be there on time. In building the situation see *real* people you know in life, whom you expect to meet there. Unless you have concrete images, your work will be vague. While you are getting ready to leave, you find a note under the door—that is all I am going to tell you now. I will put a real note there. Do not think about it until you read it. Then think what you did when you experienced an analogous emotion in life, or what you would do.

JACK: There will be something written on the note?

S.M.: Yes. And you must make a decision after you have read it. It is important for you to be at the reception, and you must know why it is important.

JEFF: You want us to mime the work?

S.M.: What do you mean by "mime"?

JEFF: I mean do you want us to do this without props?

S.M.: No, this is an improvisation. I have asked you to always use props except in the sense-memory exercises. Sense-memory exercises teach you to be so thoroughly concrete that we will be able to see objects that don't exist. But in all the other exercises and improvisations, if you do not use real objects your actions are vague and you destroy the concreteness we are trying to learn.

JACK: What I meant is that I wanted to put in my contact lenses, which is the last thing I do before I go out. Do you want me to do that?

S.M.: No, I do not want you to do it!

(*laughter*). . . . Don't think *how* you are going to do the improvisation before you have built the circumstances. The way you dress would depend on where you were going and whom you were expecting to meet; think whether it is an influential agent, or maybe a producer. Concentrate. Go on stage as soon as you are ready. When you are on stage, begin to think what you would do if this were happening in life. And do not tell us afterward what you were doing! We must understand this from your actions. Now, after you read the note, do not tell anyone else what it says.* Go on.

(*Improvisation by Michael*)

That was good, Michael. The note obviously disturbed you, and your rushing out with your tie still undone was very expressive. You know, little by little you begin behaving on stage like normal human beings. Almost everyone has some extra skins that must be shed. You are beginning to look like your own selves. The System helps you to reach the core of your own personality. Only when you reach yourself will you be able to build other people. Did you see real people in your mind? Good. Who is next? Put the note back where it was there on the floor. Thank you.

(*Evan performs the improvisation.*)

Stop. You are not concentrating.

EVAN: I know.

S.M.: If you had made an effort to see real people and real places, you would have been

---

* The note read: "Your best friend has been in a serious auto accident, and is at Roosevelt Hospital. Hurry."

concentrating, and you would not have laughed. You must learn to concentrate on the inner objects and find the right physical actions. Who is next?

(Improvisation)

Mary, you did not seem interested in what you read in the note. And why did you take your book along with you?

MARY: Well, I take this book everywhere with me.

S.M.: Well, carrying a book does not help to project that you are going to a reception. Only actions that help to express the situation are artistic; the rest only confuse the audience. They say Stanislavski once asked Rachmaninoff what accounted for the mastership of a pianist, and Rachmaninoff answered, "Not touching the neighboring key." And the actor's mastership is in not using anything beyond what is strictly necessary.

(Improvisation by Sally)

Sally, you too just walked out without giving a thought to what you read in the note. Your tempo-rhythm did not change at all. In life the slightest change of circumstances changes the objectives, and it stirs a different tempo-rhythm. After reading such news in life you would stop and decide what to do. I would like to see it again, please.

(Sally repeats the improvisation.)

Now that was much better.

SALLY: Not good enough.

S.M.: Right. You should have taken a little more time to evaluate what has happened and decide what to do, even if the decision had to be a quick one.

Let us work on *The Three Sisters* now. All I want you to do is consciously watch whether you are using the images while you are speaking and using the inner monologue between your own lines and while others speak, and whether you are making an effort to overcome the resistance of your body that must express the inner processes in your mind when you are silent. And you must know why you are saying your lines so that you can project the subtext—the meaning. Watch *what* you are doing, not *how* you do it. Let us see the scene between Andrei and Ferapont.

(Scene)

Well, this is surprising progress for both of you.

JEFF: In the beginning I did not have the inner monologue.

S.M.: Right, but I am happy because I saw a real effort to concentrate on inner objects. By the way, Michael, "bliny" means pancakes, and they are delicious.... Jeff, what are your thoughts when Ferapont talks about the rope being stretched across Moscow?

JEFF: May I explain something about my inner monologue?

S.M.: Of course.

JEFF: When Ferapont talks about the rope, I hear him for the first time, and I am trying to understand and follow what he says—this is what I'm thinking.

S.M.: Good. And yet, Ferapont's story about the rope would amuse Andrei. Well, give it a thought. Oh yes, your yawning at the end came as a surprise. I wouldn't do it. It is true that I have seen people yawn when they were nervous, but I have never seen Russians do this *(laughter)*. The most important thing is that you were able to use the inner work and you have made good progress with your body. Did you feel that the correct movement of the body involves the inner processes? I think that you were able to see a great many images. Is that true?

JEFF: I think that I have started to be able to.

S.M.: Now, Mary, did you finally write a biography of Masha?

MARY: No.

S.M.: You must do it. And Sally, did you work on your images and inner monologue? I mean with pencil and paper?

SALLY: I did it in my mind.

S.M.: That's no good at all. It is impossible for me to convince you at this point how right Stanislavski is. No lecturing will prove this. Only using the rules Stanislavski gave us will prove what it does for you. When you have assimilated the use of inner monologue and images, you will know what happens to you. And the biography is not my caprice. You must know a great deal about the character to express its essence. Since you did not do the work I asked you to, we shall move on to the scene between Tusenbach and Soliony.

(Scene from Act Two of The Three Sisters— *Evan as Tusenbach, Jack as Soliony)*

S.M. *(interrupting)*: It is not interesting to see you sitting there, Evan. You do not have any inner monologue at all. You were trying to improvise something right here. This is not the way we learn the technique. You must write it down at home. Here you should use what you have prepared at home.

EVAN: I am tired of sitting all the time. I feel like moving around.

S.M.: I do not mind if you move, if there is a

reason for it. But don't tell me that you feel like moving. You must do what is logical and right. Really, I would prefer to see a tiny bit of the scene with all the necessary thorough work than the whole scene with so little work done.

(The scene continues.)

Tusenbach, when you come in, please mumble your inner monologue. You know, this is the only time mumbling is allowed in this studio! . . . Every time there is a pause, say your inner monologue in a low voice. Sometimes when I ask the actors to do this, all the pauses disappear. . . .

EVAN: But how can I have an inner monologue and talk at the same time?

S.M.: You must not have an inner monologue while you are speaking. When you speak, you should know why you are saying the words. You must project the meaning of the words, the *subtext*, and you must see the images. You have the inner monologue during pauses in your own lines, when other people speak on stage. Wasn't that clear? Oh, Evan, when you say "Let's drink," and you clink glasses, why don't you drink then?

EVAN: I would like to know more about how Tusenbach feels about Soliony. I am not sure what kind of a man Tusenbach is.

S.M.: Tusenbach is a very good man. He sees good even in Soliony. But don't you think you should read the play again and find out for yourself?

EVAN: I was ready to scream at him.

S.M.: *You* might scream, but Tusenbach would not. Tusenbach is always in good spirits, and he radiates goodness. Yes, in order to give Soliony a justification for saying, "Don't be angry, Aleko," you must react in a psychophysical way to what he has said. But Tusenbach is not angry; Soliony just annoys him.

(Evan tries the scene.)

That is good. This slight movement is enough to justify Soliony's words. And you, Soliony—from the moment you start talking about yourself, there should be a total change in your behavior. Soliony has never talked this way before; it is a sort of confession for him.

EVAN: Is Tusenbach really happy to go to work?

S.M.: Yes, he is honest in his desire to work. Soliony, when you begin to talk about yourself, your body does not express the effort you are making. Remember the psychophysical process? Think of the pose your body would take when you change your behavior. Move your torso before you begin to speak truthfully of yourself. An action begins with the body, the torso, and ends with it. The verbal action depends on the physical action.

class 7

SONIA MOORE: Listen carefully to the numbers I give: Your neck is number one; shoulder, number two; arms, three; torso, four; hands, five; legs, six; feet, seven ... *relax* number seven; relax number one; relax number three; relax number six; relax number four.... This exercise also helps to develop your concentration.

Now we will test your powers of observation. Each of you please put one personal object under this tablecloth. No one must see what it is. Then you will have to guess to whom the objects belong, trying to guess what is characteristic for each person. All right, take off the cloth.

STUDENTS *(talking all at once)*: Oh, this ring must be yours. This is Mary's watch; no, Liz's. No, the brush is hers. I think the brush is Nina's. The wallet belongs to Joe, and there is even a check inside it.

S.M.: Don't acknowledge what is yours. I want to have everyone's opinion.

STUDENTS: The lipstick is Mrs. Moore's. No, I think the pen is hers. I am sure the lipstick belongs to Nina because I've seen her using it.... I think the watch is Meg's and the pen is Liz's. I think the compact must be yours.

S.M.: And whose watch is this?

STUDENTS: I think it's Jean's.... Yes. Shall I tell which is mine?

S.M.: Don't, if you want to prolong the exercise....

Well, that is enough, and now, Evan, you must name all the red objects in this room in the time it takes me to count to ten. Peter, don't look around, because you will have to name objects of another color.

EVAN: Your sweater, this bench, letters on the studio plaque on the wall....

S.M.: Will someone please count how many objects are called out while I count to ten?... Albert, name the beige objects.

ALBERT: Picture frame, Sally's stockings, part of Liz's dress....

S.M.: That is enough. Evan and Sally, come on stage. You are at the opera together. Think of real tunes. Try to see images of a specific opera. Ken, come here. You are at the same opera, but you are alone. You happen to see Sally's face, and you are trying to remember where you could possibly have met her. While trying to remember, you must see real places, real people you know in life, parties you have attended.

KEN: While the opera is going on?

S.M.: That is right. While you are trying to remember where you could possibly have met her, you are unable to concentrate on the performance, and you are disturbing Evan and Sally by looking at Sally. You two, decide on the situation: who you are to each other—you may be engaged, you may be husband and wife.... I'm sure that your reaction to Ken will depend on what you are to each other, too. React to the person who disturbs you in the opera as you would in real life.

> *(Improvisation. Sally and Evan take seats side by side, glance at their programs, "listen." Ken sits near Sally, looks at her, evidently in the hope that she will look at him; he drops his program to gain attention. Evan and Sally, pretending not to notice him, change places....)*

EVAN: May I say something? I couldn't keep a straight face during what Ken was trying to do. I just felt like, oh, he's giving Sally a dirty look. When I looked at Sally, I started to laugh, too, and as a result I did not work enough.

S.M.: That is because your concentration is still weak. It is not easy to concentrate on inner objects. When you learn to do this, nothing will disturb you or divert your attention. Your mind will gradually become more and more ready for such work. We are sort of massaging our brains to prepare them....

You cannot imagine how many actions, thoughts, and images you will have to keep in your mind. It will become easier and easier as you have more control over your body. The slightest correctly selected movement of the body stirs thoughts and images which have dictated such movement. And when your psychophysical apparatus is involved, you will not have to worry about what to do with your hands because you will behave naturally. You have already learned something. Every day we see some improvement.

One more improvisation. You are "looking over an apartment that you want to rent." You may need an apartment for different reasons. You probably have looked for an apartment; if you have not, use the "magic if." Do not think about how to do it until you know why you want the apartment. Are you getting married, or have you quarreled with your parents or your roommate? The situation will dictate your actions. Is anyone ready? . . . Albert, go on.

(Improvisation)

s.m.: *(whispering to Michael):* Are you ready? Then go into the same apartment while Albert is in there looking it over.

(Albert and Michael are on stage looking over the apartment.)

Albert, you should know better than to make faces. If you had really thought and your body had expressed it, we would understand whether you liked the apartment or not without your making faces. You know, Michael came on stage and walked around for a while, and you behaved as if he did not exist. It was as if Michael were a ghost. I assure you that if you were really looking over an apartment, and someone else came in who wanted it, you would behave in a different way. If I had liked the apartment, I would have tried to guess what the other person thought of it. But you didn't even see him. Who else is ready?

(Other students perform the improvisation.)

I cannot succeed in keeping two people on stage. As soon as someone else comes on, the first person disappears! I want two or three people together, so please don't run away. You must learn to be aware of other people. Stay for a while, then make up your mind about the apartment, and leave.

(*The improvisation continues.*)

That is enough. Let us perform an improvisation about the characters in *The Three Sisters*. All in their rooms, washing, and then having breakfast in the dining room.

(*Improvisation, all together*)

Now, let us work on the beginning of *The Three Sisters*. Please, no cheating. Do not speak until your body expresses what is in your mind and brings you into the words.

(*Liz and Sally begin the scene.*)

Olga, don't turn to Masha, who is not there. Speak to one of us. Go on now, and see that you use the images you have prepared at home. Do you understand what a strong will you must have in order to be able to discard your own thoughts and replace them with those of the character? Let us do the scene.

(*Scene*)

LIZ: Is it all right to see a person in mourning when I speak to Irina?

S.M.: If you did not look at Irina, it might be all right. But what you did is wrong. You must see Sally, who is our Irina. It is terrible to try to see someone else instead of the person who is in front of you. It is obligatory to *see* the actor who is performing with you, but to *treat* him as the character in the play. You do not have to look at her when you talk about her white dress, because she is your sister and you have seen her all morning. You can look at her afterward to admire her again, and then you see that her face is beaming. I hope that you have it straight that you may have images of people who do not appear *on* stage, but with a partner you must see *only* him or her. When you work at home, you can see a real person in your mind and find the typical actions that express your feelings. On stage, use those same actions to project your attitude toward your stage partner. I must emphasize this because I know that some of our actors do try to see people other than those with whom they are performing. Do you have any questions?

ALBERT: No, I don't, but I have a general awe of everything.

s.m.: Don't expect too much from yourselves. It is impossible to do everything perfectly all at once. All I want now is your effort. Work at home selecting the images and thoughts.

JACK: You know, I had to change my image because the girl I used for Natasha was better than I wanted.

s.m.: You see, it is good that you know that you must change it.

(Scene)

Your images are pale, Olga.

LIZ: I swear I saw them.

s.m.: I am sure you did, but now I am not satisfied with only seeing them. You must paint them so that your sisters will also see them.

ANNE: Don't you think that Masha is interested only for a moment in what Tusenbach says, and then she goes back to her book?

s.m.: Yes, you are right. And Olga, too, listens only for a while and then continues correcting her papers. Irina is the one who is listening attentively to the baron. Now your face becomes really radiant, Sally. But still you must change your inner monologue somewhat. The audience must see at the start that you are daydreaming. Your face becomes radiant only during Olga's speech. Why don't you try to use the same thoughts at the very beginning? And you do not have to *tell* your sisters that your brother "will probably be a professor." They know this. You are dreaming aloud.

Before we go on to Tusenbach's entrance, I want to see this scene again, with Nina as Irina.

(Scene)

Nina, you look tortured. Remember that you *want* to stand there. Nobody ordered you to.

NINA: I can't think of anything.

S.M.: Did you try to write down your inner monologue?

NINA: Yes, but I am unable to change it more.

S.M.: You must try harder.

NINA: I've already changed it several times.

S.M.: Change it again. This is the normal process. I am delighted that you know that you have to do this. You are trying to create the inner world of a person, and it is serious work. Now Tusenbach's entrance.

(Scene)

It looked very good, Michael. If you work honestly, your instrument develops; every time it will be better, and your role will grow. What you are doing, Michael, is very good.

MICHAEL: I don't think so.

S.M.: You don't think so—that is good. There is always room for improvement.

MICHAEL: I do see images, and I do think.

S.M.: You are doing beautiful work, and it will grow because it is honest work. Now you already have something to depend on.

MARY: Mrs. Moore, as I told you, I may have to

leave the Studio in February. Will I have learned by then how to build a character? Or will you start working on building the character next semester? You know, I would like to be a director....

s.m.: We have already started the work on building the character. Purposeful actions, images, and inner monologue are essential steps in the process. But, of course, you will not have learned to build the character by February. And you will not have learned it by February of the next year, either. You will learn a great deal, but there will be much more.

MARY: After this term, I mean after the sixteen weeks, is there anything new to learn?

s.m.: Yes. There will be something new all the time.

MARY: Then if I leave I will not learn it all.

s.m.: Do you expect to learn your profession in sixteen weeks? How about learning it in four years? In the United States, acting is not always a profession. Almost anyone can audition and sometimes be cast in a leading role if he or she looks "right" to the producer and the director. It is almost as ridiculous as engaging a violinist because he looks the part. And there are always foreign actors to help out.

MARY: Oh, that's terribly discouraging.

s.m.: After sixteen weeks you will understand many things, and I hope that you will have assimilated some of the technique. I am sure that it is obvious to you that after sixteen weeks of studying dance, you would not be able to dance a solo....

Let us see the scene between Andrei and Ferapont.

JEFF: Ferapont is not here.

s.m.: Who will help us out?

MARY: I will.

s.m.: You as Ferapont? Fine! Let us hurry up. *(Scene)*

Oh, Mary, that was just awful. You could throw off anybody.

MARY: Yes, I know.

s.m.: The awful thing was that you tried to *be* an old man. I thought I had made it clear how complex the process of building a character is, and you want to become the character the first time you read this part. It is a miracle that Jack didn't smile once. That shows how concentrated he was.

MARY: I didn't know that you wanted me just to read it.

s.m.: Oh, come! You know I did not expect you to be reincarnated as Ferapont on the spot. ... Jack, there was a big pause before you said, "I don't drink, I don't like saloons." It was dead. If you do have a pause, you should fill it in. Why do you think Andrei starts talking about bars and drinking?

JACK: I thought that when he talks about the sisters he feels ashamed and maybe wants to get drunk.

s.m.: Yes, but then why do you have such a long pause? Andrei may also think of how lonely he is in his house, and that may make him think of Moscow. Then you could have the pause, but fill it with an inner monologue and images expressed by your body that will logically bring you to your lines.

Let us have the same scene again.

JEFF: Could Mary read Ferapont's lines slower? She is reading so fast I do not have time for all my inner monologue. *(Laughter)*

s.m.: Mary, speak slower.

(Jeff and Mary perform the scene.)
You are trying hard, Jeff, and I like it.

Now I would like to see the opening scene of *The Three Sisters* with Meg as Olga.

(Scene)
I think it was very good in the beginning. Did you see images?

MEG: Oh, yes.

S.M.: Honestly?

MEG: Yes.

S.M.: It's very good, but there are some empty moments when you stop talking. Your body, the torso, must continue to express what is in your mind after you stop speaking. But perhaps your inner monologue is wrong and you must check it. It looks wrong.

MEG: That is where I get confused.

S.M.: When Irina speaks, your thoughts in reaction to her must be changed. However, I think that you have done very good work in a short time. Make sure that you truly see images; do not try to cheat me, because it is you who will be cheated.

Tusenbach, you seem to labor with your images.

ALBERT: This is the first time that they came so easily.

S.M.: Well, good. I don't mind your laboring at this stage. When the resistance of your body has been conquered, you will not have to labor over the images. A correctly chosen logical movement of the body will stir the images and thoughts.

class 8

SONIA MOORE: Today we shall perform an improvisation with music. We'll play a record—Beethoven's First Symphony. You are all on the beach of a fishermen's village. There has been a terrible storm during the night. Dawn is breaking now, and you are waiting for—your husband, brother, father, son, friend? Think also of your relationship to those who are on the beach with you. Listen to the music and use it as the circumstances. This is an improvisation for everyone together. Watch your blocking. Do not block others, and see that you are not blocked.

(Improvisation)

It is early morning; you have been waiting on the beach for hours. . . .

All right, thank you. You could have used the music in a more effective way. I purposely played it soft and then loud, but only Peter paid attention to this—he ran forward and started waving, as if he heard voices. Liz, you were so busy being "sad" that when you sat next to Sally you didn't notice that she was crying. You did not pay any attention even when she asked you for a tissue. This proves that we still do not quite know what it is to react to the world around us as we would in life.

And now you will prepare a room in the house where you work as a housekeeper. Your employers are expecting guests. You may not have worked as a housekeeper, but you may have had to do something for someone you disliked. Think of the physical state. Think of an analogous emotion. The situation does not have to be the same. Are you ready, Jean? Go on. . . .

(Jean performs the improvisation.)

That was good, Jean, but did you see real people whom you work for? I want you to make sure of this in every improvisation. Maybe these people's children are always leaving the room dirty, and you constantly have to clean up after them. When the Moscow Art Theatre was here, their director came to see our work, and later he said to me, "Sonia, please continue to concentrate on simple actions in concrete circumstances." And he also said, "I know that you are doing the right thing, because your students' eyes are alive." If you fulfill an action without using the circumstances, it has no meaning. If your physical actions have been selected thoroughly to disclose the circumstances you have built, you will not have failed to see the images. In this improvisation, if you like the people you work for, your cleaning will be different than if you hate them. It will be different if these people have parties all the time and you are tired. You will do it in a different way if you have decided to quit working for them. *How* you do it will make the audience understand what is taking place on stage.

(Liz performs the improvisation.)

S.M. *(to the other students)*: What did you understand?

NINA: When she looked at those shoes, I thought they were some other woman's, and when she looked at the bottle, I thought she wanted to finish it, but it was not clear.

S.M.: That's right. There was a hint of that, but not enough to project it clearly. Liz, did you like the family you worked for?

LIZ: I was hired to clean a bachelor's apartment, and it was a mess, and I saw that pair of woman's shoes.

S.M.: That is an interesting story, but remember that, whatever situation you have built in your mind, your audience must understand it. In life, seeing those shoes, you would express your attitude spontaneously, but on stage you must consciously find the external form that will express it. You must use your body. And don't be afraid that it will be an "indication." If you fulfill the psychophysical action, it is never an "indication." These improvisations force you to think logically and thus you also develop your imagination. Without a fertile imagination, your work on stage is impossible.

Next, clean your *own* room. Your action is the same but in different circumstances. Select logical physical actions. . . .

Now you are "packing." Where are you going? Why are you going? Are you going alone? Are you packing at home? In a hotel? Build all the details you can imagine and then find characteristic actions of packing to reveal the situation to us. In a play,

your role is not ready until you know what you are
doing and why you are doing it at every moment on
stage.

(*Mary performs the improvisation.*)

I would like to understand what you were doing.
What was there near the window?

MARY: A painting. I had to leave right away,
and I wanted to say something to my friend, and she
was not there.

S.M.: What does all this have to do with
packing?

MARY: I was leaving this place, and I wanted to
bring in the circumstances.

S.M.: I am trying to understand your way of
thinking. You seem to have a conviction that
whatever you do on stage, people will enjoy it. But it
just does not happen this way. And why on earth did
you lie down on the floor?

MARY: Maybe I just associated lying on the
carpet and looking at the painting with this whole
place.

S.M.: But your actions were a total mystery to
us. None of us understood what was going on. What
you did only cluttered the situation and confused us.

MARY: I just didn't know how to get the
relationship to the apartment. I didn't know how to
relate the things to the packing.

S.M.: I think I understand from what you are
saying that you did not want to part with the
painting. You must make an effort to find physical
actions that would project this. What you thought
up is very good. Your imagination is good. But you
are not convinced that you have to make all this clear
to the audience.

MARY: Yes, I am convinced. I was looking for the means to express what I thought up, and I didn't know how to find these means. I didn't take enough time to bring it all out. I was thinking of music and of some of my friend's things which might be among the clothes. Just too many things, and they didn't coordinate.

S.M.: As you know, I am fighting here the nonsense about "Never mind the audience—it is what I feel that's important." What you are doing may be some kind of psychotherapy, but it is not Stanislavski.

MARY: I failed because I was not concentrating on specific actions.

S.M.: Right. The choice of typical physical actions is difficult, but you can learn if you make the effort....

Something else before we work on the scenes. Come into the room; stand on the chair; go down on your knees; and run out.

ALBERT: We enter the room.... Why?

S.M.: That is up to you to decide.

ALBERT: You mean we have to find the reason?

S.M.: What is the matter with you? You look as if you are hearing for the first time that you must have the circumstances and the objective. Build your circumstances, justify every movement, and make sense of it.

PETER: We go down on our knees on the chair or on the floor?

S.M.: On the floor. Are you ready? ... Go on. *(Anne performs the improvisation.)* What were you doing? I did not understand.

ANNE: I was looking in the mirror.

S.M.: I understood that, but after that you seemed to be praying.

PETER: Yes, she was—weren't you? I thought she was going somewhere important.

S.M.: Were you going to your wedding?

ANNE: Well, I was going somewhere that was important to me and that could change my whole life. I wanted to make sure that everything would be all right, and so I prayed.

S.M.: I understood that you were looking in the mirror and that you were praying, but I didn't understand why. It could have been more specific. The problem is to find expressive actions.

(Jean performs the improvisation.)
What was it? A mouse?

JEAN: Yes.

S.M.: I don't believe that you would do in life what you did just now. You would probably run away or get something to hit it with. You don't go down on your knees when you see a mouse. . . .

And now a sense-memory exercise, which, of course, is done without objects. We will "carry a full pail of water" across the room. You must see the pail in your mind, feel its weight, handle it so truthfully that we will see it too.

(Jeff carries an imaginary pail of water.)

S.M. *(to the other students)*: Are you satisfied? *(No answer.)* Well, I am not. I do not think it was full at all.

JEFF: It was half full.

S.M.: Then do it again with a full pail *(laughter)*. . . . That is much better. Were you carrying water to help put out a fire? Or was it for the operating room of a hospital? You must learn to build interesting situations; you must have an objective and overcome obstacles on the way to it.

JEFF: How do I project that I am carrying this pail across the room to wash the floor, say, or something? ...

S.M.: Couldn't you, for instance, sweep the floor first or pour water on it? This would help us to understand what you wanted to do. You must choose actions that will disclose what is taking place on stage. Why were you standing there with the pail?

JEFF: I misunderstood.

S.M.: Every improvisation should help you to learn to fulfill a simple action in concrete circumstances. The circumstances influence the actions. This is the central point of your study: Number one, a psychophysical action makes the situation in a play clear to the audience at every moment; number two, a purposeful action will involve your inner experience if it is truthfully fulfilled, with the same concentration necessary in life, with the right relaxation, in the right tempo-rhythm. For example, you know that there is a child in a house on fire, and you are bringing the pail of water to help extinguish the fire to save the baby. If your physical actions are truthful to the circumstances, you may involve your emotions, even in this sense-memory exercise. We are trying to learn to do consciously what we do spontaneously in life. A spontaneous state is the creative state on stage. This is how important it is to learn to fulfill a simple physical action in given circumstances. And number three, you build the character with actions. If, for instance, you see a fire and don't care, your actions will project a certain kind of person; and on the other hand, if you see the fire and rush to help, you project another kind. If you throw things around, you project one character; if you are neat, you project another. Actions are for actors what paint is for painters.

I think I have made it clear why even in sense-memory exercises I want you to build the circumstances. . . . And I warn you again, you cannot neglect physical training. No matter how well your psychological instrument is trained, this is only half of your preparation. By now, you know how much the body resists you onstage. Your voice, speech, and body must be under your control.

Let us do an improvisation on the characters in *The Three Sisters*. Everyone is in his own room: Andrei, Ferapont, Olga, Masha, Irina, Tusenbach, Soliony, Anfissa. Try to think what you do as the character in situations that are not in the play. Meg, you started working on Anfissa. Think about how Anfissa, the nurse, who is trying all the time not to show how old and weak she is, would behave when she was alone.

MEG: In a production there is makeup. Here there is nothing to help.

S.M.: That is true. . . . You should watch old people in life. Observe what happens to their legs, the way their knees are bent, the way they bend their shoulders. And try this here, in this role.

MEG: Could I speak with an accent?

S.M.: Why? This play is performed in English, and no accent is necessary. Go on with the improvisation.

(Improvisation)

Jeff, think harder, what does Andrei like to do? He has many interests. All you did was read a book. Remember, the play makes it clear that he also plays the violin and carves picture frames. The role is ready when you can improvise as the character in different circumstances. When you know his desires, how he eats, drinks, dresses—his everyday behavior—then the character becomes a live person.

Now I would like to see the scene between Andrei and Ferapont.

JACK: I did not work at all.

S.M.: I hate to hear this. Everyone must bring work done at home to every class. This is the only way you can progress. I do not like to see a scene that has not been worked on. This will be an exception.

(Scene)

You have many empty pauses, Jack. If you pause, it is because Andrei is .thinking of something. So each time you stop, please, say your inner monologue aloud.

JACK: I stopped because I was trying to get the image in my mind.

S.M.: In that case, I am ready to be patient at this stage of your studies and wait until you "catch" it! You don't have to rush. If you move your body logically expressing your attitude to the image that you are trying to "catch," you will achieve it more easily. But it is the logical movement that is important, not just moving because I insist on moving your body. When your body obeys, the images, the thoughts will flash through your mind as they do in real life. Unfortunately, actors like pauses. A pause keeps them on stage longer. They do not realize that in dead pauses *they* are dead—they do not exist on stage.

JACK: May I work at home and not do it again now?

S.M.: That is a good idea. I hoped you would

suggest it. Let us do the same scene with Jeff as Andrei.

JEFF: You know, I have finally written a detailed biography of Andrei.

s.m.: Well, I hope it made you study the play. If you build Andrei with a behavior which is wrong for him, you will have built an entirely wrong character.

(Scene)

Jeff, you are doing good work. Your leaning back in the chair, with your arm on the back, was very expressive. I am happy because you are really trying. In order not to hear Ferapont's story about "bliny," you must concentrate even more on your inner monologue, and I would suggest that you continue to lean back, so you are not so close to him. Jeff, Andrei talks because he has no one to talk to. He is saying his inner monologue aloud. He does not cry yet. You make Andrei into a little boy. You have your inner monologue and your images, but they are not yet quite what they should be. Also, you go through a stage when you exaggerate your inner monologue. It does not have to be that long. But this is a normal stage in our work. Sometimes only a word is enough, or a short sentence, which brings you logically to your next words. Revise this too.

Let us hear Olga's speech.

(Scene)

You too, Olga—between the time when you said, "You are already wearing a white dress," and the next line, "Your face glows," your inner monologue was like a long speech.

LIZ: I know.

s.m.: Don't worry, you will learn to make the inner monologue just the right length. Sally, your

images must be changed again. You are still looking
uncomfortable and unhappy. And Mary, I would
give another penny for your thoughts when Olga
said to you, "Don't whistle, Masha." Your look was
totally blank. And Liz, it seems to me that you have
not worked at all since last time. It was truly
beautiful then, and now most of it has disappeared.
When you hear the clock striking, it brings back
memories of last year. Your action changes, and you
must change your pose. And it is not a funeral. You
are dragging it out, and, believe me, the spectators
would fall asleep. Everyone is in a good mood; only
Masha is bored. But even Masha may smile. You can
find a justification for her smiling once or twice. I am
sure that Masha would smile when Olga scolded her.
Olga, when you looked out the window and said that
the birches haven't any leaves yet, you looked and
looked as if you had to make sure. But Olga knows
this. She goes outside every day. It looked terribly
overdone. For Olga everything in Moscow is
wonderful, and everything here is bad. You even
pretended to be surprised when you looked out the
window. What are you thinking at this moment? Let
us do this moment again.

    (Scene)

That was much better. When Tusenbach says in the
dining room, "Of course, nonsense," Olga reacts as if
he had meant it as an answer to her "I wanted
passionately to go home." That makes her mood
worse, but only for a moment. Olga is good, and she
has great inner strength. Irina, what passes through
your mind after you say, "Why remember?" Irina
does not stop daydreaming even then. Be sure that
you use your body before you say it and after you have
said it.

class 9

SONIA MOORE: Ken, please go into the front room and close the door after you. (*Whispering.*) Let us make some changes here. Liz, take off your jacket and put it on the chair [etc.]. Ken, come back now. Look around carefully and tell us whether you notice any changes. This is not just a game. It is a way to develop your ability to observe. There is unlimited material for observation around us in life. What you register can be material for you to use.

KEN: Mary put on her coat. Didn't she put her coat on?

S.M.: No.

KEN: Evan was holding a book.

S.M.: He still is, Ken.

KEN: Albert is sitting on a pillow.

S.M.: He was sitting on that pillow all the time. Do you give up? But first try again to remember.... Don't you see that Liz and Sally exchanged chairs?

SALLY: And we put an ashtray on your chair.

S.M.: All right. Now you go, Meg....Anne, put this jacket on. No, don't put Meg's coat on. She would have to be blind not to notice this. Come back, Meg.

(Meg does not notice any changes.)

s.m.: Do you give up?

meg: Yes.

s.m.: Don't you see that Evan, sitting there next to you, has rolled his sleeves up? Both of them? *(Laughter.)*

meg: Oh, yes, and Anne put on this jacket.

s.m.: Right, and one more thing: Everyone is participating, so look at everybody. You see, I am trying to help you.

meg: Oh, there is a suitcase on this table. And you took off your bracelet.

s.m.: Good. Next, please.

(Everyone performs the exercise.)

Let us perform a sense-memory exercise, "to hang a picture." In this exercise without objects you also must build the circumstances—what kind of a picture it is, a Renoir, a Raphael, or a cheap reproduction.

(Michael performs the exercise.)

Was that the *Mona Lisa* or another famous painting that you stole from the Louvre?

michael: Yes, yes.

s.m.: You used a great deal of imagination. Everything you did was crystal clear. However, don't you think that your picture changed size every now and then? All right, who is next?

(Peter performs the exercise.)

What do you all think of that? Don't be afraid to criticize. You will all be criticized; it makes you observe and learn.

MEG: What was he pounding into the wall? It did not look like a nail.

PETER: No, it was a thumbtack (*laughter*).

S.M.: Can you hang a picture on a thumbtack? You see how we forget the simplest things on stage?

PETER: I didn't forget. Gouldn't it have been a long tack with a head which you had to screw in?

S.M.: All right, any other criticism?... Who is next? This is a very important exercise because it helps you to learn to fulfill an action thoroughly and concretely, using all the elements such as imagination, concentration, measure of truth, relaxation, and tempo-rhythm. This is what you must do in a role. Everything must be specific and expressive.

NINA: Let me tell you what has been happening to me since I have been doing these exercises. I notice the gestures I make while I am working. Even if I only pick up a book from the table I find myself analyzing. If I have to cross the room I feel as if I were performing right here in the Studio. I am very much aware of everything I am doing.

S.M.: That is very good.

NINA: Before, I would just walk across the room. Now I think (*laughter*).

S.M.: You will see how that will help you when you start to work on roles. Observing and studying yourselves and others is most important for your work....

Now you are "coming home after a day in a mine."... Yes, you have spent a whole day underground. Build the circumstances. There may be different reasons why you were in a mine. Where are you, in your home town, on a trip? Are you living alone? And so on. While working on an improvisation, never try to "act." Think of an analogous emotion. Think what you did or would do in such circumstances in life. Think hard about what you would do if you had been in a mine for eight hours. If you want your action to be truthful, include all its elements.

(Evan performs the improvisation.)

Evan, why were you looking at me every now and then? Obviously you were not concentrated on what you were doing.

EVAN: I have never been in a mine.

S.M.: But I am sure that you have done some heavy and dirty work at some time. Well, who is next?

(Several students perform the improvisation.)

What do you think was wrong with Liz's improvisation?

JACK: I thought she looked sad instead of tired. I think when one is tired, he is not sad, but has kind of a blank look.

S.M.: Liz, what you were doing was pretending to be sad. You must not try to be sad, but do what you do when you are sad. If you can remember your physical actions at a time when you were sad in life, they may stir the emotion of sadness in you now. We reach emotions through actions.

(More students perform the improvisation.)

What do you think was wrong with that?

MICHAEL: I did not see any difference in Meg walking toward the sink to wash and walking away afterward.

S.M.: I thought it was wrong that she walked into the house in those dirty overalls and then took them off and put them in the drawer. . . . Yes, that was funny. It was clear to us that those were the overalls you worked in. Maybe you were too tired to take them off before coming home. But you do not go to the table in dirty clothes, and you do not put them in the drawer or whatever it was under the table. Don't you think you might have taken them off outside? It was not believable. You would never behave this way in life. In addition, you touched the chair and the table several times with filthy hands, and only after that did you go wash them. . . .

Nina, your improvisation was very good—really good. Only I wish you would use props. Obviously I have not made it clear enough that the only exercises which we do without props are the sense-memory exercises. By being so vague in what you do, you destroy the concreteness we are trying to learn. Who is next?

(Improvisation by Michael)

You seemed to be wiping your hands on your shirt. You looked quite brisk, and then all of a sudden, you seemed tired and went outside for some reason.

MICHAEL: I went outside to brush off my clothes.

S.M.: Don't you think that you should have done that before you came in?

(Improvisation by Sally)

ALBERT: She looked as if she had just seen an accident in the street.

EVAN: We couldn't tell at all that she was in a mine.

SALLY: I saw a man killed in a mine.

S.M.: Was he a man you really know in life? You know that you must use images of people you really know in all the improvisations. . . .

This time we shall "burn a letter." What kind of letter is it? Who sent it to you? Why are you burning it? See real people in your mind. . . .

KEN: I don't believe we see images in life all the time. Now that I'm talking to you, I don't see any at all.

S.M.: If what you are saying were true, you would be dead. We really should trust Stanislavski, who studied human behavior for forty years. We are ordinarily unaware of these natural laws, but if you think about it, you will realize that this is what happens to us in life. Perhaps someday, you too will make an important discovery, but before you do, study what has already been discovered. Would you reject what has been discovered in any field and arbitrarily insist that you knew better?

(Improvisation by Mary)
What were you burning?

MARY: A letter from a close friend.

S.M.: Why were you reading that book before you burned the letter?

MARY: Well, I was trying to study for an examination.

S.M.: Mary, tell me what the reading of the book has to do with burning the letter?

MARY: Nothing, I guess.

S.M.: If you projected that you were trying to concentrate on the book in order not to think of the letter, that would be fine because you would be overcoming an obstacle. But actions that do not help to project what has to be projected only distract the audience's attention.

JEFF: Now I understand what you meant by saying that we must not have too many objectives.

S.M.: I beg your pardon? Did I say that?

(*Laughter.*) In a play we have the superobjective of the author, and all the actions—the *through line of actions*—must contribute gradually to disclosing it. Every action must have an objective or it stops being human behavior. The same thing on a smaller scale applies to an improvisation. How do the spectators understand the play? Through consecutive, logical, and expressive actions. If an action is not helpful, eliminate it. Keep only those which project what has to be projected. If you want to read the book because you have to study for an exam, it is perfectly all right, but we here must understand that you are unable to concentrate on the book *because* you are disturbed by the letter. Your superobjective is "to burn a letter."

JEFF: I thought at first that she was going to find the letter in the book.

NINA: You know, I thought that she was trying to be very cool and calmly sit there and read the book while the letter was burning. I thought she was trying to prove something to herself.

S.M.: Everyone here had a different idea of what you were doing.

EVAN: Her main action was reading the book, not burning the letter.

S.M.: Right. That is what came through. . . . Can you imagine what it means on stage to know how to choose the right actions? Anybody else ready?

(*Improvisation by Sally*)

What was that, Sally? Are you a spy?

SALLY: It was from a woman for whom I worked.

S.M.: It is very important that you yourself know all the circumstances, and they must be expressed. The people in the audience must not have to strain to understand what is taking place. Every action answers three questions: what, why, and how. The *how* will make the *what* and *why* clear to those who watch you. You must think of the *how*— adaptations. The *how* will depend on the circumstances, and that is why you must know all the details before you decide on the adaptations. You will burn the letter differently if it is from a lover than if it is an important document that is dangerous for you to keep. The richer your imagination, the richer your adaptations will be, and the more interesting your work will be. For the moment, I am happy if you are able to project in the simplest way what is taking place in the circumstances that you have built. But, as I have already told you, in the theatre not every truth is interesting. You know, the great actor Michael Chekhov wanted to be a writer before he became an actor. He wrote a story and showed it to his mother, who read it and said, "It is very truthful, but it is not interesting." (*Laughter.*) The more your imagination develops, the more demanding I shall become.

(*Improvisation by Meg*)
Why were you looking at the door?

MEG: I know that I was not getting it across. My lover was waiting for me, and this was a note from him. My husband and my children were in the other room.

S.M.: Your looking at the door was not convincing. I am sure that if this paper were something you weren't supposed to have, you would either close the door or at least make sure that no one was near. Would you really burn this if your husband and children were in the next room?

MEG: But you said that we must not indicate. I knew all the circumstances, but there was no way I could show them to you without indicating.

S.M.: You are wrong, you have to project those circumstances with physical actions, and the purposeful actions will never be indications if they are dictated by the circumstances.

(Improvisation by Ken)
And what did you burn?

KEN: I didn't know whether I was going to burn it or not.

S.M.: I assure you that in life you would not be sitting the way you did as if nothing in the world touched you. You must project the physical state.

KEN: I was just going to ask, isn't there a difference between the way you do something normally with nobody looking at you and the way you would do something if you were trying to show someone what you were doing?

S.M.: I have told you many times that in life we are often not aware of our exact behavior. This is what we are learning to become aware of. I am sure that, on the contrary, because you are alone in your room without anyone watching, you might have done a great deal that would have expressed your inner experience. I want you to make an effort to think either what you did in such a case if it happened to you in life, or what you would do if it should happen. I see that you are skeptical, but what I am telling you has been confirmed by such scientists as Pavlov and Sechenov. It is a fact that in life the whole complex inner world of a human being, every inner experience, is always expressed physically. On stage you must learn to find small, simple physical actions that will convey the turmoil inside you. If you find such physical actions and know how to fulfill them, they will also stir this inner turmoil. If you fulfill only the physical side of an action, it will be dead, and if you are interested only in the inner side, it will be equally dead. You are learning to involve your psychophysical apparatus. When you succeed, your whole nature will be involved: your senses, your memory, your will, your thoughts, your body. Then you behave on stage as a living human being. When you achieve such a state, you have created the best conditions for possible inspiration—the goal of the Stanislavski school of acting. The goal of the "method of physical actions" is to enable you to achieve involvement of your whole psychophysical apparatus.

KEN: Well, maybe in life you don't show expression. I know people like that.

S.M.: Take it for a rule, Ken—there always is some physical expression, even if it is only the movement of a finger or a slight movement of the head, or complete immobility.

KEN: That's what I mean. In life, you wouldn't do everything that Michael did. You could watch every movement someone made, and you wouldn't have the faintest idea what he was doing. But if you were doing it on stage, there would have to be more of it.

S.M.: If you mean that on stage it should be more interesting, and more expressive, you're right. I hope that you will start watching yourself in life, because it is difficult to convince you with words alone. I am certain that if you were alone while burning the letter, you would be doing much more than just sitting there with a blank expression in your eyes.

KEN: In my circumstances, I cannot show it to you.

s.m.: What do you mean, "show"?

KEN: Just because it's theatre, why do I have to walk around and make a lot of unnecessary movements to show you exactly what I'm doing when I'm not interested in showing anybody? (*Laughter.*) I am just sitting here and reading the letter, and I'm trying to decide whether I'm going to burn it or not, and I finally decide I'm going to burn it, and that's exactly——

s.m.: But nothing came through, Ken. You seem to be one of those actors who think that people should be content to see Ken sitting there for no reason at all, and they should applaud just for the "pleasure" of seeing you. Watch yourself in life, and the day may come when you will say that Stanislavski was right and you were wrong. I am afraid you are like those who say that they know Stanislavski backward and forward, or those who think they have gone beyond him, without really knowing what he teaches. So many people are satisfied with minimum knowledge and antiquated data about his work. Stanislavski verified everything thousands of times, experimenting with himself and with his students, and sought confirmation from scientists. Learn his technique, and only after you know what it does for you may you experiment further, because from nothing can come only nothing. The only reason for your being on stage is to make everything crystal clear to your audience, and if you do not, you will not satisfy them or your director.

KEN: The audience knows the circumstances, they know what has gone before.

S.M.: You will soon learn that there is often a great deal in a play that is more difficult to project than the reason why you are burning the letter. This is why we are preparing our imagination and our ability to choose and fulfill an action.

KEN: I'm not trying to argue with you, but it seems to me that it is absolutely impossible to make clear to the audience all the details of a situation.

S.M.: It may seem very difficult, but these demands will be useful to you later. I would be satisfied if I at least understood why you were burning the letter. You criticized Michael for a great many unnecessary movements. I disagree with you, and I see that there are others in the class who also disagree. Michael made it clear that he burned a letter that he didn't exactly enjoy reading.

KEN: Would he really act like this?

S.M.: I don't think everybody would, but Michael might.

MICHAEL: You don't know me! (*Laughter.*) If you would only see me burning a paper in my own room. . . .

KEN: If you were in your own room, you wouldn't have to be sitting there and trying to show . . . you would just burn the letter.

MICHAEL: I was trying to do what I remember I really did once.

S.M.: Well, let's leave it at that. Ken, you are fighting the necessity of fulfilling actions to project what you are doing. What comes across is. "No matter what I do, it should be interesting for the audience." Well, it is not interesting, Ken. . . . Stop worrying about "indications." If you have the inner side of your action, if you have an objective, and if you do not overdo the physical side, it will never be an indication. I remember in another class—I think you were there, Liz—a student did a great many interesting things, and I told him that it was indication from beginning to end. His movements and gestures were all mechanical. This was the other extreme. Maybe Michael overdid it in some moments—the physical expression must be as economical as possible—but he made a good effort. If you do not try to project what and why in these simple improvisations, you will have a great deal of trouble in your roles. As you must not move a chair or open a door without knowing why, where, and so on, neither can you be preoccupied with only the psychological side of an action. Your behavior will be dead in either case. The stage is not for the satisfaction of your own ego. You are here to learn to serve the play.

Now I would like to see the scene between Tusenbach and Soliony.

(Scene)

Please, Jack, do not try to impress us. Soliony is not funny, and no one laughs at him. He has an impenetrable face. Just use your inner monologue. Make sure that you are thinking as Soliony.

(The scene continues.)

There is not enough contact between you, and this is also proof that your inner monologues are not in reaction to each other. Soliony, immediately before you say, "When I am alone... ," you must have a transition, and you must move your body, the torso, to begin a new action and to express your inner monologue. Soliony suddenly becomes sincere and confides in Baron Tusenbach. Since your inner behavior has changed, your pose must be in accord with it. I would like to see the scene again.

JACK: I know what my inner monologue is at this moment, but obviously it doesn't come through.

(The scene starts again.)

S.M. *(interrupting as soon as Tusenbach—Jeff—enters after Soliony)*: Jack, did you hear Tusenbach's footsteps?

JACK: No.

S.M.: You must have heard them. I did.

JACK: I didn't hear because I was thinking.

S.M.: I was thinking, too. We are always thinking in life, but we still see and hear what happens around us.

JACK: I heard some movement.

S.M.: There must be a slight physical reaction. Otherwise, you seem deaf and dead. Soliony has become annoyed with Natasha and with himself, and has left the dining room and wants to be alone. But as soon as he sits down, someone comes in after him. His inner reaction to this must have a physical expression. On stage, actors are often paralyzed, and this is why you did not hear Tusenbach coming in. Jeff, your inner monologue is wrong, or there is no inner monologue at all when you sit near Jack. Your objective is not clear. You look as if you were telling Soliony, "Well, go ahead with your lines, so I can say mine."

JEFF: I'm thinking that he is a strange fellow. Should I change it?

S.M.: It does not come through. Your inner monologue must logically bring you to your words. And Jack, I never know why you say, "I am strange, and who is not strange?" It is your reaction to his words, isn't it? You must study not only your lines, but also Tusenbach's, and know your reaction to what he says. Jeff, your Tusenbach is too gloomy. The baron is always in high spirits. He is intelligent and has a sense of humor. Will the two of you please meet and work more on the scene? It's a pity you do not work enough, because both of you show good potential for these roles. Let us do a run-through of the first scene.

(Scene)

You're not mourning any more, Olga, but now you're overdoing it in another direction, and I don't believe you.

LIZ: The whole thing to me is that although it had been cold and snowing, now it is warm, and this excites me.

S.M.: You cannot be excited just because you have decided to be. You are overdoing it. Remember what we call the measure of truth.

(Scene)

That was very good, Liz.

LIZ: My images are becoming much clearer.

S.M.: Yes, especially in the beginning and the middle of the speech—I'm sure of it. It is because you moved your body correctly. This time you really worked. You have made definite progress. Work more now on *transmitting* the images to your partners. Masha, I didn't watch you. Be honest, did you have your inner monologue?

MARY: Not continually.

S.M.: I appreciate your honesty and would be even more appreciative if you worked. Soon you will have to prepare scenes yourselves, and apply some of these techniques before you show the scenes to me.

class 10

SONIA MOORE: Now, one of you go on stage. Enter a room ready to "meet an unknown person." As always, build your circumstances. Concentrate. ...All right, Peter, I see that you are ready.

(Improvisation: Peter enters and pantomimes speech.)

Please do not talk to anyone who is not there.

PETER: How do I know that he is not there?

S.M.: Can't you see whether someone else is there on the stage? *(Laughter.)* Try to behave as you do in life. If no one is there, you have no one to talk to.

(Nina performs the improvisation.)

Whom did you come to meet? It was not very clear.

NINA: A friend.

S.M.: Didn't I say to "meet an unknown person"?

(All the students perform the improvisation.)

The next improvisation will be "two people who are not on speaking terms." Talk over the situation between you. First decide whom you will do it with. Know your relationship—why you are not on speaking terms. Do not speak or pantomime.

There should be no need to talk. As soon as there is an organic need to speak, the improvisation is finished. After you have built the situation, go on, and do not "make an entrance." Come on stage for a purpose. Life goes on off stage and must continue on stage.

(Evan and Jack perform the improvisation.) Well, I am sure you would not be glancing at each other all the time as you did. What was it, anyway? Did you want to make up after a quarrel? Were you friends living in the same room?

EVAN: The way I imagined the situation was that he had dated my best girl friend, and I did not know it, and then I found out. I couldn't find anything to do and tried to concentrate on my feelings.

S.M.: Instead of concentrating on your feelings, you should find physical actions which would tell us what has happened. These actions might express your feelings and even make you feel.

EVAN: Without saying anything?

S.M.: I know it's very difficult.

EVAN: I found it difficult to concentrate because of my tremendous anger and hurt.

S.M.: Oh, you think that you were angry and hurt? An actor can be hurt or angry without a personal reason *if* he has learned the technique of involving his whole psychophysical apparatus. You certainly have no personal reason to be hurt, because Jack really did not take your girl friend away from you. What you think were your emotions was only physical tension. If you had a girl you know in mind, you could have found some physical actions for such a situation which might have stirred your emotions. And how on earth do you think we could have understood your story? If, for instance, the girl's picture were there, or you were tearing up some letters, or.... Well, you could have found actions that would have given us some idea.

(Jeff and Nina perform the improvisation.)
My, how stingy you are!

JEFF: Mrs. Moore understood it! Was it clear that I hated writing all those checks?

S.M.: Yes, the way you looked over at her as you wrote them made it clear. But Nina, are you really a spendthrift, or is he just stingy?

NINA: I'm not extravagant. I don't even have the money to buy a pair of stockings.

S.M.: This was not projected. If you had felt a run in both your stockings, for instance, and couldn't find a good pair, we might have an idea that he does not give you enough money. This is only an example.

Next you will be a "thief in a dark room." Make sure you know what you are stealing, and why. You may be starving and want a piece of bread, or you want someone's jewelry, or a document.... Go on as soon as you have built the situation and remember an analogous emotion. The situation does not have to be analogous, you do not have to have stolen in your own life. You must remember an analogous emotion, as, for instance, hunger, revenge, greed, etc.

(Albert performs the improvisation.)
Were there any people in the house? Did you know this room?

ALBERT: I knew it fairly well. There was one person in the apartment, but definitely not nearby.

S.M.: All this might have influenced you. If

there had been people around, you might have gone to the door first to make sure no one was near. You might also have barricaded the door with some furniture. You would be overcoming obstacles to your objective. Next, please.

(Peter performs the improvisation.)

Where were you?

PETER: I was in a room with a lot of antique books. I was tempted to steal a book with a leather binding. I smelled it. *(Laughter.)*

S.M.: I did not understand why you smelled it.

PETER: Some antique books have a certain odor.

S.M.: All right. Did you take what you wanted? How can I impress on you that everything you do on stage must be understood by the spectators? All you have to do is build interesting content and find an interesting form to express it.

ALBERT: That's all? *(Laughter.)*

S.M.: You remind me of something else. One director said at a conference that some actors will soon abolish the audience because they disturb their performance! ... Let us go on with the thief.

(Liz performs the improvisation.)

What was wrong with that?

MICHAEL: First of all, in a dark room the tendency is not to squint as she was doing, but to open your eyes like this—as wide as possible. Also, after a certain period of time your eyes will have adjusted somewhat to the dark.

LIZ: If I am going to be in a blind situation, I shut my eyes, and I imagine how it would be. I try to feel how a blind person would feel.

S.M.: Why would you, as a blind person, run as you did? You knew exactly where you were going.

LIZ: I just ran into the corner.

S.M.: How did you know there was an empty corner?

LIZ: My first reaction was to get out of the center of the room.

S.M.: What kind of a room was it?

LIZ: It was a room on the first floor of an abandoned house on Twenty-second Street in New York. My story was that I had seen a little bench there, and I wanted to take it for my apartment. Even if I were breaking in at night in complete darkness, I would have known roughly where it was.

S.M.: I am beginning to tire of telling you that you should not have to tell us this interesting story, but find actions to express what you have thought up. It certainly is impossible to project a Twenty-second Street address. But your rushing around proved that you forgot that you were in the dark, and it was not even truthful. Please, keep asking yourself, "What would I do *if* ... ?" It is fantastic how much this "if" helps, especially because it helps you to find what is personal to you.

Now we shall begin *oral improvisations*, because by now you have an idea what it is to be thinking on stage. With no words to hide behind, you have had to think. This is an important step forward in your studies. Words are physical verbal action. Like all physical actions, verbal action is a means of expressing inner life. Work on words is work on the inner world of the character and on his relationship with the world that surrounds him. The effect on the audience depends on what you put into the word. The images in your words must stir images and associations in the spectators. The great singer

Feodor Chaliapin made the spectators all but perspire with one word, "Fire!" When we speak in life, we are usually trying to influence someone's imagination. Sometimes you are trying to influence the emotions of the other person—when, for example, you speak of something tragic. As in life, you must evaluate the other person and watch him in order to see whether you are achieving the expected results. Let us say you want to change the other person's mood. For instance, you are talking to a girl who is sad, and you want to cheer her up. While you are talking to her, you may watch to see whether she smiles. This will create communion on stage.

Now you will "persuade another person to do something you want him to do." Choose your partners. You must know your motivation. It must be important to you. Know who you are to each other. Think of an analogous emotion in your own life. The circumstances you build will tell you how to achieve your aim. Overcoming obstacles to your objective will influence your tempo-rhythm and give color to your actions. As in the silent improvisations, do not think of the *how* before you know *why, where*, and so on. Try every possible way to persuade your partner. These ways or adaptations create the inner and physical communion on stage. If one way does not work, think of another. Watch your partner to see whether you are succeeding. That is what we do in life. Do not just talk purposelessly. There must be a counteraction and a conflict in each improvisation. You must know why you want it, and the other person must know why he refuses. . . . Evan and Jack, go on stage. I shall give you the situation. Evan, you are talking Jack into robbing a bank. You understand, the situation does not have to be a life situation. It is the analogous emotion in life that is important to remember. In the situation I gave you, you want a lot of money. In life you might have wanted something else. Please, remember that the body begins the action. Your body must "speak" before you speak the words. And your body must continue to "speak" after you have spoken your lines. And your hands move only after you have felt the current from your spine culminate in your fingers' tips.

    EVAN: . . . Does it have to be a bank?

    S.M.: If you want it to be an individual who has enough money to satisfy you, that is all right.

    (Improvisation)

Well, Jack, if you refuse, you must have a reason. Why didn't you want to take part in the robbery? You kept saying just, "No, I don't want to." Was it because you are an honest man, or simply because the job wasn't important enough? It was not clear at all. Evan was quite convincing in painting a beautiful future for you—the cruises, and the beautiful women you could take along. But you expressed no attitude toward what he said or your reasons for refusing.

    Let us see the scene between Irina and Soliony.

    (Scene)

    S.M. *(interrupting)*: What are you writing, Irina?

    SALLY: I am copying from the book.

    S.M.: That's wrong for this particular moment.

    SALLY: I was trying to get my mind off my troubles with the book and paper.

s.m.: You might try to concentrate on the book, but you look too busy. Irina does not know what to do with herself. Jack, is the argument you had with Andrei still on your mind when you enter this room?

JACK: Yes.

s.m.: Sally, you don't react at all when he asks, "Nobody here?" You look as if you were waiting for your cue. Don't you think that you should answer his question even if you have no lines to say? You do not know that he will say something else. There is such a thing as inner monologue in reaction, and maybe a slight movement of your head would be the physical expression of this. And give him your right hand, not your left. Jack, your standing there upstage is too prolonged.

JACK: When she says good-by, do you want me to start leaving?

s.m.: Yes. What you're doing is fine, but your moment of hesitation is too long. And Irina, you'll have to change your inner monologue and your body, because the other actor doesn't behave the way you expected. You must coordinate your behavior. That is what ensemble work means—continuous inner and external reaction to each other. Let us start the scene again.

(Scene)

Just a second. What you do, Jack, would be right for you or for someone else, but not for Soliony. Soliony never bends. He would think this was undignified. He has no experience in speaking of love. He is very stiff. He always looks like a soldier on guard. Irina, you want to get rid of him. But Irina is a lady, and she doesn't shout. Jack, justify your standing upstage. Is it because you do not dare look her in the eye? Let us start it again.

(Scene)

(Interrupting again) Say your inner monologue aloud when you enter and cross the room, to be sure that you have it. Go on. . . . Now it looks good, Jack. But promise that you will write down every thought that passes through your mind when she speaks. This is more important than memorizing the lines, which really could only be harmful at this stage of your work on the role. The right inner monologue will bring you to your lines, and you may have entirely different intonations. However, there has been definite progress since I saw it last time, because then you were just coming in out of a blue sky every time you said a word. Now it is much better, but still vague. Write your whole inner monologue down on paper so that you will have something concrete to correct and change. All right? When I see your discouraged faces every time I insist on it, I can't help thinking of what happened to the Habima Studio. After the leaders of that group had talked with Stanislavski, they told their actors, "We must close our theatre and study." Most of the actors were disappointed and left, but those who remained built one of the best theatres in Moscow. I wish Stanislavski could talk to our actors. . . . Soliony, you are standing there without any reaction to her.

LIZ *(interrupting)*: Only now do I know what it means to react to each other on stage. I have been told for years that I must react, but no one ever explained how.

S.M.: Some people think that ensemble will be achieved when we have repertory theatres and people have worked together for years. Well, I saw some actors who had had such good fortune, but there was no hint of an ensemble work in their performances. It is when the expression on one person's face changes the expression on another that you can call it ensemble work. Without this technique it will never exist, no matter how long a group of actors may have performed together. Ensemble is the actors' inner and external reactions to one another in a mutual endeavor to project the superobjective of a play.

Now you, Irina....

SALLY (*interrupting*): I've come downstairs because I have nothing to do, so I just sat down.

S.M.: All right, but don't you hear Soliony's footsteps?

SALLY: I heard footsteps, but I thought it might have been Natasha.

S.M.: Would Natasha's steps sound like Soliony's? Natasha does not walk. She flits around like a butterfly. But even if you thought it was Natasha, wouldn't you react in some way? And here all of a sudden Soliony appears. You did not know he was still in the house, and yet you don't react at all. This is what I was trying to make you understand with the oral improvisations and earlier in those silent improvisations when there were more than one of you on stage. You must watch each other, sense each other, hear and see each other. Every role depends on all roles. You must know what the other one is doing because your own behavior depends on it. You must react to Soliony's entrance. I don't mean you should jump up, but have in your mind something like, "Who is this?"

Now I want to see Andrei and Ferapont. Have you worked, Ken?

KEN: Yes.

(Scene between Andrei and Ferapont)

S.M.: Are you sure you have an image for your wife, Natasha?

KEN: Oh, yes.

S.M.: Well, if you do have an image, it is the wrong one. Read the play again to understand what kind of a woman she is and what has happened to you, Andrei, during the time you have been married. I do not believe, either, that you have the right images of people you care about and whose opinions are as important to you as Andrei's sisters' opinion is to him. Ken, it does not come across. You speak about your wife and sisters, and there is no difference in your attitude toward them. Your images should be deeper, clearer, by now. It is the correct use of your body that will achieve this. *This is how, through the "method of physical actions," we stir the inner processes.* And when you pause before you say, "and lonely," it looks as if you want to project that you realized this only now. But Andrei has been lonely for quite a while, and he knows it. Please, do not create unnecessary pauses. I shall be happy when you can fill the necessary ones! In such cases your sighing disappears. But if you cheat yourself and do not have any images or inner monologue, your instrument does not develop, and you do not move forward. You know, if you don't practice the piano, you don't progress, and this is exactly the same thing. In some of you, who are honestly trying, I see tremendous progress in mastering these difficult steps toward building the character. The whole System is based on the willpower of the actor. The more honestly you work each time, the easier it will be for the next role. And we can move forward.

KEN: But I do use my inner monologue during my speeches.

s.m.: Just a minute—again this confusion. When you speak on stage, you must know your subtext, which is the meaning of the lines. And you must have images for everyone and everything in your subtext. Stanislavski called it the "illustrated" subtext. You must have your inner monologue during silences on stage, while others speak, and during pauses in your own lines.

class II

SONIA MOORE: Before proceeding with the exercises, I want to know what scenes you want to do next. I told you we were using *The Three Sisters* as an example of work on a role. It is a difficult play, but it is perfect for our work because there are many pauses and silences in Chekhov's plays. That is why actors who do not know the inner technique, which you are learning, should not attempt to perform in them. Now we must take another step. I want to see other scenes, but do not abandon *The Three Sisters* until you actually begin working on a scene from another play.

SALLY: May I work on *Blood Wedding*?

S.M.: Garcia Lorca is one of my favorite dramatists and his writing is pure poetry, but at this stage of your studies I would prefer something in simpler language. I do not think you will be able to do thorough work on it. Lorca's clarity is often subordinated to the musicality of verse. Keep it in mind for your next scene. How about working on Abigail in Arthur Miller's *The Crucible*?

SALLY: Oh, I would love it.

MARY: May I also work on Abigail?

s.m.: Good. I like to see several people working on the same scene. You learn a great deal by watching others. Liz, would you like to work on Goody Proctor in *The Crucible*?

LIZ: Yes, I love the play. Which scene?

s.m.: The scene where she insists that John go to Salem, and they have a quarrel. And Evan, I think you should work on John Proctor. Jeff and Anne, how about a scene from *Another Part of the Forest*? Do you know the play? It is by Lillian Hellman.

JEFF: Yes.

s.m.: Maybe you also know *The Little Foxes*? *Another Part of the Forest* is about the same family, but twenty years earlier.

Begin your work on new scenes by reading the play as many times as you can. Try to understand what the author wanted to say. For instance, Regina and Ben in both *The Little Foxes* and in *Another Part of the Forest* are ready to cut each other's throats for money. You must build characters who will be symbols of greed. We should try to project such a phenomenon through those people. You must penetrate to its roots. Is it nourished by life in the South? Ask yourself what you want to project; what kind of atmosphere; what you want to say; why you like the play. After you have studied the play and have an idea what it is about, write your character's biography, as you did with *The Three Sisters*. Think of what your character is striving for in life, what his main action—his superobjective—is. The next step is to analyze your particular scene. If the scene is one episode give it a name—a noun—that will characterize the scene. If there are different important episodes in the scene, each one must have a characteristic name. In the improvisations that we have done, you built the situation, or I gave you the situation. In a play the author gives you the circumstances, which you must understand thoroughly. An important event, or an episode, must have a characteristic name. For instance, if you call a moment on stage "war," this will dictate certain behavior to you. Decide on the superobjective of the scene; only then do you begin analyzing your actions.

LIZ: How about images and inner monologue?

S.M.: Certainly they are still there. They are essential parts of the psychological side of an action. In her book, *The Directing School of Nemirovich-Danchenko*, Maria O. Knebel, head of the State Institute of Theatre Art in Moscow, says that Russian psychologists have greatly developed the teaching on inner monologue, which is understood as the condensed and unexpressed form of speech. The inner monologue is essential for transforming a thought into a speech. In life, people continue to argue, persuade, and so on in their minds even when they are silent. In literature, Nemirovich-Danchenko pointed out, good novelists frequently introduce us to the innermost thoughts of the characters—the thoughts that bring them to their decisions and actions. Mrs. Knebel mentions one of Chekhov's stories, "He Quarreled with His Wife," which consists almost entirely of the thoughts that go through a man's head after he has complained to his wife that the supper was not good. At almost the end of the story the husband speaks for the first time since his complaint. He says to his wife, "Stop crying, my little darling." This story shows what a great deal in inner monologue can lie behind one spoken sentence. I hope you will read it. Playwrights seldom describe the thoughts of their characters, so it is up to the actor to create an inner monologue to complete that part of a character's life.

Now, you must find names for the events and choose your actions. This is also the beginning of your use of the Stanislavski *analysis of the play through events and actions*. It includes finding the superobjective and the through line of actions—the chain of logical, typical, consecutive actions which gradually disclose the superobjective. It will also help you to have a clearer idea of your character's superobjective. Take some time to do the preparatory work, and meet with your partner. You must coordinate your behavior; you must understand your partner's actions and write them down as well as your own. Perform as many improvisations as possible on the situations in the play, or on some that may not be in the play, but which could have happened. Only after a great many such improvisations may you perform improvisations on every action in your scene, using your own words. Reread the play and the scene you work on, following the actions in your mind. This will enable you to have a better idea of the superobjective of the play and of your character. Then perform more improvisations. Only after such thorough work may you use the author's text. And then you must be faithful to the text. You must not distort it. And I remind you again—do not memorize your lines during the first stage of work on the role. Keep away from playing the result. Fight in yourself the temptation to do superficial work, which will result in cliché only. Show the scene to me. We shall continue to work on it together until we have brought it into the best possible shape. Ultimately, you must make sure that you have selected the best means to express the character. In your next scenes you will be able to do more independent work. Remember that each scene must have a beginning, a development, and a conclusion.

JEFF: How do I determine an action? Do I use my own judgment?

S.M.: First study the play. You choose an action to achieve an objective. Improvisations on an action will help you determine whether the action is the right one.

And now let us proceed with our improvisations. This chair is "a vicious dog." He is on a chain, but he can reach you and could still tear you to shreds. For some reason of your own, you must cross the yard. The reason should be important. For instance, you may be a doctor who is bringing medicine to a dying patient. Do not try to believe that this is a dog. Build the circumstances and then choose your actions, or what you would do in life in such a situation. You must treat the chair as if it were a dog; do not force yourself to see a dog there. Is that clear? It is what you do that will make us believe that you are trying to avoid a dog. Let us concentrate and build the imaginary circumstances.

(All the students perform the improvisation.) Good. Albert, I like your idea of using a hamburger to distract the dog, as Jerry did in *The Zoo Story*.

Now this chair is a "throne." Again you must build the situation and treat this plain old chair in such a way that we will believe that it is a throne.

KEN: In a play this would be much easier because of the sets and the right props.

S.M.: Yes, in most cases. The audience would

see a throne, but even then you would have to treat it as one.

MICHAEL: Must we be a king or a queen?

S.M.: Not necessarily. Build circumstances in which you would be in a room where there is a throne. . . . Ready?

(Some students perform the improvisation.) Ken, if you know where you are, we would like to know too!

KEN: You mean you must know what country I am in?

S.M.: No. We do not have any idea that it is a throne.

MICHAEL: Are you a king?

KEN: Yes.

S.M.: I don't think that kings sit on the throne all the time. Not nowadays, anyway. You must have some special occasion for this. If you were King Lear, for instance, and I hope some day you will portray him, then you will have the occasion to sit on a throne.

KEN: It is very difficult to project. I was a king in the nineteenth century.

S.M.: It is doubtful that in the nineteenth century a king would sit on a throne doing nothing. I am sure that such a king would sit on an ordinary chair when he signed papers. A king might sit on his throne when he made a declaration or received ambassadors.

KEN: I was honest and I believed and I fulfilled what I believed.

S.M.: Oh, it is always I, I, I! You must realize that there is no place for you on stage unless you are capable of projecting what is taking place. The audience must be affected by what you are doing. Otherwise you can stay in your own room and "feel" and "believe" for your own enjoyment.

(Mary performs the improvisation.)

That was very good, Mary. . . . It was clear that she was in a church. I saw her in Saint Peter's church in Rome. Stanislavski said that the only things that an actor can do honestly are simple physical actions, which are miraculously expressive. Mary took some water, and made the sign of the cross, and went down on her knees, and she fulfilled very simple actions which could be performed easily and truthfully by any actor—and they were not indications. Such purposeful actions help you to achieve complete concentration of your body, mind, thoughts, and emotions, your whole psychophysical apparatus. This is what the Polish director Grotowski calls "the total act."

And now the *same* chair is an "electric chair."

EVAN: Do we die in it or. . . .

S.M.: It depends on what situation you want to build. Concentrate and go on. . . .

(The students perform the improvisation.)

Very good. Jack, at first I expected you to be executed in this chair.

JACK: No, I was a guard checking the wiring.

S.M.: Yes, you made it clear afterward. Liz, you made it clear that you were in some sinister museum, and that you wanted to touch the chair but did not dare. Well, don't you think we are improving and our imagination has developed quite well?

Let us perform an oral improvisation on an action "to make another person leave."

ALBERT: To get rid of someone?

s.m.: Yes, but not physically. Talk over the situation with your partner—decide who you are to each other, but do not tell your partner why you want him to leave. And your partner should not say how he will react. I want this to be unexpected for each of you. When you realize that he wants you to leave, react accordingly—the way you would in such a situation in life. Remember an analogous emotion in your life. Where are you going, Evan?

EVAN: Don't we have to discuss the situation with each other?

s.m.: Oh, fine. Make sure you watch each other carefully. I may have you reverse your parts and then each of you will have to repeat exactly the words and movements of the other.

(Improvisation. After speaking a great deal about how much work he has to do, Evan tells Albert he has a headache, and takes a pill. Albert at last is convinced, and leaves. Then Evan rushes to the phone.)

That was good. When Evan went to the phone, we knew that he had gotten rid of Albert in order to make a call. Do you understand that I gave you the physical side of the action? Yes, don't look so surprised, this—"to make another person leave"—is the physical action. The psychological side is your reason for wanting him to leave, the images of people, places, and events in your mind. You must add the psychological side. After you have done this, go on stage to fulfill the physical action "to make him leave." You must select and fulfill a chain of small physical actions leading to this, and use your words—the verbal physical action. And if you fulfill the selected physical actions leading to your superobjective truthfully and energetically, you will stir your inner life. I hope that what I say is becoming somewhat clearer.

(*Other students perform the improvisation.*) I must say that few of you really projected the reason for wanting the other person to leave. When we want someone to leave, we have a serious reason. Try to think hard what you would do. . . . Don't sit all the time, but don't move as you did, Jack, without a real reason. Your movements must be of help, and they will be if you have a reason for them. . . .

Let us see some scenes from *The Three Sisters*. (*The scene between Andrei and Ferapont*) That was beautiful work, Jeff. Your objective was clear. Now that you say Chekhov's words, please stretch all words and bring out your attitude in important words.

May I see the scene between Irina and Tusenbach?

(*Scene*) It is really quite lovely. Sally, in the beginning you were too aggressive with Tusenbach. Now you have changed considerably, and you are much more Irina, who really likes Tusenbach. Everyone likes this man. She is not in love with him, but Irina is not annoyed by him either. I would like to see the beginning scene from Tusenbach's entrance.

(*Scene*) Meg, I am not convinced that you have all of Olga's inner monologue while Tusenbach speaks.

MEG: Mrs. Moore, you said I can go back to correcting papers.

S.M.: Yes, that is true, but you still must think. I do not insist that you should think all the time in

reaction to what he is saying, but you must think as
Olga without interruption. And the same thing
applies to Masha. You don't have to listen to him all
the time, but that does not mean that there can be
dead moments. The only one who was listening and
thinking in response was Irina, and it was good, too.
Tusenbach, stretch your words more and project
your attitude to them. You must choose the
important words in every sentence and say them
almost as if the person you are talking to does not
understand your language.

class 12

SONIA MOORE: We will perform a difficult exercise. I shall ask you questions and you must answer them without hesitation. The answer should be logical. This is another way to "massage" your mind. You need an alert, fertile imagination. Liz, somebody told me they saw you with a baby in your arms, near Park Avenue and Fifty-third Street, at five in the morning. What were you doing there?

LIZ: It was my friend's baby.

S.M.: But why at five o'clock in the morning?

LIZ: Well, there was some trouble with burglars and I had to——

S.M.: The policeman took the baby away, and they told me that you began to run.

LIZ: Yes, yes. I remembered that mother was going to call from Canada and I had to be home....

S.M.: And Sally, I saw you with an old gentleman yesterday at eleven in the morning. Who was he?

SALLY: An old gentleman?

S.M.: Don't try to gain time. Answer right away.

SALLY: Oh, he fell, and I was taking him home.

S.M.: Why did you run?

SALLY: I saw a taxi and ran after it.

S.M.: But, when the taxi stopped you refused to use it and called a policeman. Why?

SALLY: Why did I? *(Laughter.)* ... Oh, because the old man started to become nasty.

S.M.: And that is why you went into a bar?

SALLY: Well, I needed a drink. . . .

S.M.: Albert, I saw a young woman waving to you, and you hid around the corner and she started to scream for help.

ALBERT: I threw the coat over my head, and she thought I was a gangster or something.

S.M.: Anne, where were you going last night with that nice young man?

ANNE: We went to a movie.

S.M.: Which one?

ANNE: *Andersonville.*

S.M.: But you came out right away?

ANNE: We were hungry.

S.M.: In the restaurant, so they told me, you threw your glass at him.

ANNE: Yes, well, we had a fight. We fight a lot and we'd just had another.

S.M.: Nina, what were you doing at Blomingdale's this morning?

NINA: Buying a hat.

S.M.: How much did you pay?

NINA: Two ninety-eight. . . . It was on sale.

S.M.: They stopped you at the door to check whether you had paid for it?

NINA: There was some shoplifting in another part of the store, and they asked me for the receipt.

S.M.: Why did you scream?

NINA: That was someone else, not me.

S.M.: And why did you go into the telephone booth?

NINA: I had to let a friend know I would be late for an appointment.

S.M.: Oh, but then you came out even before you started to talk?

NINA: No, I was talking, but my friend started to yell that I am always late, so I hung up.

S.M.: Peter, who was the girl you were walking with near the Four Seasons?

PETER: Near what?

S.M.: A restaurant, the Four Seasons. Who was the young girl?

PETER: A girl friend.

S.M.: What is her name?

PETER: Olga.

S.M.: Why were you there at six in the morning?

PETER: Well, we like fresh air. *(Laughter.)*

S.M.: Why were you arguing?

PETER: Well, she did not want to get up at five in the morning, but I said, "If you want to get out by six, you have to get up by five." ...*(Laughter.)*

S.M.: Mary, I saw you in a restaurant with a middle-aged gentleman with glasses. Who was he?

MARY: Who was he? ...*(Laughter.)*

S.M.: Answer, don't try to gain time.

MARY: He was a man from a film company.

S.M.: He did not behave very nicely.

MARY: What happened? ...

S.M.: He threw a bottle at somebody. It seems that I am answering your questions! ...

MARY: Oh, I insulted him.

s.m.: What happened?

MARY: I told him he made second-rate films.

s.m.: So he threw the bottle at the bartender?

MARY: He missed me, I ducked.

s.m.: Jean, I saw you with a young man at ten in the morning. First you kissed each other, and then you slapped him. What was the matter?

JEAN: Well, you know how it is.... *(Laughter.)* It is a very personal thing, and he started to be extremely fresh.

s.m.: Did you know that they took him to the police station?

JEAN: Oh, I am delighted to hear that....

s.m.: Did they let him out?

JEAN: Well, yes. They let him out. It was all a case of mistaken identity. Somebody had stolen a dog, apparently an expensive French poodle, and they thought he was the man.

s.m.: When they let him out, where did you go with him?

JEAN: We went to this crazy pub where they have German beer.

s.m.: Jeff, you answer. As soon as you entered the pub, someone asked you to come out again.

JEFF: That was my mother.

s.m.: Where did you go?

JEFF: She wanted me to catch a cab and come straight home. She did not approve of the girl I was with. *(Laughter.)*

s.m.: Well, that is enough. *(Students express their relief.)*

Next, we will "eavesdrop." Build the circumstances: why you eavesdrop, where, when, all the possible details. . . .

(Ken performs the improvisation.)

You said you were in an agent's office? How do we know that?

KEN: But this is terribly difficult.

S.M.: Yes, it is. Give it a thought. After all, we are your audience. We don't know where you are, what you are doing there, nothing.

KEN: I am just sitting and smoking in an agent's office.

S.M.: You must know that on stage nothing can be only "just." You can also sit and smoke in a doctor's office. Why did you come here? Did the agent call you and tell you that there was a leading part for you in a movie? Or is this the first time you have been in an agent's office? *(Silence.)* Well, what do you all think was wrong with this?

JACK: His physical actions did not express anything.

ANNE: His tempo-rythm was wrong.

S.M.: That is right. In life, when anything happens, we do not have to think whether we should move fast or slowly; we do it spontaneously. And you were only thinking, and it was still dead, because you must function psychophysically to be alive. I want you to know that in your body-movement class also you must think of psychophysical action. You are given the physical side, and you must bring in the psychological side. You are learning this technique, and you must use it in your dance class, and also in your speech classes. There should be no movement or word without justification, concrete circumstances,

an objective; without images or inner monologue.
Do you remember the exercise we did where you had
to justify and connect three movements? [See page
74.] Justifying movements in the dance class will also
develop your imagination at the same time, and you
will put life into the movements. All great dancers do
this. They use their movements to express the inner
content. When you see a great dancer, you think that
what he is doing is the only way to express the
content. In every art the most important is the
spiritual content expressed in an artistic form. A
good portrait breathes life. You can see life in the
faces, in the hands. It is the same thing with music. I
think that the pianist Sviatoslav Richter is extraordinary. It is difficult for me to keep up with his images.
He says so much. And yesterday I heard a violinist—
some people say he is very good. Well, maybe he is a
great technician, but to me he seemed dead. In this
studio, whatever you do there must be inner content
expressed in laconic, eloquent external form. In your
dance class use the music as the given circumstances.
The various nuances will give you ideas. Listen to
music, try to understand what the composer wants to
say. In life, the smallest change of circumstances
makes a difference in our behavior. We behave
differently in the morning and at night, in the rain or
sunshine. Our behavior in life is *spontaneously
psychophysical.*

Who is next to "eavesdrop"?

*(Albert performs the improvisation. He sits
and types, then stops, puzzling over the paper
in the typewriter. He gets up and goes to a
closed door, pauses, and moves nearer to
listen.)*

That was good, because you established that you were in an office, that you had to ask your boss about something, but there was someone with him, and you became interested in their conversation. That was clear. Who is next, please?

(Evan performs the improvisation.)

s.m.: What did you all understand?

MEG: It was clear that he had his blood taken for analysis and naturally wanted to know what they were discussing in the doctor's office.

s.m.: When you looked under your bandage, it was not a mechanical action because we could see in your eyes that you were thinking and wondering.

(Everyone performs the improvisation.)

You see how different all of you were at eavesdropping? No two of you did the same thing, because of the different circumstances and because you are all different people. This shows that no two characters are the same. Every character has a different psychological and a different physical behavior.

Now there will be three people on stage. Albert and Jean, you are spies, and one of you must pass an important document to the other spy. Meg, you are a detective, and you are at the place where the spies meet. Build your circumstances. Know who you are spying for. To be caught may mean life imprisonment.

ALBERT: Do we know that she is a detective?

s.m.: No, you do not know, but I think that you would not dare pass the document in anybody's presence.

(Improvisation)

Well, spies with an important document would probably pretend not to know each other in the presence of a third person. The way you behaved would attract anyone's attention, not only a detective's. This is an improvisation in communion on stage, without speaking. You must catch each other's glances, each other's movements. And the detective should not let them see that he is watching.

ALBERT: We were at the bus terminal, and there were other people around. I think that you couldn't get away with false pretenses like reading a magazine.

S.M.: We did not believe that you were aware of the danger if you were caught. Am I right? Two spies seeing another person, especially someone behaving as suspiciously as Meg did, would not sit next to each other. I want you to sense each other, to catch each other's looks, barely perceptible signs, which the detective would not discern. Maybe you could put the document where the detective would never suspect you could have put it. You did not think of your physical state. It would have influenced the tempo-rhythm, and a special atmosphere would have been created.

ALBERT: Couldn't I have put it in her pocket as I did?

MEG: Oh, I thought you put it under the chair!

S.M.: A real detective would have seen where he put it. Don't you think so?

MEG: Yes, I do.

S.M.: It was not convincing, and that is that.

JEAN: I thought that the obvious thing for us to do was to pretend that we were not afraid, and thus fool her.

S.M.: Suppose that Albert is a dangerous spy and his face is known to the FBI. Would you have wanted to be seen with him? And anyway, I want you to be some distance away from each other because this is an exercise in communion, and you must attract each other's attention with glances or barely perceptible signs. We are facing again the problem of selecting the right actions. All the actions which will lead you toward fulfillment of your main action— "to transmit the document"—may also be considered in such cases as adaptations. Stanislavski said, "Adaptations are our 'paints.'"

MICHAEL: I don't think that a spy would look too suspicious, would he?

S.M.: Don't you think that Jean was acting too suspiciously? By the way, when I tell you that the improvisation is not an oral one, that does not mean that you can pantomime speaking. You should know better by this time.

JEAN: I did not pantomime.

S.M.: You started doing something like that. Don't ever do it. Meg, they should not have known that you were watching them, you want to catch them *en flagrant délit,* in the act of transmitting the document. Therefore, you should have given them a chance to do it and then arrested them. You should have looked very busy with something else. Incidentally, how did you justify that you were here before they came in?

MEG: I knew that they were coming here, that this was their meeting place.

S.M.: All right.

MEG: I knew the time and the place.

(Anne, Michael, and Evan perform the improvisation.)

S.M.: Did you get the piece of paper? I thought

it remained in that little hollow coin or whatever it was.

MICHAEL: Oh, no.

S.M.: I thought that you left the money here and that the document was in it.

MICHAEL: Oh, no. I got it.

(Everyone performs the improvisation.)

S.M.: And now, the one who has the document is entering his apartment. Let us see what you would do.

(Several students perform the improvisation.) You did not even lock the door, Sally. No one thought of windows you could have been watched from.

SALLY: The windows in my apartment face a wall.

S.M.: I still think that you would have put the shades down.

JACK: And I was in a room without windows. *(Laughter.)*

S.M.: If you don't have windows, that's that.

Let us proceed with an oral improvisation. The action is "to encourage." Choose your partner and decide on the situation. Know your objective. Think of an emotion that should be stirred in this situation and remember an analogous emotion in your life. Do not rush; the more circumstances you bring into the picture, the more interesting your actions will be.

JEFF: Mrs. Moore, if I encourage, what is the other person's reaction?

S.M.: If the other person lets himself be encouraged right away, then you will not have to make any effort. The other person must have counteractions to create obstacles. His resistance will create a conflict. We do not realize that in life we are constantly overcoming obstacles. There must be dramatic conflicts on stage; otherwise theatre is dull. Here, in your improvisation, everything depends on the circumstances you build. Do what is logical, what you would do in such a situation in life. Never forget the "magic if." Concentrate. The means to be used will depend on the other person's reaction. In life, we try one way, and if it does not work, we try another, more persuasive way. . . .

(All the students perform the improvisation.) Shall we see the scene between Irina and Soliony?

(Scene)

The beginning looks better. Still, Irina, I am not sure of what you are thinking when Soliony appears. Then, when Soliony says, "Oh, my heavens," and so on, you should look at him and after that he says, "Such magnificent, wonderful, marvelous eyes."

JACK: When I am saying my inner monologue, should I look at her or away?

S.M.: Jack, I don't want to tell you everything. By now you have an idea of what the psychophysical action is. Why don't you try to think what would be the logical thing to do? We shall see how this works. Your standing upstage for such a long time still looks unjustified, but I agree that you should be upstage. Think more about it, and find the justification. Also, when you threaten, "I'll kill any rival," it must be more convincing. I want the audience to wonder why Irina does not take this more seriously. If she did, this might have prevented Tusenbach's death. Soliony is dangerous because he senses his inferiority. Such people may try to destroy those whom they consider superior. It is tragic that none of these nice people understands Soliony, and they simply witness the tragedy. Let us go on with Andrei and Ferapont.

(Scene)

Now, Jack, you are very convincing in establishing how you feel about Protopopov. And now you are used to thinking every second....I mean as the character! Yes, at the command of your will, you think. When Ferapont says that they didn't let him in, do you think of Natasha's new regime in the house? Your body was expressive. It was clear that you were evaluating; your body became completely still for a moment, and then it changed. This is what we do in life.

JACK: That's what I wanted to think—that it humiliates me the way my wife treats the servants.

S.M.: You know, your sighing disappeared when you were really thinking. Do you realize that it is much easier to think when your body moves?

Let us work on the scene in which Baron Tusenbach enters and says, "You sit by yourself all the time," and so on. By the way, Anne, I meant to tell you that you have done fine work as Masha, and it would be good if you started to work on Masha's confession in the third act. Well, let us go on with Soliony and Tusenbach.

(Scene)

Ken, do not look at Tusenbach when you start the confession all of a sudden.

KEN: I am supposed to talk to him.

S.M.: Yes, you should be talking to him, but you do not have to look at him. We don't always look at a person when we speak to him. And before you

say, "When I am alone, I am all right," you must
have an inner monologue that will bring you
logically to these words. It is sort of a decision;
Soliony softens and talks about his troubles to
another man. Then, when you see that Tusenbach
agrees with your self-criticism, you fall back into
your usual self and tell him that you are not any
worse than he, Tusenbach. You must learn to react
continuously to each other in a psychophysical way.
You must study your partner's lines and know your
reactions. Though you look at him, Ken, believe me,
you are not talking to Tusenbach. As usual, you are
yourself, not interested in anyone or anything. You
have not yet projected an action in any improvisation. Whenever I ask you what is taking place, your
answer is the same: "Oh, it's not important to
me. . . ." When I asked you whom you were waiting
for on the beach after the storm, you answered, "Oh,
for no one specially important to me." You look
nonchalant in everything you do, whether an
improvisation or Soliony. There is no way for us to
know what you are saying or doing, and why. You
isolate yourself; you lose contact with your partner
and everything around you. If you do not project the
action, then, first, you will never involve your
psychophysical apparatus; second, the audience does
not know what kind of a character you are; and,
third, the audience does not know what is happening
on stage. Thus your presence on stage makes no sense
at all.

    KEN: Then you want me to forget everything I
learned during the five years I studied with other
teachers?

    S.M.: Actions are your means of expression,

and if you don't know how to choose and fulfill them, you know nothing about acting....I don't think you quite understand that you must learn to stir your own organic nature to work *for the character*.

KEN: Why can't I stir the emotions of the character?

S.M.: Because a character in a play is dead until an actor's own emotions, will, memory, thoughts, and body are involved. This is your material for creating another person. You seem to be doing nothing but imitating a Marlon Brando posture.

KEN: I don't think we have to try to bring out an actor's emotions, because an actor always has his own emotions.

S.M.: Yes, when it concerns his own personal interests. When the interests are those of the character in a play, an actor's emotions will not come to the surface spontaneously. The Stanislavski technology will give you the possibility of making your own emotions work for the character. You say that you have studied for five years. But Stanislavski studied for forty years. He never hesitated to demolish the means that he himself had established when he found better ones. If you don't change your attitude as quickly as possible, you will be an amateur for the rest of your life. That is a pity. One more thing. You also resent that we dwell on the same scene for a long time.

KEN: I do—because it becomes stale.

S.M.: This is what I wanted to answer. With the Stanislavski technique, a role can never become stale. It is when you mechanically say your lines, repeat only the physical form, that it is dead and will become worse and worse. But Stanislavski says, "Today, now, here." If you do all the work anew every time, it will be always fresh, and your role will grow. You will find more and more interesting things. Stanislavski gives an actor unlimited possibilities.

(Scene)

Please, everyone, it is time for you to pay more attention to the words you speak. Different words have different values. Stretch all the words and choose those that you think are more important and emphasize them. For example, "Tomorrow is Friday, I don't *have to attend*, but I'll *go* anyway. ...It's *boring at home*.... How *strangely* life changes and deceives us."* You should start working on a new scene as soon as possible, without discarding this one. This scene should serve as an example for your further work. Also, there are still possibilities for improving it.

Let us have a run-through of the first scene.

(Scene)

There has been a tremendous improvement. Tell me soon what you want to do next.

JEFF: Yes. Could I do Ben in *The Little Foxes*?

S.M.: I think you are too young, and I would prefer you to do Ben in *Another Part of the Forest*.

EVAN: I have started to work on *The Crucible*. I mean I read it twice. Do I start working on images and inner monologue first or on actions?

S.M.: On actions, actions! Inner monologue and images are part of an action. But wait a moment.

---

*Students use *Logic of Speech* by T.I. Zaporojetz, published in Russian in 1974, and translated and adapted by Sonia Moore.

First you must try to understand the play and its message. Then write the biography of John Proctor. Then think of what Proctor's superobjective is.

EVAN: You mean in the scene?

S.M.: First his superobjective in the whole play, and then in your scene.

EVAN: I've already started to work on images.

S.M.: This is wrong, Evan. The circumstances and your actions will suggest the right images to you. Do you know what the scene is about? You must know what you have to project. Find the name for the scene. In this case the scene is one event. And this event will dictate your actions to you. Do not think about images before you have done this work.

EVAN: May we show you next time at least a little bit of it?

S.M.: Yes, if you do some more preparatory work. I would rather see it before you are sure that you have done such magnificent work that you would resent criticism.

class 13

*(Class begins as usual with group exercises
and vocal exercises.)*

SONIA MOORE: Now, one oral improvisation
on a concrete action in given circumstances. The
action is "to blackmail." Choose your partners.
Build the imaginary circumstances; know your
objective and your relationship. Think what emotion is to be stirred and remember an analogous
emotion experienced by you in life. Then go on stage
and think only of physical behavior. You must find
the unique physical actions that will fit the inner
world you have built. In life our physical behavior is
unique for expression of our inner world. This is
what you must achieve on stage in the imaginary
circumstances. Only then will your whole psychophysical apparatus be involved and your emotions
stirred.... Ready? I don't want to rush you. On the
contrary, I am ready to wait because I would like you
to build interesting circumstances with as many
details as possible. And please do not speak until you
evaluate what you have heard or what you intend to
say. "Speak" with your body, before you say your

words. Your verbal action depends on the physical action.

(All the students perform the improvisation.) Most of you were so concentrated on yourselves that you ignored your partners. Don't you want to obtain a result from your blackmailing? For instance, Michael, you looked so happy with your idea of threatening to divulge this woman's past to her husband that you totally forgot to watch her reaction and see what effect you were having on her. I see only one way to remedy such a situation. We shall exchange parts in every oral improvisation. This will make you watch the other person.

MEG: But this is impossibly difficult. How can I think of my action and watch him at the same time?

S.M.: This is exactly what we do in life. When we want to obtain something from another person, we observe him closely. Of course, in life we do not have to make any effort, and on stage we have a great deal of conscious work to do. You are already able to do things you couldn't do a few months ago. Your "instrument" is only beginning to become adjusted to this work....

EVAN: May we show *The Crucible* now?

S.M.: Have you done enough work? This is your first independent work on a scene. Do you know what the play is about? I hope that you remember that, though you are only working on a scene, you must know the superobjective of the play.

(Discussion of the superobjective of Arthur Miller's The Crucible *and its relationship to McCarthyite "witch-hunting."*)

Did you both write the biographies of your characters?

EVAN: You know, I told you that I started working on images first of all.

S.M.: And I told you that this was wrong. Did you think about the superobjective of the character you will portray? Let us see what you have done.

EVAN: We will only show you a little bit because there really is too much to be done. Is that all right with you? If we are on the wrong track, it is better to find it out at the beginning.

(Scene between John Proctor and Abigail)

S.M.: Well, what is the scene about? What has to be projected in it? Though it is a short scene, we should treat it as a whole play, and we must always remember Arthur Miller's superobjective.

SALLY: It is a confrontation between two people who are attracted to each other, but finally Proctor's decency takes over.

S.M.: Do you agree, Evan?

EVAN: Yes, I think we must project the idea that no matter how involved a man is with someone, he can still be good.

S.M.: Well, if it is so, let us try to project it. What name have you given to the scene?

SALLY: I was wondering whether we should give one name to the whole scene or whether we should divide it into several units?

S.M.: Many years ago a play, the acts, and the roles were divided into many small bits, but not anymore. If the whole scene is one event, one episode, you don't have to subdivide it. But your actions may change a great deal in the course of the same event. What did you call the whole scene?

EVAN: "The meeting of two people attracted to each other."

s.m.: Could you think of one word for it?

EVAN: This is very difficult.

SALLY: Could it be "pitfall"?

s.m.: Let us try with this. But think about it carefully, because it is the event that influences your actions. Let us see. You both agree that Proctor and Abigail are attracted to each other. Sally, you are convincing in this. But, Evan, how on earth do you expect us to know that you are still attracted to her? Let us start from the beginning. Maybe you should cover your lantern, Proctor. You do not want anyone to see the light, do you? What is your first action?

EVAN: To wait for Abigail.

s.m.: Fine, but you can wait for different reasons and in different circumstances. And since you consider this event a pitfall, as soon as you enter we must know that Proctor is waiting in the circumstances of a pitfall. Also, you must make us understand that this is a forest, that it is night, and that you are not eager to be seen. These are also your circumstances. Your physical state will project it. We must create atmosphere. Now enter again. From the moment the curtain goes up, the spectators must understand what is taking place at that moment.

EVAN: Oh, I'll have to change everything.

s.m.: Of course. You did not expect to have everything right! That is what is so wonderful about the Stanislavski System. It gives us unlimited possibilities to change and grow. Isn't it wonderful that you have already learned something about changing and improving your work? As soon as I reminded you about the circumstances and asked you what your first action was, you began to have ideas. We are beginning the famous Stanislavski analysis of a play. The more deeply we analyze the events and the actions, the more the essence of the play will be brought to the surface. You must understand the play thoroughly to convey it to the audience. You must also know why you wanted to work on this play, what attracted you to it, what your super-superobjective is, i.e., what you wish to contribute with your work. Did you read the play again before you wrote your biography?

EVAN: Yes, and I saw things I hadn't noticed before.

S.M.: I am sure of that. And if you read it again, you will see more of what you did not see before. Writing a biography forces you to read and study the play. Only in this way will you understand what kind of people Proctor and Abigail are. You cannot depend only on me, and you must argue with me if you think that I am wrong. You must learn to work independently. Since last time, both of you have realized that Arthur Miller is a dramatist with strong convictions. You know that Proctor is a good man. You also told me, Evan, that Proctor was afraid of his attraction to Abigail, and that is why he had postponed seeing her in order to persuade her to stop the horror.

EVAN: Right.

S.M.: All this has to be projected. We study the second plan and write the biography with the sole purpose of learning about the character and to be able to build him. Do you understand this?

SALLY and EVAN: Yes.

S.M.: But is Abigail's house so close to this spot in the forest that she runs right after Proctor? Doesn't she have to put something on? She was already in bed. Delay your entrance a little. Sally, you ran straight to him. Did you know where he was standing?

SALLY: I saw the light of his lantern.

S.M.: That is right. I'm glad you thought of that even though we don't have a real lantern. What is your action?

SALLY: I think that he has finally come back to me. The action is "to hug him"—I know, I know, in the concrete circumstances! *(Laughter.)*

S.M.: Right. But I do not think it is right for Proctor to embrace her. He has come here for a serious purpose: to save people from burning or hanging. Don't you think, Evan, that you have decided to do your best to fight her?

EVAN: If I start fighting right away, she may go.

S.M.: Yes, but still do not embrace her at this point. You may want to, but fight yourself at the beginning. And that is why you tell her to sit down. Let us see it.

(Scene)

Well, you will have to work on this. Now that you know what your first actions are, fill in the images and the inner monologue. Every verbal action begins with evaluation and the body expressing the inner processes. Abigail, what is your next action?

SALLY: I am worried that he has come for a different purpose.

S.M.: You know better than that. To be worried is not an action. What do you do when you are worried? As Abigail, in these circumstances?

SALLY: I may think that I am trapped and try to test it.

s.m.: Fine, then listen. Go on, Sally, listen, really listen. You may think that there are people hidden behind the trees with knives waiting to attack you. Abigail has many enemies, you know. And then when you ask him to come closer, you recognize his look, and this is when Proctor loses control for a while.

evan: Yes, that is what I figured out. Proctor is really jealous of Abigail. Don't we have to give this episode a different name?

s.m.: I am not sure. Your action changes, but it is still the same episode. But what do you want to call it?

evan: "Jealousy."

s.m.: All right. Then what do you do, as Proctor, when you are jealous?

evan: I accuse her, reproach her.

s.m.: Fine. Shall we see it again?

sally: I would rather work on it first before we do it in class again.

s.m.: I quite agree. I don't think you gave enough thought to an analogous emotion experienced in life. Remember, this is essential in your work. Shall we see the scene from *Another Part of the Forest*?

liz: We have not done much work on it.

s.m.: What did you do?

jeff: I read the play three times, and I think that I know what Lillian Hellman wants to say. What horrible characters!

s.m.: What about you, Liz?

liz: I am in the middle of my third reading, but I wrote the biography.

jeff: I wrote the biography of Ben after I read

it twice, but when I began to read the play the third time I made a lot of changes.

LIZ: Yes, I changed it too.

S.M.: Good. What else did you do?

JEFF: Liz and I met, and we lost a lot of time trying to decide on the name for the scene.

S.M.: I don't agree that this is losing time. A word that will tell you clearly what the whole scene is about is of great help, because then you know what the audience must understand. Disclosing the essence of an event is the gradual disclosing of the play's theme. You achieve this with actions dictated by the event. Eugene Vakhtangov said, "A unit in a role or a scene is a step in moving the through line of actions toward the goal," or the superobjective. What name did you give it?

JEFF: We decided that it is "greed." Then Liz and I worked on actions.

LIZ: We also worked on our inner monologue and images, but not very much.

S.M.: That is understandable. You cannot do it all in such a short time, but I am delighted that you started your work on a scene the way it should be done. Let us see the scene and stop talking. Many people still think that Stanislavski discussed the play for months, sitting around the table. This was true before he developed the so-called method of physical actions. As soon as Stanislavski discovered ·the psychophysical process of human behavior, he sent actors on stage after they had read the play and briefly discussed the main events and actions. Stanislavski realized that the discussions at the table artificially divided the actor's physical and psychological behavior. I think that you have done enough work now to begin moving, improvising on the stage. When you have learned the analysis through events and actions, and how to use the given circumstances, you will not waste time on long discussions. Analysis through actions must be done with all the psychic and physical forces of an actor. When you act physically in the given circumstances, you are forced to think of inner problems of the character. Since Stanislavski developed the method of physical actions, we analyze the role and the play *in action*.

(scene)

Yes, I realize that you did not have enough time to do thorough work. But one thing upsets me. We talked and talked about the play: You decided on the name for the scene; you wrote the biographies; you said you knew the main objectives of your characters; you said that you searched for your actions, i.e., that you improvised on actions. But where is all this? It seems to me that the analysis you did, the study of the characters, the biography, and the rest, is only academic work for you. Obviously it is still not clear that all this work has only one purpose: to project to the audience what you have learned about the play, about the characters, and about this particular scene. Stanislavski said, "An actor becomes an actor when he masters the choice of actions." Nothing you did, not one of your actions— and I must say this to both of you—proves that you really searched for expressive actions. But to be frank, this should have been expected. To understand the System theoretically is one thing, but to make it work is another.

Stanislavski said that unless you *assimilate* the technique, you don't really understand it. If you did assimilate the whole technique you would already be accomplished actors. When you have learned the artistic process of the choice of actions, you do not have to come here to study, only to practice.... I am not joking. When this is taught in all drama schools and in all drama departments of our universities, there will be an acting profession in the United States. Now the majority of actors are only people who have made up their minds that they are actors. Real actors are those who can build characters in a play with their own psychophysical resources. Well, that is enough of this for today.

Jeff, Ben, who was badly mistreated by his father and his sister Regina, obtained some horrible information about his father's activities during the war. With this information he blackmailed his father for his whole fortune. If the father had refused to give it to him, Ben would have reported to the authorities that his father made his fortune at the expense of many lives. The blackmail took place this morning. Now, the father is in the next room signing the necessary documents to transfer his possessions to Ben. Ben is the boss for the first time in his life. And Regina, who had everything she wanted from her father, who adored her, now has nothing. Liz and Jeff, from the moment the curtain goes up, the audience must understand that something is taking place in the other room, that Ben is "drunk" with his coup. Your body must express it. Not a second on stage can be empty. Everything you do from the beginning must disclose the situation and help to reveal gradually the superobjective of the play. You must build these characters, Ben and Regina, who are capable of blackmail, of literally cutting each

other's throats for the sake of money. There is no
crime these people would not commit for greed.
They are like animals, you know, like those
rhinoceroses in Ionesco's play. When the lights go
up on this stage, the audience must understand at
once that someone is in the other room and that you,
Ben, cannot wait very long and that you are
thinking, "Better hurry, or else..."

JEFF: What can I do?

S.M.: What is your first action?

JEFF: To wait.

S.M.: Right. But the circumstances, your
objective. There must be psychological meaning in
an action. You can wait in a hospital for a diagnosis;
you can wait in a restaurant for a friend; and you can
wait for your father, whom you blackmailed to
transfer all his possessions to you. The only way to
find what to do while you are waiting is to perform
an improvisation on "to wait" in the circumstances
of the play and of this scene. An improvisation on an
action is the way to find out whether you have
projected your action and whether you have chosen
the right one. Say your own words, forget the
blocking you and Liz have found. Strive to find a
better more expressive blocking, better adaptations.
Think of only one thing: to project the action of
waiting for the money you have wanted all your life,
so that you will be able to humiliate those who have
humiliated you before. It should really be done at
home, but let us try it.

   (Improvisation)

Don't you think that this was very helpful? You did
not think before of going to the door to see whether
your father would be ready soon. Now, having your

action in mind, you did it and it was expressive. I think we should keep your standing at the door in the scene. Do you have an image for the father?

JEFF: Oh, sure.

S.M.: Good, your feeling about him is quite obvious.

JEFF: Could I have a ledger, a book for figures, and be sitting and adding the figures first?

S.M.: Yes, or you could start at the door with the ledger in your hands, and maybe a pencil. It might help to project what you are waiting for. Then you could sit down to count your money. Also, I would like you to project that now you want to sit where your father used to. There should be at least three chairs at the table, not one. And if you project that while starting to sit down at your usual place, you change your mind and sit down at the head of the table, where "the boss should sit," it may be of help. Let us see this.

(Scene)

Yes, and I like your pushing your chair away with your foot and glancing toward the room where your father is. You see, all this establishes the situation. Now Regina comes in, Regina the boss. She has no idea that she is not the boss anymore. Do you remember that at the end, when Regina is convinced that Ben has all the money, she moves her chair away from her father and sits next to Ben? They are absolutely horrible people. Please do not try to sweeten them. Some actors do not like to be seen as nasty characters. This is a mistake. You must expose their nastiness. Liz, when you came in, nothing projected what you are. You were only walking around saying your lines. Search for typical details that will help make your character the quintessence of greed. What do you see when you come in?

LIZ: I see that Ben is sitting on Father's chair. But my first action is to come and have my morning coffee.

S.M.: All right, you see something strange, and your action changes. What is your next action?

LIZ: To boss him?

S.M.: Right, because you do not know yet what happened. You may think he is drinking at this early hour. Well, how about an improvisation on your entrance? Do anything and say anything to project that Ben, whom you despise, sits on your father's chair, and you think this is arrogant.

LIZ: Will my action be "to understand" what is going on?

S.M.: Right.

(Improvisation)

Good. In the scene, when you enter, Liz, don't be afraid to stop and think, "What is the matter with this idiot?" Project your evaluation with your body. And Jeff, you start ridiculing her in anticipation of giving her the full blow. All this talk about building a new house is obviously to shock her. Watch Regina to see whether you are achieving the result you want.

Well, I think that this gives you an idea of the beginning. We must make the play, or in our case the scene, alive. Give it more thought; think of analogous emotions; think of actions to project that this house, everything, is yours now at last. Jeff, sitting at the table mumbling words does not project the play. You only looked bored. Ben is not bored; he is sitting on top of the world. Watch your tempo-rhythm, Jeff. It is wrong at the beginning. You look too comfortable, and no one would guess that you were counting money you never had before.

JEFF: You mean my tempo-rhythm when I do not move?

S.M.: Yes, when you do not move. There is a tempo-rhythm inside us too. And in this particular scene, you do not sit without moving. You are counting the money, and the tempo-rhythm of your body does not correspond to what is inside you. You must work on your physical state. It will stir the correct tempo-rhythm. Is this clear?

JEFF: I guess so.

S.M.: What is your next action, Jeff? When she sits down.

JEFF: To belittle her.

S.M.: But you are not belittling her. Project your action. Use the words. Move your body before you speak, because the verbal action depends on the physical action. I think we should stop right here. Work on this, and also go further. These were only suggestions, and I hope they will help you. Perform improvisations on other situations not included in this scene.

LIZ: I must change my actions and my inner monologue.

S.M.: Good. I like to hear that.

Well, I hope you have not forgotten *The Three Sisters*. Let us see it from the beginning.

(Scene)

It really looks good. But, Meg, you must trust yourself. Do not push your inner monologue. When we think, we often do not want other people to know what we are thinking. You are forcing, and your face is tense. Of course, you are not yet at the stage when thoughts and images of the character flash through your mind, but you must not push them. Sometimes you look as if you are saying, "Look here, I'm thinking." Nina, you look radiant now as Irina. But please do not "announce" to your sisters that "Brother will probably be a professor." They know it. Masha, Anne, you are very good. Hold your book higher. No, not so high as to hide your face. You know, the women wore stiff corsets, and she wouldn't be able to bend as you do. Tusenbach, I am satisfied with your description of Vershinin and his family, but I do not see any difference between your attitude toward Irina and your attitude toward Olga and Masha. What is your objective?

ALBERT: I come to tell about Vershinin.

S.M.: That is right. Irina, the girl you are in love with, is in the room. This is part of the circumstances. And, as you know, the circumstances influence your actions. Describing Vershinin would be different without Irina. What does her presence add to it? Think more about it. Let us see the third act of *The Three Sisters*. It has been a while since I have seen it.

(Scene)

That was absolutely beautiful work.

MEG: It is substantially the same inner monologue, but something was wrong before, and it was my own fault. I guess it wasn't strong enough.

S.M.: Anne and Meg, both of you almost made me shiver—your inner monologue was so convincing. Now it is all there. Very good.

MEG: It is not any of my business, but it seems to me that Irina should talk more *to* Masha.

S.M.: She does.

MEG: Does she?

S.M.: She does not look at Masha all the time, but she turns to her whenever it is justified. You are backstage most of the time when this happens, and that is why you don't know. Nina is very well aware of Masha's presence, whether she turns toward her or not. Do not worry about this.

MEG: Besides, I think that Olga may also be interested in Vershinin.

S.M.: Olga is dissolved in others.

MEG: I don't believe that. I think she would like to get married.

S.M.: Yes, that may be very true. But when their mother died, Olga became the head of the family.

MEG: She was even playing mother to their father....

S.M.: Well...*(Laughter.)*...By the way, someone asked whether the father died suddenly or had been ill for a long time. And then someone said that it must have been sudden—otherwise, if the father were ill, there wouldn't have been a party in the house at the time. I said that there is no reason to think there was a party, but as usual there were a great many people in the house. You do not know the Russians; there are always many people in the house. Tusenbach, Soliony, Rodny, Fedotik—there is no doubt that they were all there as they were every day.

class 14

SONIA MOORE: One oral improvisation: "to belittle." I think we had this action in *Another Part of the Forest*. Let us see whether we can project it. Choose your partner and build the situation. After you have built your imaginary situation, think of the emotion that should be stirred in it. Then think of an analogous emotion which you experienced in life. When you are on stage, think of the physical behavior that will be expressive of what you have built in your mind. The one who is being belittled must have a counteraction. Do not forget the relationship between you. Watch each other and react with your body.

(The students talk over the situation with their partners and perform the improvisation.)

Do you see that it is possible to hear what your partner is saying and go on thinking at the same time? In life we always see and hear another person's words and gestures without interrupting our own train of thoughts. Of course it is not easy on stage, because we must think what has to be thought, at the command of our will. Your body still resists. You,

Jeff, push your body almost with every word, and it is during silences, before speaking and after speaking, that we must make the effort. The action begins with the body expressing what is in our mind before we speak, and it continues after we finish speaking. Your hands must not move so much. Only after you feel the current from your spine going through your arms and culminating in your fingers do you move your hands. Then your gestures will be needed and alive.

Let us see *The Crucible* now.

EVAN: We did an improvisation on that "jealousy" scene, and it seems to work.

S.M.: Good. May I see it?

(Scene from The Crucible*)*

It does make more sense now. Evan, when Abigail says, "Please come closer," don't you think you could move closer so that she could recognize the look in your eyes? She must see that look. Your reproaching her is good. Proctor comes to his senses when she shows him the "wounds" on her leg. He attacks her furiously because he is angry at himself, too. What is your next action?

EVAN: To force her to save Elizabeth.

S.M.: And your action, Sally?

SALLY: I realize that he has not come for the reason I thought and I accuse him. I think at that stage Abigail believes what she says.

S.M.: You mean she has gone so far that she herself does not know when she is telling the truth and when she is lying?

SALLY: Yes, and she fights him because she does not see any way out and she wants him.

S.M.: Your tempo-rhythm at the end is too

slow. Laugh more. And why should Abigail brush the shawl? Cut it. Your ending is quite effective. I hope you realize that there is still much work to be done.

EVAN: Oh, yes.

SALLY: Since last time I have completely changed not only my actions but all my images and inner monologue.

S.M.: Of course, your images and inner monologue depend on your actions. This scene will be very exciting.

Shall we see *Another Part of the Forest* now? *(Scene. Mrs. Moore occasionally interrupts.)* Jeff, when you say, "warm outside," you must emphasize the word "outside." Emphasize it. Bring out your attitude. He means that inside she is cold, that she looks warm, but is not. Your speech is not good, Jeff. You mumble. I don't believe you have images. If you had images, you would not mumble that way. Do you have images?

JEFF: No. *(Laughter.)* You know what happened? When I started to work I did have images, and now that I think of it, I don't. I was so engrossed in actions that I forgot about images.

S.M.: Because your body did not move. When your psychophysical instrument is ready, this will not happen. But now you did not have any images at all.

JEFF: No, that is not entirely true.

S.M.: That is not true? Well, let us see the moment when you say, "The man who thinks you behaved very badly," and so on. Can you honestly tell me that you have continuous images? There is no color whatsoever in your speech, because you have no attitude to them; we do not understand what you are saying; you do not project the attitude to the subtext or to the images.

JEFF: I know very well what I mean.

S.M.: So you think we should be satisfied because *you* know what you mean? Jeff, I am not after you. You are the "victim" for today, and in a way I am glad this happened. It will be helpful for everyone. Go on.... Ridicule her because she has lost everything she had planned so carefully. Ridicule... ridicule, Jeff. Do it with your body before you speak and after you speak. And when you say, "And do it quickly," you really are chasing her out of the house. Your tempo-rhythm must change here.... Good. That is better. Jeff, you still walk as Jeff, not as Ben. Yes, your hands in your pockets, that is better already. Liz, not going to Chicago is a shattering disappointment for Regina. Don't forget this. It is fine for you to grab the book from him. Jeff, when you say, "Marry him this morning," remember that this morning is a special one. Can you imagine what kind of an image you must have? The speech is interesting; please work on it. This encounter with her brother has probably made Regina perspire.

LIZ: Oh, I could wipe my face.

S.M.: Right.

JEFF: What if I am too high before the high point of the scene?

S.M.: Go down before this point, and then up again. Let us see the beginning again.

(Beginning of the scene)

Jeff, your standing at the door looking at your father in the other room looks as if you were sympathizing with him. Your pose does not express your inner action at all. You should not stand at the door so long, either. Go to the coffee table, take your coffee, and on the way to the table look at your father again. In the beginning if you stand at the door, this should be only for as long as it is necessary for the audience to take in you and the room. Think of tempo-rhythm. It helps to connect the inner experience with the physical behavior. The mutual interaction of inner and external rhythms explains many mysterious motions of the human psyche. Express what is inside you with your pose. Fine. That is very good. You begin to look like a gangster already. *(Laughter.)* This is what Lillian Hellman intended. Ben is not like you, the shy Jeff. Since our goal is to achieve reincarnation, which means changing your own peculiar qualities into those of the character, you must analyze your behavior in the given circumstances. Analyze it in actions, not in qualities— that is what Stanislavski demanded. Do it with your whole psychophysical apparatus and you will reincarnate gradually. Reincarnation occurs when you are able to think, feel, and behave as the character. This is the highest level in theatre art, and is what we must strive to achieve. And remember, Stanislavski said, "The character is not someone, sometime, somewhere," but "*I*, now, here, today." Now, whatever you do, you do in order to challenge your father. Think of what you would do in Ben's circumstances.

JEFF: I think, no matter what kind of a person Ben is, he would always think, "Should I, or shouldn't I?"

LIZ: Oh, I don't think so. That's wrong.

S.M.: I doubt that Ben would hesitate. This is

the moment he has been waiting for all his life. The thought that he is finally the boss never leaves his mind. "Why shouldn't I sit at his place now?" he thinks. The moment when you evaluate this is good, but then after that you look like a nice little boy again.

JEFF: Yes, I should find better physical actions.

S.M.: Also, when you are writing, it is not clear that you are counting the money so that he does not cheat you. Your pose is wrong. The whole beginning is not clear yet. We must pay complete attention to disclosing the play, and the beginning is especially important. We should approach the beginning of the scene in the same way. It must be energetic. The blocking we found today is not obligatory—it is the best we could do today. Your work during a rehearsal or a performance may sometimes be better, sometimes worse, but it *must* be the best you can do that day. When you work alone, without me, perform improvisations on your actions, and you will find better blocking. Show me what you find. This is how you will also learn to direct. I cannot overemphasize the usefulness of improvisations on actions.

PETER: We want to show you *Desire Under the Elms.*

(Scene)

That was good preliminary work. Peter, when you enter the courtyard, you do not see her, and she does not see you or hear you, but both stop because you sense each other's presence. . . . Yes, right, but you must fill it with inner monologue. Anne, would you please move your chair a little more upstage to give him room to cross the yard?

ANNE: Like this?

s.m.: A little more. Fine.

PETER: How long should I stand here?

s.m.: You must know what is going through your mind, and let us see how much time it will need if it is justified.

PETER: I am trying to control myself and cross the yard, pretending not to pay any attention to her. I think, "I am going to the village, no matter what. I must not let her see how much I want her."

s.m.: Fine. Now say your inner monologue, and we will see whether it is right.

(*Peter performs the beginning of the scene again.*)

That is right. But something is wrong when you stop at her laugh. You anticipate it.

ANNE: Could I start laughing as soon as he starts moving even if he is still behind our screen— I mean the wall?

s.m.: Yes, that is the right idea. You may see him as soon as he moves. Let us see that again....

Good, that is just right. Peter, please work on your inner monologue during her long speech. You need tremendous concentration to justify standing there spellbound for such a long time. Anne, I like what you are doing in your speech. Of course, your images must become deeper, but you have only started this scene, and I think you are on the right road. Show it to me again soon.

class 15

(Mary as Julie and Ken as Jean perform a scene from Strindberg's Miss Julie.*)*

SONIA MOORE: Mary, why were you standing at the door?

MARY: To see whether Christine [the cook—Jean's mistress] was still asleep.

S.M.: *You* know this, but we have no idea of it. Ken, in this scene, as usual, you are "not interested."

KEN: I think Miss Julie, my boss's daughter, is interested in me, but I'm the butler, and I am not interested in her.

S.M.: This is wrong, Ken. Jean and Julie are both attracted to each other. An actor's art depends on his ability to bring new characters to life. You have "typed" yourself as your own cliché, and your real personality is lost. The great director Nemirovich-Danchenko said that it was not important how many roles an actor has performed, but how many characters he has created. Ken, what you do does not work, believe me.

MARY: I know that he wants me very badly and

doesn't want to give up what he has started. That is why I only pretend to wake up Christine.

s.m.: Yes, that is right.... Mary, when you offer him the drink, it does not come through that you want to make him feel that he is an equal .... Well, I do not know whether there is any sense in discussing it further until Ken changes his mind and begins to work the Stanislavski way, not his. Why don't you take Laurence Olivier for your ideal?

ken: Laurence Olivier is all external. He has said himself that he goes from the external.

s.m.: Olivier is not external. He achieves the psychophysical behavior. He gives great attention to the external form, and that is how it should be. It is absolutely incredible that some people in this country think that Stanislavski influenced the American theatre much more than the English theatre. It is amazing, because English actors *really* use what they know about the Stanislavski System, while our actors follow the American "method" cult. I have heard American experts raving about the performances of English actors, and I cannot understand how they can fail to realize what our actors lack. Stanislavski's teachings are almost entirely ignored in America.

Now, back to *Miss Julie*. The man is losing control, but all we see is your usual impassive self. Have you found a name for this episode? *(Silence.)* ...After you do give it a name, then think of the physical actions. I hope it will be very different when you show the scene to me again. No one can do anything all by himself. No matter how talented an actor is or how good his work is, he will not be able to project what has to be projected if the others do not contribute actively.

KEN: Is stating a fact an action?

S.M.: Sometimes it may be. But do not go through the whole role stating facts!

KEN: It is one thing to have an action and another to project it.

S.M.: Yes, but it can be learned if you *try*. Nemirovich-Danchenko said about Tolstoy, "What courage to be so simple!" But he also said about some actors, "Simplicity can become insolence."

What else do we have today?

MEG: Jack and I would like to show the scene between Proctor and his wife from *The Crucible*.

S.M.: Very well, but only if you have worked on your biographies, on the name for this exercise, know your objectives, have analyzed your actions, worked on images and inner monologue, have performed some improvisations.

JACK: We did, but of course we have not worked enough.

S.M.: Let us see it.

(Scene)

Well, that is very different work and I am happy. Now let us see it again, and I shall interrupt you for notes. To start with, Jack, what is your objective?

JACK: To avoid her.

SM.: Good, and your action, Meg?

MEG: I thought that he went to Salem, and I am waiting for him to tell me about it.

S.M.: This came across quite well. But I think that after you hear her singing, Jack, you don't have to move so cautiously. You know that Elizabeth will

come in to give you your supper. Meg, when you
enter, stop for a while and wait for him to tell you
what happened in Salem. He doesn't say anything,
then you ask him, "Why did you come so late?" . . .
What happens next after he answers you?

MEG: I am disappointed.

S.M.: To be disappointed is not an action. In
life when we describe an experience we always speak
of actions. We reach an experience through an
action. What do you do when you are disappointed?
What would you do if these were the circumstances?

MEG: I would reproach him.

S.M.: Right. You may want to say something
like, "But you said . . ." and this should be expressed
with your body. Then stop, and go to the stove
saying, in reproach, "Oh, you've done this."

(Jack and Meg repeat the scene.)
You actually have no lines when you begin to
reproach him. But your psychophysical action must
express your reproach. What you did now was
overdone. You should work on this. Jack, if you want
to project that you are avoiding her, you must move
away not toward her. When Meg moves to empty the
basin, when she moves toward you, go to the table to
avoid her. . . . Right, that looks good. What happens
next?

JACK: My action is to talk to cover up.

S.M.: Yes, and Meg, your action?

MEG: Well, we both talk just to talk, but I am
waiting for a moment to attack him.

S.M.: Finally we have a scene on which Meg
and Jack have worked in an "educated" way. I am
truly delighted. Now, Jack, don't you think that you

stand up too soon? Don't you think you can defend yourself and still continue to eat? After all, you have been in the fields all day long. When she says that Mary Warren is an official of the court, this is shocking enough for Proctor to stop eating.

JACK: Yes, right.

S.M.: It is a very good scene. . . .

Let us see *Another Part of the Forest*.

(Scene)

There has been a tremendous improvement since last time. I am quite impressed by the work you have done.

JEFF: And last time you were very worried.

S.M.: Yes. Because what you did last time, Jeff, was only external. But now it is quite different. And now, Liz, I also see your efforts to build Regina the way she is. I was worried about your insisting that Regina was not that bad. I felt that you did not even want to work on this role. You are not the only one, Liz. I know many examples of actors trying to build positive character because they don't want to appear "bad" on stage. This is a terrible mistake. You, the actress, must know your opinion about the character. I am sure, Liz, that you cannot think that Regina is a good person. I don't mean that there may not be anything good in her, though I wouldn't know what. And, it is all right to *try* to find something good in a negative character. But Regina is a horrible woman, and since you, the actress, know that, you must build her that way. Lillian Hellman has not given her any attractive characteristics. You were trying to make Regina a person with whom people would sympathize, though you yourself do not sympathize with her. This is a distortion of what Lillian Hellman wanted to say. Nemirovich-Danchenko said, "While living the emotions of the character, an actor should be his prosecutor."

But last time there was practically nothing, and today it is so much better. I am sure that you know the value of improvisations on different situations. Let us do it again, and I shall stop you. First of all, Liz, your through line of actions is not clear; it seems as if you have only one action.

LIZ: Isn't there one overall action?

S.M.: There is the superobjective of your character. The through line of actions—the chain of consecutive, logical, purposeful actions—gradually discloses it. You tease him, you ridicule him, you mistreat him, and you challenge him, right?

LIZ: Right. Doesn't it come through?

S.M.: Your actions are not concrete or expressive enough.

(The scene starts again.)

(Interrupting) Jeff, when you stand there with your back to us, your back looks wrong. . . . Yes, I mean it. You don't look very aggressive, only stiff.

JEFF: Well, I was conscious of the stiffness in my body, but I thought it was right because for the first time in my whole life I had the upper hand.

S.M.: It does not seem to be in the right tempo-rhythm.

JEFF: I realize this.

S.M.: While you are standing there, you should be challenging your father in your mind and saying something like, "Hurry up, you damn fool, and sign those papers. Don't try my patience." Maybe a little laugh at him would help. Just before you turn.

JEFF: I did laugh.

s.m.: Obviously your body was not involved in your action, and therefore the laugh was not projected. We must insist on the psychophysical process of an action, also because otherwise your emotions will never be involved.

jeff: May I perform an improvisation on "to challenge"?

s.m.: Let us see it. It must be in these circumstances, when you have the upper hand for the first time.

(Improvisation)

Did you see what happened, how suddenly your body became expressive? This is what you should do in the scene. I don't mean all of it, but your figure, at the door, throwing back your head, should be in the scene. Your going away from the door and then looking through it again was excellent.

liz: I still don't think that Regina should be just bad, just black.

s.m.: Everyone has good and bad qualities, but some people have much more bad in them, and some more good. Regina, as conceived by Lillian Hellman, is a negative character, and I cannot understand why you argue about it. Today I thought you did understand it. I suggest that you reread the play. Now, when you enter, you go for your coffee, and then you see Ben sitting at your father's place.

liz: No, I see him first.

s.m.: All right. Let us see how this works.

(The scene continues.)

Jeff, what is that book you are holding?

jeff: It is supposed to be the ledger.

s.m.: Oh. Keep the pencil ready. I still think that your struggle with Regina when you put your foot on your father's chair was more interesting and more expressive than what you are doing now. I would appreciate it if you would put it back in the scene, unless you can bring something that is more interesting. Liz, during the scene you must find moments in which you will project that you resent his arrogance, and when he puts his foot on your father's chair you explode. It should come to this gradually. You don't project the moment when you begin to realize that "something interesting has happened here this morning." Let us see it again.

(Scene)

I would like less shouting, Liz, when you say "with carnival trimming." Don't you think it will be more convincing and impressive if you do it without shouting? I would also like to suggest that when you make the decision to try another approach with him you stand with your back to the audience. We must sense this, and when you turn around we should realize that you have made a decision.

(Liz continues.)

That looks very good. I can read your inner monologue clearly.

LIZ: Do I have to look out there?

S.M.: What you did was just fine. It was very expressive.

class 16

s.m.: Let us begin with a silent improvisation: "shake hands with different people."

liz: What do you mean?

s.m.: Each of you decide on a relationship between yourself and each of the other people here. Don't tell us, but you must decide for example, that Evan is a king, Meg is a person who has hurt you, Sally is someone you owe money, Michael is your best friend. . . . Do not rush. Let me remind you that you have to see the people who are here, but treat them as those you have built in your imagination.

(The students concentrate for a while and "shake hands.")

s.m.: The theme for an oral improvisation is to "push another person into something." Build the circumstances, know the relationship between you; know why it is important to you, and other details.

peter: I think we have already done something like this.

s.m.: Yes. Therefore you must build a different situation now. We can repeat the same improvisations many times, but each time in different circumstances.

EVAN: And what is the other person's action?

S.M.: It depends on the persuasiveness of the one who pushes. I don't think that I should give you hints. Everything must depend on the situation you build and how it develops. And please, move around—not just to move, of course; but do what you would do in such a situation in life. Choose your partners, then concentrate to remember an analogous emotion, which should be stirred and which you have experienced in life.

(Students perform the improvisation.)

JEAN: We want to show you *Separate Tables*.

S.M.: Fine.

(Scene)

What is the play about?

JEAN: It's about people who don't belong.

S.M.: Why did she come here? What did you say the name of the event was? Was it "peace"?

JEAN: No, "negotiations."

S.M.: This seems more characteristic. But first I want to know whether both of you have written biographies of your characters.

JEAN: Yes.

S.M.: I am sure that this made you go back to the play for a more thorough understanding of it. Where does the scene take place?

MICHAEL: In the lobby of a resort hotel.

S.M.: Your behavior in a hotel lobby is different from what you would do in your own house. We have performed many improvisations, but as soon as we do a scene from a play, most of you forget that the circumstances influence your actions. Here in the lobby, people may come in any time. The conversation began a while ago. Nothing you did helped to project this. What is your objective when you ask him, "Why did I marry you?"

JEAN: I am trying to convince him that I love him, and I want to know whether he is still in love with me.

S.M.: Right. Michael, you become somewhat alive when you say your lines, but to be quite frank, even then, you are more dead than alive. You are rushing as if you want to get it over with. Your body is dead. I do not believe that you have many images. It is a question of willpower, Michael. You must be able to control on stage the work you have done at home. I am quite certain that you have worked at home. You must make a true effort in class. I don't mind if you do only a little bit of a scene, but there must be actions, images, inner monologue, and the body that expresses these inner processes. Your speech is good. But without images and your attitude to the images and to the words, it is dead.

JEAN: Every time I show a new scene I am scared.

S.M.: I am more scared of you than you are of me! Sometimes I am afraid to see new scenes because some of you think what you show is perfect. It's difficult to give you constructive criticism without upsetting you. And when I praise someone, others are upset. I think you show very good promise and there is nothing to be upset about.

JEAN: I am upset because I work and work, and then everything is wrong.

S.M.: But how long did you work on this scene?

JEAN: About six or eight hours.

S.M.: And you think that this is a great deal. Do

you realize that you must give birth to another human being? You neglect to penetrate into the character and are playing your most primitive impression of it. You are playing the result, instead of building it step by step. Anyone in the audience who has read the play may know as much about it as do you. But actors must have much richer knowledge and bring out more of its essence.

The theme of this play is worthlessness, loneliness, humiliation. In this small suburban hotel people are assembled mostly by chance and are cut off from life's currents. Some are here to get away from problems, and for others it is the only place where they can afford to live out their lives. As in most of Rattigan's plays, the characters are middle-class people. They are broken by life, lonely and not very strong emotionally. These people look for peace in ordinary, everyday pleasures and preoccupations. There are no heroes; Rattigan is interested in ordinary man.

MICHAEL: You know, when I staged a play at the Community Center, I asked an actress what her action was, and she answered, "I feel sad." I told her, "I don't care how you feel. Just fulfill your action."

S.M.: Good for you! The truth is that an actor does not feel a thing until he succeeds in involving his psychophysical behavior. By now you have learned something about the use of the emotional memory without any damage to your nervous system. This is achieved through the method of physical actions. When you find the unique, purposeful physical actions in the given circumstances and are capable of fulfilling them, your psychophysical apparatus is involved, and then you *feel.* Jean, you are doing very well and you must not expect your scene to be ready in such a short time. We are not preparing for summer stock. I expect you here to be pioneers of high-level professional theatre in the United States. But it is hard work. I never promised you that it would be easy. And, all of you, please do not show me a scene unless you have worked on the superobjective of the play, the superobjective of your character, the name of the event or events, your objectives, your actions, inner monologue, images, and your body. I do not expect it to be in final form, but a great deal of preparatory work must be done before you show me the scene.

The worst thing is that you have already memorized your lines. Is that the great deal of work you have done? Then it is a great waste of your time. I thought I made it clear that you must not memorize the lines until you have done improvisations on your actions with your own words, until you are sure of the objectives, actions, inner monologue, images, and the body. Then you must memorize your words, and they will sound fresh every time. It will be very difficult for you to change your intonations now. I wish everyone's physical instrument were as well-trained as yours, Jean. But what you have been doing so far belongs to the school of the theatre of representation, identified with Coquelin, rather than with the living theatre of Stanislavski. Theatre of representation is also art. But, as a rule, its actors do not live the inner experience; they demonstrate only the external form. When actors are true artists, this may be very beautiful. They impress with refined taste, magnificent speech and gestures. But this great skill is used only to illustrate text. An actor remains only himself.

JEFF: Does Brando belong to the school of representation?

S.M.: Oh, no. Marlon Brando does not belong to any school. Marlon Brando could be one of the greatest actors of our century. But he stayed with his own inventions and never learned the technique. I am always upset when I think of this. It is very sad. I have told you before that the Comédie Française is a fine example of the school of representation. They do beautiful work, but usually actors of this school never stir the audience's experience; they don't affect anyone. It is only a beautiful spectacle. You know by now that I am not an admirer of the school of representation. Some actors of this school have said that being on stage was torture for them. I can understand why. To be on stage without living the character's life does not give any satisfaction to either the actor or the audience. But when an actor lives the emotions, it is thrilling for both. Stanislavski demanded that the actor exist on stage as the character, not just illustrate him.

And now back to the scene. I cannot understand the stubbornness of some of you who insist on working on long scenes. You know, at auditions sometimes they allow you only a three-minute scene. I do not mind if it is five or seven minutes, but a scene of twenty minutes is too long. We can do much better work on a short scene, and I beg you to cut it. While cutting, be very careful not to distort the scene. Pay attention to the essential lines. I shall be glad to sit down with you and help you with the cuts.

JEAN: I feel like dropping the scene.

S.M.: That is up to you, though I don't like you dropping what you have started. You can do it very well, and you have some good moments. Do some more work, and then we shall see.

(Scene from Saint Joan, *by George Bernard Shaw—Albert as the Dauphin; Mary as Joan)*

s.m.: Oh, Mary, stop, please. You don't have any inner monologue.

mary: It is his moment. I must let him have his moment.

s.m.: Yes, but that does not mean that you must die. He will have his moment also if you continue to think! . . . Go on, now.

(Scene)

You must try to bring out Bernard Shaw's humor. Albert, you are doing beautiful work; I congratulate you. But you look absolutely ghastly today.

albert: Evan and I stayed up until four in the morning arguing with some stupid people.

s.m.: What about?

albert: About Stanislavski. . . .

s.m.: What about *A Month in the Country*? *(The scene from* A Month in the Country, *by Ivan Turgenev)*

It is a beautiful scene. It is about two women in love with the same man—the tutor Beliaev—and this must come across. But Nina, watch out. It sounds as if you like the other man, who is interested in Liza.

nina: Really? I didn't mean it. May I laugh while I speak about him?

s.m.: It may be helpful. Both of you are doing excellent work, though it is not yet completely Turgenev. I do not understand why you are reluctant to kiss Natalia Petrovna's hand. It would be approrpiate and would help to project that you are not her equal. Keep on working; it is a lovely scene.

class 17

SONIA MOORE: Liz, some of your ideas during our discussion of *The Children's Hour* absolutely stunned me. It had been a long time since I had read the play, and so I reread it to see whether I had a wrong idea. I must remind you that we must be careful about the interpretation of every play. We must read and reread to try to understand the author's idea.

SALLY: I think we have been distorting this play. Lillian Hellman intended the little girl to be evil and the two women to be victims. Even if Martha had an unnatural feeling toward Karen, she kept herself under control.

LIZ: I still think it wasn't only Martha. It also crossed Karen's mind. Karen leaned on Martha as if she were a man.

S.M.: I would appreciate it if you read the play again. I don't know where you see this.

SALLY: I always thought that Karen was the strongest one.

LIZ: Do you know any woman who would invite someone to go along on her honeymoon as Karen did?

s.m It may seem very unusual, but remember that Karen felt sorry for Martha and did not want to leave her alone. I know that Chekhov invited his sister to join him and his bride—she was the actress Olga Knipper—on their honeymoon. She did not accept the invitation, and it is possible that Martha wouldn't either, if the marriage had taken place. I am certain that Karen did not have the ideas you are trying to impose on her.

SALLY: I think Martha did not fully realize her feelings toward Karen until all this happened. She is honest when she says, "You need . . . this girl . . . to realize what was in you all the time. . . ."

LIZ: If this is so, I don't think that Karen would have been so shocked about her fiancé's suspicions.

s.m.: I cannot agree with you. On the contrary, Karen is shocked because she couldn't imagine such an idea crossing Joe's mind. I hope that you will read the play again and change your mind about its theme. But let's see the scene now.

(Scene)

After watching Joe leave and then pulling that imaginary window shade, you sat down without justification. It looks as if you were sitting down because the director told you to, and you had néver heard about using the circumstances or knowing why, where, when. . . .

LIZ: I don't think that Karen should pull the shade down.

s.m.: I don't understand what you have against this. It symbolized your break with Joe. Sally, did you know that Liz does not pull the shade down any more before your entrance? Since we don't have a real shade, you may not know. But you must change your reaction at your entrance.

SALLY: Yes, I know, but it seems to me that I can react the same way, because I see at once that Joe has left.

S.M.: All right. Did you change your inner monologue? . . . Good. Why do you speak about the darkness and the supper?

SALLY: To make conversation. I sense what must have happened between Karen and Joe.

S.M.: Good. When you speak about giving supper to the "duchess," you must project your feeling toward her. After all, she is the one who started all your trouble. Do you have the right image for her?

SALLY: I sure do!

S.M.: Then project your attitude toward her. Also, Sally, you do not watch Karen enough. While setting the table, and later, you must keep your eye on her and notice that she is going to pieces. That is why you say, "Go back to Joe. . . ." You realize then that you should move out of her way. Let us see the beginning again.

(Scene)

Since we will forget about your ideas that Karen is a lesbian, your action changes, and therefore your inner monologue is wrong and must be changed. Karen may even laugh when she says, "Other people have not been destroyed by it," because she is so far from "it." And Sally, you too must change some of your actions and some of your inner monologue. We must come back to what Lillian Hellman wanted to say in this play.

LIZ: Then you don't want what we found the last time any more?

s.M.: Definitely not. At first, when Martha talks about her feeling toward you, you must be so concentrated on your inner monologue that you do not hear what she says for a while. Your answers should be automatic. I believe at this moment Karen is engrossed in her thoughts and decisions about Joe. Oh, your sitting down at the beginning still does not look justified. You sit down either because your legs are shaky or because you hear Martha coming and do not want her to see how disturbed you are. There must be a reason for your sitting down, and we in the audience must know the reason. It looks like only the physical side of an action. Would you please work on this? Sally, when you are lying to her, you should not move toward her but away.

SALLY: I agree, but I can't understand why she does not tell the truth right away.

s.M.: Maybe because she does not know how to say it. Liz, don't you think that it is logical for Karen to be thinking of Joe at this moment? After all, she is in love with the man. At this moment you are not interested in what Martha is saying, and your turning away from her looks right.

LIZ: You know when Martha tells me how she feels about me, I would give her a "look" and go right to her.

s.M.: *You* would, but would you if you were Karen, in this situation? We are learning to build a character, not to be ourselves all the time.

LIZ: I think this is what Karen would do.

s.M.: I agree with you. I only wanted to check

on you. I think this is a good idea. Let us see how it works.

(Scene)

That was good. It looks better and better. I believe in doing the best we can every day, so don't think that this is the best. That would not be like Stanislavski. On the road he gave us, there is no end to improvement. I am certain that next time you will bring some good ideas. Then I may be able to improve on what you have brought until all of us have exhausted our possibilities. And even then, that will not mean that it is the best it could be. (Laughter.) Really, some moments in this scene look very good.

Now let us see *Another Part of the Forest.*

(Scene)

Liz, you must change your action at the beginning. You do not project that you think you are still the boss. Ben knows what has happened, but Regina has no idea. You must treat him as you always have, which means to mistreat him. In the beginning you wouldn't let him upset you. But now, I believe you when you are speaking about Chicago. It is clear how much the trip means to you. What is not clear yet is why these people are the way they are, why they are ready to cut each other's throats for the sake of money. It is an important message, which we must try to project. I admit, it is very difficult to achieve in this play, especially in only one scene. Both of you have done excellent work since I saw this scene last time. That does not happen often ... and I am delighted.

JEFF: I want to say only one thing. You said

last time that I must project the ugliness of the character, and at the same class we came upon the business with the newspaper—you know, the one Regina throws on the floor and I give it a good kick. Did it come off now?

s.m.: Very well. This is what the physical actions are for. You were really involved because your whole psychophysical apparatus was involved. It looked very convincing. I really congratulate you on your work.

jeff: And did you get the feeling that Ben is stronger in the beginning?

s.m.: Definitely.

jeff: Mrs. Moore, couldn't we do it without the fight over the chair? What if I grab her arm?

s.m.: Now that you have made me so happy, I am ready to give in! Let me see—oh, Liz, when he says, "You're not going to Chicago," don't you think you should stop moving?

liz: I pulled away from him on this. Didn't it work?

s.m.: Let us see it again.

(Jeff and Liz perform again.)

That was somewhat overdone. By the way, Jeff, don't you think that it is time for you to go to the door again to check why it takes your father so long? ...Watch him looking at your father, Liz. Try to understand. You go into the other room, and when you come back you are a different person because you have realized that something serious has happened.

liz: Now it seems that everything is wrong again.

s.m.: Not at all. What you did just now is very good. Your actions are right, but it never hurts to revise them. I have never tried to hide from you that there is no end to improvement in this work, but it was very good. After she comes back, she has lost her superiority.

LIZ: Yes, in the beginning she is strong and only tries to find out what is the matter with her father. She is actually a strong girl.

S.M.: Yes. When you begin to anticipate the "catastrophe" and begin to weaken, watch your tempo-rhythm. It should change with every slight change in the circumstances. And the opposite happens to Ben—the more Regina is shaken, the more arrogant he becomes. Revise it.

LIZ: You know, I tried hard to think of something as important to me in my own life as Chicago was for Regina, and then I thought, "What would I do?"

S.M.: That is good. That is how we use our emotional memory. The right physical actions will stir your inner experiences. It is a great satisfaction to me that you found many interesting things in your blocking, thanks to the improvisations on your actions.

LIZ: Shall I go to the door when I say, "I shall make him say"?

S.M.: Try another improvisation on your action, and you will find the answer. Maybe it will be helpful—or maybe, on the contrary, it will be stronger without moving toward the door. The only way to know is through an improvisation. Liz, I remember how terribly overdone it looked when you tried to be frantic without having any inner monologue. Your face used to look distorted, and now you are beautiful in this scene.

Now that Liz has told us about digging back into her life to find something as important to her as the trip to Chicago was to Regina, you must know that you must go through the whole role that way. Then you will gradually build *your own theme*. Find your own experienced emotions which are analogous to those of the character you are creating, remember your behavior, and use it for the character. Then you will merge with the character, and it will be difficult to know what is yours and what is the character's, because you will also be revealing yourself. This involves the audience, and they either sympathize with you or are antagonistic toward you. You will be sharing your own suffering, your own joy. Seek your own theme from the beginning to the end of your role. I do not know what Liz found in her own life, but if, for instance, she had been promised a leading role in a film, and then she learned that someone was trying to ruin this unique chance, this might be analogous to Regina's feeling about Chicago. But don't try to become emotional thinking of this. You must think of *actions*, of what you did when this happened, or what you would do if this should happen. After you find the actions, you don't have to think about Hollywood anymore. You think of it in the process of your work in order to find the right actions. Later, you treat Chicago as if it were Hollywood.

ALBERT: For instance, if Jeff and Liz don't hate each other, but Ben and Regina do hate each other, they have to find people they hate in their own lives and then find the right actions.

s.m.: Yes. I am sure we all have someone in our life whom we cannot stand. It is not always easy to find analogous experiences, but with effort it can be done. In addition to our own life there is an inexhaustible source of material in the life around us. Stanislavski urges actors to observe and analyze what they see around them in life. You must observe and store your impressions. A well-developed emotional memory is the most important require-ment for an actor.

JEFF: Do we use what we found for our own theme on stage?

S.M.: Yes, during rehearsals the stage situation becomes finally the stimulus for your emotions. Then you use the physical *actions* that you have selected when working on your own theme. If you succeeded in selecting the right, logical, typical physical actions on the basis of your analogous emotions, and if you are capable of fulfilling them truthfully, if you honestly communicate with your partner, you will involve the psychological side that dictates these actions to you. Your own organic nature is involved then, and you will really feel and live the life of the character.

EVAN: Do you mean that we must work at home on the psychophysical actions and then on stage think only of the physical side? Is that it?

S.M.: Yes. The truthful execution of the physical action will involve the psychological side of the action, i.e., emotions, images, inner mono-logue—everything that dictates the choice of a physical action. You understand that a movement of your body, even the slightest shrug of your shoulders, is a physical action. We are speaking of the *method of physical actions.*

KEN: But if you stir your own emotions, then

you are playing yourself and not the character.

s.m.: Oh, no. Please, all of you, listen carefully. It is *always* your own emotions that you are trying to stir for the character. A character in a play, for instance Regina, is only a dead character until the actress's own emotions are stirred. You are your own material, your own instrument. You, your own personality is the material with which you create different characters in a play. If you study the play, the events, the actions, the thoughts, the images, the subtext, the physical behavior of your character, you do not have to worry that you will always be playing yourself. You will always be a different Ken because your psychophysical behavior will be different for different characters. You will be a character in a play while remaining yourself because it is your own organic nature that is involved. But, if you don't do all this work, then you will always be Ken as Ken, not Ken as the character. There are as many nuances of emotions as there are different physical actions.

ALBERT: Then you don't have to sit backstage trying to become emotional, like some actors?

s.m.: Those actors are satisfied with the antiquated data that Stanislavski revised a long time ago. They oversimplify the System and forget that its goal is "reincarnation." They don't want to understand that the heart of the Stanislavski System is his method of physical actions, which enables actors to stir different nuances of emotion, not just emotion in general. To receive a good role or to buy a new dress may both make you happy, but it is happiness with very different nuances. Therefore trying to stir your emotions in general does not help to build the character's life. Without such a differentiation of emotions, the spectators will never understand the interests of the character and what kind of a person he is.

JEFF: If money is not very important to me, what shall I do for Ben?

S.M.: Something else may mean as much to you as money means to Ben.

JEFF: It takes a lot of work at home.

S.M.: It certainly does.

KEN: You know, if I have to be in love with my partner, and if I see a bunch of flowers in my mind, this helps me. *(Laughter.)*

S.M.: Jack wants to say something.

JACK: When I was working on Andrei, I was thinking about my grandmother all the time, until I realized that I was moving away from the play.... I realized that I did not know the play, and that this image was wrong. My actions did not stir my emotions. I became more and more dead.... I did not have images that fitted the play.

S.M.: Did you use the image of your grandmother for Natasha or for your sisters? *(Laughter.)* It certainly seems to be wrong for any of them.

class 18

MICHAEL: Mrs. Moore, we have a surprise for you. Meg and I have been working on the scene between Irina and Tusenbach in the first act of *The Three Sisters*. May we show it to you?

S.M.: Of course. You know I love this play.

(Scene)

I hate to disappoint you, especially since you have put in a great deal of excellent work. You have objectives, actions, the inner monologue, images, good control of your body, but your actions are all wrong for Irina and Tusenbach. You have built totally different characters. You have built a Soliony rather than a Tusenbach—and Meg, Irina would never be rude to Tusenbach. She likes him very much. Everyone likes this noble friend. Michael, Tusenbach does not know that Irina doesn't love him. He is so in love with her and he is such an enthusiast that he does not hear her until the fourth act, when she says that she will be a faithful wife to him but cannot love him. This is just before Tusenbach goes to the duel with Soliony. And this is what kills him before he is actually killed in the duel. There is no sense talking much about it, because you must read the play over and over again to understand it and its characters. Your impression of these people is wrong. You must change your objectives, your actions, images, and inner monologue.

MEG: Maybe we should show you the scene with Olga, Anfissa, and Natasha. It is better to know right away if we are on the wrong track.

S.M.: Maybe. Let us see it.

(Scene)

It is good work, but—as often happens—the role of Natasha is misinterpreted. She is hard, down-to-earth, a complete contrast to the spirituality of the three sisters. Her petit-bourgeois insolence is a degrading, frightening force. In the Russian production staged by the remarkable Tovstonogov, according to a critic, Natasha is like a moth flitting through rooms snuffing out candles. It is impossible to get rid of her and it is impossible to live with her. Natasha should be mercilessly but gradually exposed. She is pretty, and she is not always hysterical. I am sure that if she were, Andrei would not have fallen in love with her. By the time of this scene, Natasha is in full command of the house. She does not scream when she can command quietly. She is self-confident, and she starts out firm and quiet with Olga, but at Olga's every move she gets more and more irritated and finally becomes hysterical.

By the way, to have "gained weight" was a compliment in those days. Natasha likes it, so you must change your action when you look in the mirror and say, "They say I have gained weight," and the rest. Olga is tired but tries to keep herself under control, but Meg, you can lose control for a moment, and blame yourself for it. It is a good scene but a difficult one. I think all of you are doing very good work in it. Without inner work, Chekhov's plays especially are absurd.

Didn't Michael and Mary say they wanted to show *Cat on a Hot Tin Roof* as Brick and Maggie?

MARY: Yes.

S.M.: Well, let us see it.

(Scene)

It is pretty good. But at this stage, Michael, I would like your images to be deeper, and your thoughts could be more interesting and of greater variety.

MICHAEL: That's right, my inner monologue has no variety.

S.M.: That is why your face looks stiff.

MICHAEL: Does it? I wanted to show how shaken I was.

S.M.: You "show" plenty by making faces, and it looks overdone because the inner side of your action is not rich enough. And your inner monologue is inactive; it should contain decisions. Brick has plenty to cope with at this moment. The physical form should be more economical. It is an interesting scene, and I would like you to do more work on it.

Now, I would like to see Proctor's scene with his wife from *The Crucible*.

(Scene)

I love this scene . . . *(Long sigh from the actors who performed it.)* Yes, I do, I love it. The beginning is just fine, really everything is good. Jack, when you drop into the chair, and then say, "Oh, it is a black mischief," it seems dragged out.

JACK: I am having my inner monologue in the pause.

s.m.: Yes, I know you are. But you do not need it. You must not create pauses just to put in your inner monologue. I wonder whether this is clear. Do not try to fill in the inner monologue if there is no need for a pause. The inner monologue is your train of thought when there is a reason to be silent. The logical thing for Proctor is to drop into the chair as you do, and say without pausing, "Oh, it is a black mischief." And also, when your fight begins, there should be no pauses, so as not to slow the tempo-rhythm. From Elizabeth's lines, "Good, then let you think on it," the tempo-rhythm must become crescendo, to the very end. Another thing, Jack, when she puts her hand on your shoulder, trying to persuade you to go to Salem, you must react. It is unusual for Elizabeth to be so affectionate, and this makes you feel even more guilty. Often when people feel guilty they become aggressive, and that is what Proctor is doing. But I do love the scene. Shall we see the other scene, with Proctor and Abigail?

EVAN: Yes. We have worked a great deal on it. We came to the conclusion that since Proctor is coming to see Abigail in order to save his wife, he would not want to make love to her.

s.m.: I agree with you, but Proctor could lose his head for a moment. He regains control when she begins to show him her "wounds." It is like cold water over his head, and he begins to fight her. Well, let us see what you have done.

(Scene)

There is no doubt that you have discovered interesting content. Evan, you said Proctor would not make love to her in these circumstances. But don't you realize that it was a love scene as you did it?

EVAN: Well, I think he is torn between his duty and his attraction to her.

S.M.: Right. But it is much more logical for such a decent man as Proctor to forget himself for only a short moment. There are quite a few very interesting moments, but you must cut seventy-five percent of the movements. There is an impossible accumulation of detail. It is difficult to follow everything, and the scene has no form. You must revise it and discard what is superfluous. It is an exciting scene, and all the essence that you have brought out is more proof of the value of the Stanislavski analysis in understanding the undercurrent of a play.

Do we have time for something else?

NINA: Can we show you a bit from *The Unsatisfactory Supper*?

S.M.: Very well.

(Scene from The Unsatisfactory Supper, *by Tennessee Williams——Nina, Jeff, and Meg)*

Very interesting. Nina, your attention on the lollipop should be exaggerated. Also, when you come in, I want to see that you can scarcely breathe —that is how much you ate. These people are caricatures of human beings, and we must try to build them like that. Jeff, you must be a contrast to her. While she can hardly move, your movements should be fast and frantic—like a nervous wreck. Yes, go on, move, move. Don't be afraid. You see, your body is in the wrong tempo-rhythm there. By the way, in the beginning, did you bang the door purposely, or was it stuck? . . .

JEFF: I did it on purpose.

s.m.: Very good. Come in again, and we want to see a nervous wreck. Stop as you enter, and make it more obvious that you are picking your teeth. This is quite characteristic for this horrible man. Yes, like that. Yes, we want to see what is in this man's soul. This is what will express it externally. Nina, you must laugh like a degenerate. Meg, your work is good; keep on apologizing. Oh, Nina, sit up from your lying position sooner, because we can't see you—Meg gets in front of you when she picks up the magazine you throw down. Then as soon as she puts it on the table, you throw it on the floor again. Meg, stay right there where you are. Don't leave. Your head down is good. Yes, you see, this expresses your inner state externally. Jeff, what is your action when you speak of the expenses that you may have?

jeff: I am trying to scare my wife with expenses.

s.m.: Right. But you must make it clear that your wife is stingy. And Nina, you must also make clear that you are stingy. It is impossible for one actor to project the situation by himself. All the actors in the play must contribute.

(Scene)

Ken, I would like to see what happened to the suggestions I gave you on the phone for your scene from *Miss Julie*. Did you work on it?

ken: No.

s.m.: That is terrible. You call me at home, we discuss it, you promise to do improvisations, and then you come to class without having done any work. We talk and talk about improvisations, but there are very few of you who really use this way of working on a role. It must be done.

LIZ: Mrs. Moore, I think I told you some time ago that Sally, Albert, and I were working on *No Exit*. After a while we gave it up, and then recently we decided to "revive" it. After a few rehearsals, we realized that we need help. Do you mind seeing it and giving us your suggestions?

s.m.: Not at all.

(Scene from No Exit, *by Jean-Paul Sartre)*

All three of you are doing very competent work, but you have not built the characters yet. I do not think that your problem is the choice of actions. I wonder whether you understand the characters. How much do you know about Sartre? Here is an example of how important it is to know the playwright's ideas. Your actions and thoughts depend not only on the character you are building but also on the mentality of the author.

Like many other modern playwrights, Sartre is preoccupied with people's inability to have healthy relationships. His heroes are lonely; they need each other but are unable to approach and reach each other. Sartre's idea is that a man is always surrounded by a wall as if he were in prison. People torture themselves with constant guilt feelings and they are also tortured by the condemnation they see in the eyes of others. The characters in *No Exit* are trapped in their feeling of shame and guilt. Their attempts to break loose from this hell are really an attempt to regain their feeling of innocence. But they cannot. Dissatisfaction with oneself makes it impossible to relate to people. The hell in the play represents the world in which a man must live whether he wants to or not. Sartre believes that a man must create for himself the values to live by. It is what a man does that defines him. By creating his own values, he creates himself, or as Sartre says, finds an exit. Sartre believes that man chooses his values and makes himself. I am sure that you know all this, but how much of it did you take into consideration when you tried to build the lesbian, the woman guilty of infanticide, and the coward? The conflicts must be developed to the limit, as, of course, they should be in any play.

SALLY: Don't you think we should stop until we have worked some more by ourselves?

S.M.: Yes, I do. I want to tell you, Albert, that I am happy to have seen you in this scene. Few people here can compete with you in your work on inner monologue. When you sat with your head and face covered, it was in the right tempo-rhythm, and your figure lived. . . .

When Eleonora Duse performed in *Hedda Gabler,* in one scene during her husband's speech she was sitting with her back to the audience. The critics said that you could tell what she was experiencing by the slight movements of her arms and head. We here know that she was living the psychophysical process of human behavior. Do not think that I am comparing you with Eleonora Duse, Albert. *(Laughter.)* But frankly, you looked impressive. Well, enough of *No Exit* for today. It is not an easy play, and if I have not discouraged you with my talk, go on and work on it. You will fully understand a play if you understand the mentality and the style of the dramatist.

class 19

(*Beginning of Scene Four in Noel Coward's* Still Life—*Sally and Albert. The setting is a refreshment room in a small railroad station.*)

SONIA MOORE: It is amusing, and will be of help as a prologue to the later scene between Liz and Jack, which I find still somewhat melodramatic. Sally, you are trying to read that magazine with such zeal. What are you trying to project?

SALLY: That I am doing something I really should not be doing. I'm a waitress, and I should be clearing the tables, not reading.

S.M.: Well, you are the one who knows this, but we do not. Maybe there should be more dirty cups on the tables, or you could have started the cleaning and stopped because you glimpsed something interesting in the magazine. But I should not be giving you hints. Think about it. What is your next action?

SALLY: Getting ready to go out with him.

S.M.: Project that you pretend not to want to go with him and let him convince you. It is not clear that you wanted that from the beginning. I do not see it at all.

EVAN: I see it.

S.M.: Then you are very perceptive! Not everyone else in the audience is so perceptive. Let us revise the circumstances in which this happens. It is getting late and you, Sally, have been working all day long. This should come through when you are cleaning the room, and then the prospect of a date with him chases away all the tiredness, and you go through the room like a whirlwind. The tempo-rhythm must be not only different but a complete contrast. Before, you are dead tired and bored, and now all of a sudden you are full of bursting energy.

SALLY: But before I go out with him, my action is still "to clean up."

S.M.: Yes, but the circumstances in which you are cleaning have changed. Before, you were tired, you walk around practically asleep on your feet, and after the talk with him you are transformed. You cannot wait to finish your work to leave for your date. It is not cleaning any more just because it is your job.

(Sally tries this out.)

Wonderful, start from this table. Then go over there, faster, faster. And again here, and again there, faster. . . . Yes, this is better, but still not fast enough. It is a wonderful little scene, but you will never do it right until you know your objective, have the right actions. This little episode can stand on its own feet as an independent scene. Albert, you are just fine. Everything is clear, only be careful to enter without her hearing you so that when you pinch her it will be a real surprise.

Let us see Liz's entrance.

(Scene)

The moment you enter we must know that this woman is distraught. We speak a great deal of actions, and the psychological and physical behavior that will project what is taking place inside you. That is enough of *Still Life* until you do more work on it.

I would like to see *Ferryboat* again, but of course only if you have worked since I last saw it. It is a full one-act play, and if we do not work as often as possible, it may take ages to have it ready. But first I would like you to tell me more about the play. Who are this boy and girl on the deck of this New Orleans boat, and what do you want to project? When you are ready I hope you do not have to tell us this because everything will be clear from your actions.

NINA: They are strangers to each other. They are both lonely and need affection. But neither of them knows how to approach people. I think that the girl is afraid of men because she saw plenty of them with her mother. You know, I even think that she is glad that the boy is so rough with her. It makes her think that he is not going to touch her as that artist did. But she needs company.

PETER: The more I study this play, the more I see not only that the boy has been hurt a great deal in life and that the worst thing happened to him in New York, but that he does not trust himself. This is one of the reasons why he brushes her off. Yes, I agree that he wants and needs affection, but as soon as he is close to a woman trouble starts.

S.M.: It sounds exciting and shows that you really studied the play.

PETER: I think that this boy might even have killed someone, perhaps in an auto accident.

NINA: We have worked together and separately quite a bit. We have performed a great many improvisations on all possible situations in their lives. I had to change my inner monologue also, because the blocking is a little different.

S.M.: Very good. Put that ladder across the stage on two chairs for the railing of the boat.

(Scene)

There is still work to be done. I hope you understand this. You know Salvini worked on Othello for ten years! What really happened to your mother?

NINA: I say it. She was run over by a car.

S.M.: When you say it you make me think that it was a shock to you, but the way you hold your foot kills this impression. Your pose does not express what is inside you. Peter, your reaction to the accident with her mother is still overdone. Didn't you say that you feel there is something mysterious about the boy and that one of the things he is hiding was that he killed someone in the same way? Your memory of this should be tragic, not melodramatic or sentimental. I would like to cut out all the sentimentality and build him as a much more hostile person. There is an undercurrent in this play that we have not discovered yet. What you say about church must be stronger to make her wonder again about this boy. Please, do not forget to think of the physical expression. Your body must help expression by moving before you speak and after you speak. The movement of the spine culminating in the tips of your fingers and toes is the preparation for the words. Your words and your movements, pose, gestures, are the physical side of the psychophysical action, remember? And it must be given as much serious attention as the psychological side. What is your objective, Nina, when you talk about the baseball game?

NINA: I want him to know that there is beauty in life.

S.M.: Good, but add to this your desire to take him out of his bad mood. Watch to see whether you achieve this. Peter, you are just starting to relax and listen to her when she asks you about New York. This puts you into an even worse mood. Do you know what happened to you in New York?

PETER: But, you know, what you are saying is entirely different from what you said last time.

S.M.: Well, I should probably apologize, because I may be saying different things for a long time, or as long as I can continue to improve on what has been done.

PETER: But last time you said it was good.

S.M.: I am amazed that after all this time you have known me, you still insist that I should always repeat what I said the last time! We will change as long as we can improve, find more of the essence, enrich the "second plan," discover better actions which will serve the play, and find more expressive adaptations and blocking. After all, we are not bound by the three-week rehearsal period. Vakhtangov said, "Art is search, not finished form." I am very much in accord with him. Last time we did the best we could, and today you and I can do better.

The New York episode was clear now, but you should prolong it a little more. It is still bothering you when you go on to say, "What are you doing here?"

PETER: When should I start to trust the girl? Could it be after we talk about the seagulls?

S.M.: That is what I thought. Obviously he is terribly lonely and homesick and begins to cling to the girl.

PETER: Oh, that is good.

S.M.: I forgot to tell you that in the beginning you picked up your book in the wrong tempo-rhythm. What are you reading?

PETER: It is a book you would read when you were depressed.

S.M.: I thought you were trying to keep from thinking about what disturbs you.

PETER: I picked it up just to be reading something.

S.M.: Your ideas are right, but you did not project them at all. Your action is wrong because of the wrong tempo-rhythm.... Yes, that is better. Now, didn't you hear her coming? It looked as if you were deaf. Incidentally, do not monopolize the bench. Nina also has a right to it....

(Scene)

Both of you have some truly wonderful moments. It is honest and interesting. Peter, come back for a moment. You have changed some blocking, and it looks convincing. I liked your not moving when she spoke of her mother's death. It was just fine because you justified it. When she puts her hand on yours, I would like your hand to be visible. Then we would know why you are looking there. You do not trust people, and here you begin to believe that she honestly likes you.

It is a good class today. Everyone seems to be

in inspiration. It is wonderful. Finally I am happy. I saw Nina and Peter really involved because they fulfilled their objectives. Both were fully concentrated psychophysically. You responded to each other, and there was no problem of communion. Neither did you need time to become concentrated or emotional, as some actors do. Did I ever tell you about two of my students who took endless time to do some relaxation exercise before they started a scene? And after all this, when they went on stage they were very tense.... Once, one of these boys took off his shoes and wiggled his feet. I thought it was a part of the scene.... Then I understood why one famous actress said what she thought of actors who make their colleagues wait until they feel they are in the right state. One of the great problems in our theatre is that some people use only one element of an action, others use another one, and the Stanislavski technique as a whole is ignored. *It is the fulfillment of the psychophysical action, including all its elements, that is important, not separate elements.*

I think Peter and Nina have given us proof that we need very little time to concentrate on an action before going on. Peter, why did you ask her, "What are you doing here?"

PETER: I know why. *(Laughter.)*

S.M.: Is it a secret?...

PETER: I am just curious.

S.M.: You know that that is not an action. And it is more important than just curiosity. Please think about whether you are still influenced by the New York episode, or do you really want to find out whether she is a prostitute, as you thought. I truly do not know yet what the right action is. Let us all give it some thought.

Michael, how would you like to work on the scene from *Mourning Becomes Electra*?

MICHAEL: Jean and I have already started to work on it.

S.M.: Good. You can show it to us next week. Today let us see Meg and Jack in it.

(Scene)

Well, it is good that we have seen it, and now we must do something about it. . . . One of the greatest faults in your scene is the unnecessary movements. This scene should be performed with a minimum of movements, as if stripped. It should be intense inside and laconic externally. Jack, your sitting at the desk looks as if you were doing homework. The urgency of what you are doing, the expression of your inner state in your pose is lacking. Your physical state is wrong. Are you sure you know every action? If you are trying to cheat me, you are cheating yourself, you know.

JACK: No, I am not trying to cheat.

S.M.: What are you writing? Wait, what was the name you gave to this episode?

JACK: "Confession."

S.M.: All right, "confession." Why did you close the door?

JACK: You want to know why? *(Laughter.)*

S.M.: Yes, I want to know why.

JACK: I don't want my sister to know what I am doing. I understand that I am writing it because I cannot stand the burden of our crimes, and also to control her.

s.m.: Right. I must say the beginnings are giving us a great deal of trouble! Will you please perform an improvisation on the action, by yourself?

JACK: Yes. I would rather do it by myself and then show you.

s.m.: Good. Now when Lavinia pushes you, and you look at her, I have no idea what your look means. I can bet that you do not have a concrete thought in your mind, and that is why you look blank. Let us do it again. You must give her a reason for apologizing....

Yes, that is better, but Jack, I want a concrete inner monologue, not something accidental that you thought up on the spot. Check on it at home. It must fit the moment, the character, the play. I like your laugh when you say, "I happen to feel quite well...." Continue, continue this laugh, go on, never mind that she is speaking, go on laughing.... Do you know why you are laughing?

JACK: Because I have a document incriminating her.

s.m.: Right. Go on.... That is good. It is right that you are almost roaring. I think this laugh should go on until she mentions Hazel. What did you call this episode?

MEG: "War."

s.m.: Then don't forget that this is war.

MEG: The war starts with his laughter, and my action is to stop it. The war stops for a while and then begins again when he says, "Wash all the guilt from our souls."

s.m.: Don't you think the whole episode is "war," but your objectives and your actions change?

MEG: That's what I mean.

s.m.: If it is "war," then attack each other. Let us try it again from the moment Orin points to the portrait.

(Scene continues.)

You want her to agree to confess, but you are not convincing. And again, the moment when she pushes you away—there is no reaction, Jack, and then out of a blue sky you begin to accuse her. It is because of your reaction that she says, "I am sorry." This is the moment when both of you are trying to reach each other. Isn't this the action you decided on?

meg: Yes.

s.m.: The action is psychophysical. What you are doing, Jack, is only physical. You go to her for protection. Then you embrace her because you are attracted to her. When she pushes you away, in your desire for revenge you begin to make insinuations about the terrible weapon you have against her.

jack: If you don't mind, I would like to make sure that I understand what we decided about the beginning. Is what I am doing as Orin a combination of confession and revenge?

s.m.: His objective is to control his sister, and the confession is the means to achieve this. What is your physical action? To confess?

jack: It is not a physical action.

s.m.: Yes it is. The psychological side is your objective, images, the meaning of your words, all the circumstances. What is the action?

jack: How about "to hide"?

s.m.: To hide what?

jack: The confession.

voices: No, no.

jack: To free myself from guilt?

s.m.: Go on and try an improvisation on the action "to free myself from guilt." *(Laughter.)*

(Jack tries the improvisation.)

You see, it is not enough to find a name for an action. You must make the action clear to the audience. All the complex problems must be reduced to a simple concrete action. When will you finally accept the fact that you are on stage for the audience? And in order for you to be able to make your action clear, it must be simple, easy to fulfill. The action "to free myself from guilt" is not easy to project. Everyone who is working on this scene: What is your first action? *(Silence.)* Well, this is nice. No one knows the first action. That is absolutely awful.

JACK: Isn't it to get the confession over with?

MICHAEL: Or to control my sister?

s.m.: I want all of you to promise me to give some serious thought to this. The right action will reveal the meaning. You also know that the right purposeful action truthfully fulfilled will involve your emotions, and the right actions are essential for building the character of Orin. Don't you think these are sufficient reasons for trying to find the right actions?

When the curtain goes up, we in the audience must know what is happening. The audience may not know that he is writing a confession because you are working only on this one scene, but they must realize that Orin is writing something very important to him which is difficult to write. They must know that you are not writing an ordinary letter or doing some homework. The choice of actions is complex, but you must make an effort, and you will find the right ones. You have no other choice: you must reveal every moment on stage. I can bet that right now Jeff has a new idea for the beginning of *Another Part of the Forest. (Jeff laughs.)* You see, I can read your inner monologue. I can read another person's inner monologue even on the phone! And you are absolutely right to give more thought to the beginning of your scene. Meg, you have done good work. I did not see any serious problems with actions, inner monologue, or images.

MEG: Only yesterday I told Jack that I have worked on this scene more than on any other scene or play in my whole life.

S.M.: Why do you think you did?

MEG: Before, it was all guesswork. Now, I know what steps I have to take. Though I think it is not as difficult for me anymore, it is still a lot of work. And now I never wait for cues because I have my inner monologue, which leads me to my lines.

S.M.: I am happy to hear that. You know, when Meg came for an interview with me, I did not think she would join the Studio. She told me she belonged to an amateur group which would become a sinking ship without her. I said, "Let it sink!"

MEG: I knew that I would join this studio when you said that theatre is for the people in the audience.

S.M.: Jack, you know how much I think of your talent, but I also know that very few talented people really make the effort to learn this technique. This is why there are so few good actors. Many talented people prefer to depend on what happens to them only once in a while without technique. I warn you that without technique inspiration happens only rarely, even to geniuses. Don't you want to learn full control over your creative state on stage? Do you want to remain a talented amateur all your life? But what a rare treat to meet a talented actor who is a thorough worker! Talent without technique is wasted, and diligent workers often become great technicians, but they don't always sparkle. Anatole France said, "Art is threatened by two monsters: an artist who is not a master, and a master who is not an artist." . . .

Well, Jack, revise your actions first of all, and then, when you sit down with the book pretending that you are reading it, look at her and see that she is looking at the closed drapes. Follow her glance. Both of you must have concrete inner monologue there. Orin must look to see where she was looking and have a reaction to this. Do not overlook this, because it is a part of ensemble playing. Tell me, Meg, why do you come into this room?

MEG: To find out what Orin was doing.

S.M.: Why do you want to know?

MEG: Because I don't trust him.

S.M.: Why don't you trust him?

MEG: Because I know that he gets fits of depression in which he is apt to tell anyone what we have done.

S.M.: What have you done?

MEG: Those terrible crimes—incest, murder. . . .

S.M.: I asked you all these questions to remind you of the circumstances in which you want "to find out." You must come to the root of your problem. It is the fulfillment of a concrete simple action in the given circumstances that is important. Yes, and another thing—do you really want him to know that you do not trust him and that you are worried?

MEG: Oh, no.

S.M.: Then you must hide what you are going through behind the door before you enter the room. When you enter, you must cover it up and pretend to be nonchalant. And why do you go to the table?

MEG: Now you are catching me off guard. Before, my action was to go and see what he was doing, but now I must find another action, since I have to hide my great anxiety.

S.M.: No, I think your action is the right one. You still must find out what he is doing, but you must use different means, or, as we say, different adaptations, to do it while not revealing it to him. Let us see it.

JACK: From her entrance?

S.M.: Yes.

(Scene)

You are walking in a terribly wrong tempo-rhythm. Your slow walk will immediately reveal your intention to him.

MEG: I always felt that she must move slowly, I don't know why. Maybe because I try to feel her long gown.

S.M.: I do not think that your walk is justified. And I have noticed that you do not move as slowly in the rest of the scene. Maybe you should give it more thought, and we shall see.

MEG: Is it right for me to be interested in what he is reading when he says, "I am reading"?

S.M.: I doubt that Lavinia is interested in his reading. From the way he says "reading," it is clear that he is hiding what he really is doing. Maybe when you go up to him you could look at the desk to check what he was doing. I think that you must almost be joking in order not to reveal your anxiety. Besides, acting so frantic makes Orin seem much stronger than Lavinia.

MEG: Oh, I don't want that, because I think he is very weak.

S.M.: And, Jack, when you said your action was to scare her, your posture was wrong. And if you insist that you want to see the book he is reading, Meg, what you do is not convincing. Your glancing at it was not enough to know what book it was. Jack, you have a problem with physical expression. You must think consciously and find the physical form. If you want to scare her, *use* the words——bring out your attitude to every word. Verbal action is the strongest action. Stretch the words, project your attitude, and prepare the words, moving your body before you speak and of course after you speak. Perform improvisations to search for psychophysical behavior. Yes, Jack, don't laugh. Someday you will overcome your reluctance, and then you will understand what a help it is. It is a demand on your willpower. Work on an improvisation on your action "to scare." If every director would go through the whole play this way, there would be fewer problems in the theatre. Some of you here have profited immensely from this way of working....

JACK: Mrs. Moore, I am convinced that Orin confesses in defiance of his father.

S.M.: Why don't you also try this action at home? Forget your blocking and say your own words, but remember the circumstances of the play. Don't be afraid of changing actions if you find that they are wrong. Your through line of actions gradually discloses the superobjective. The through line of actions is the movement of the inner life of your character, and through this the play is understood by the spectators. The analysis you are using is the most efficient way to decipher the play. The action brings out the meaning of each moment of the play as the subtext brings out the meaning of the words. This analysis that Stanislavski developed, and which you must do with all your psychological and physical energies, is vital to actors and directors. It enables you to understand the experience of the character and to build his physical life. It also teaches playwrights how to construct the mechanism of a play. And this analysis provides the criteria for evaluating plays, acting, and directing.

I would like to see *The Little Foxes.*

(Scene)

I must be honest and tell all three of you that not enough came through. I did not understand *why* you say, "Only a few Saturdays, only a few Sundays." Really, we talk and talk and then we forget about the concreteness we are trying to learn. We have run-throughs without enough work done at home. We should not let this happen. Now, all of you know what you must do by yourselves. Why don't you do it? Don't you want to become independent in your work?

EVAN: Mrs. Moore, you know, Liz and I work full time and it is impossible to get together.

S.M.: Always the same thing. But nothing will convince me that it could not be arranged somehow. Couldn't you stay after class and work? And Regina, at the end of your speech find a justification to move downstage before Alexandra begins her speech.

class 20

(Scene from The Wingless Victory *by Maxwell Anderson, followed by applause)*

SONIA MOORE: Evan, I am glad that you finally realized that Nathaniel is not such a good man. After all, he abandoned Oparre. Nathaniel married this native princess, and you know that her father disinherited her and exiled her as a result. Nathaniel abandons her under pressure from his relatives, who cannot accept his marriage to a native woman. I do not think that there is anything that can excuse him. Believe me, he is not a hero at all. Oparre has no place to go, no solution, and she poisons her children and herself. It is Nathaniel who is culpable, and by projecting this we will expose the whole problem of interracial relations. On the whole it is good work, but the speech—oh, the speech! Sally, you push your words. If you do it to project the images, you could not be more wrong. Now, sit down and explain something to me. It looks as if you had twin babies.

SALLY: She has two children.

S.M.: Yes, but not the same age. The little girl can walk. You cannot create the impression that

Oparre has twins. I like your pacing the room with the baby in your arms. It is very expressive of your inner state.

SALLY: Maybe we could do this scene with one child?

S.M. Maybe. I also liked your figure leaning on the door, the way you closed it—it is really very good. You see, this is what is expressive. You are on the right road, Sally, because you try to grasp the psychophysical action. However, when you hold the baby at the beginning of the scene, it looks as if you were going to nurse it any minute. You have poisoned the baby, and the audience must understand that the baby is dying and that it is dead when you hear knocking and take the baby away. If you cannot project something, there is no place for it on stage. When you bang the door, it seems to me it would be stronger if you did not scream. It would be unexpected and expressive.

You have done a great deal of work. It is quite amazing how the scene has developed and improved, thanks to your efforts. Your improvisations on actions had very good results. Did you all see the blocking they found? This is what you must learn to do; then you will need very little help from your director. If you have learned this, you will bring your own blocking to a rehearsal. This probably will be changed by the director, but, who knows, sometimes you may even give a director some ideas, and teach him something! Don't you think their blocking is good?

But I want to say something else to you, Evan. When I stopped you, it was because your way of walking is not right for all the turmoil inside you.

(Evan tries a different walk.)
Yes, this is much more what it should be.

EVAN: But my inner monologue is not the same now.

S.M.: Your objective has changed, and that means that you have to change your inner monologue. Well, this is a good proof that we are learning something. What is next?

JEAN: *Mary Stuart.*

(Scene)

S.M.: It is an exciting scene. But you are meeting your archenemy—Elizabeth. Look into each other's eyes. This is a fight for power. Let us start it again.

(Scene)

(Interrupting) Jean, please say your inner monologue to yourself. You have many gestures, but you do not begin or finish the action with your body, and this is why you have little inner monologue or images. You are forcing your emotions. Do you know your every action? When you screamed, everyone here should have shuddered, but nobody did. It is naked screaming. You do not fulfill your objective, and that is why your emotions cannot be stirred. This is Schiller, and you have a tremendous responsibility. You speak and move beautifully, but in this scene you and Meg seem to be actresses of entirely different schools. She lives the experiences, and you imitate them. You have shown very good work lately. But please, promise me that you will work on your actions, inner monologue, and images. Remember that Mary Stuart changes from humility and hypocrisy to attack. She reads in Elizabeth's eyes that she is finished anyway.... Unfortunately, in

staging classics, our theatre usually only *illustrates* history, and this does not stir the audience. Though the environment, the clothes, and so on, are entirely different, the conflicts must be true for all times. The conflict between Mary Stuart and Elizabeth is totally contemporary, but you must bring it out sharply. Of course, we must be careful not to distort history. But the conflict must be made clearly contemporary. Dressing actors in modern costume will not make a play contemporaneous. This play is classic because its theme is the eternal universal human theme. And what is more contemporary than jealousy or the struggle for power? Well, let us start the work on it in a serious way and try to make this play alive. Remember, speech in a tragedy must be simple, not pompous, even when it is in verse, when the rhythm must be preserved. And your voice for Mary should be lower.

ALBERT: Mrs. Moore, did you see *Marat/Sade*?

S.M.: I saw the play in London and found it interesting.

LIZ: It was beautifully done, but it was as far as you can go in a certain direction and still be good.

ALBERT: The leading characters were not convincing.

S.M.: Well, I don't know. It was a good production, believe me.

ALBERT: I liked only one character, the one on high heels who chased the girl. He was the only one who was convincing.

LIZ: I thought that those actors were using the technique you are teaching us. When they were sitting they were able to think all the time. I was watching for that.

ALBERT: I am not speaking about the people in the background, but about the leads.

LIZ: So am I. And they are not trained in the Stanislavski System.

S.M.: I would not say that. They are trained in Stanislavski. You know there is no other acting technique in the world besides the Stanislavski System. And they use it, though not all of it. They are doing much better work than the American actors also because they realized early that the inner, psychological technique alone is not enough. And we know how beautifully trained the British actors are in voice, speech, and body movement.

ALBERT: Let's take the girl playing Charlotte Corday. How does she go about building an insane girl who is playing Charlotte?

S.M.: You mean how would an insane person build a character?

ALBERT: Yes.

S.M.: She would not. *(Laughter.)*

LIZ: If I were to play this crazy girl, how would I go about building her?

S.M.: You know that we build a character with psychophysical actions, and you must select the actions, the psychological and physical behavior of the insane girl. No two human beings are alike, and insane people also vary. It is the play, the events of the play, that will suggest the right actions to you for the character you must portray.

ALBERT: I still say there was only one person I believed, and that was the man on high heels.

S.M.: I saw the play in London, and I am not sure that all the actors were the same. But they received very good reviews here. Often critics say totally different things about the same play and the same actors. This is what happens when there are no criteria for judging the acting and directing. There must be common criteria for judgment in the theatre, and the Stanislavski System teaches them. I hope that everyone in our theatre will learn them. The critics will benefit enormously when they learn about analysis, psychophysical action, the actor's "own theme," the inner monologue. . . .

NINA: I want to ask you something about *Ferryboat*. When he stands at the railing of the boat and is aware that I am there upstage, I just have no courage to talk to him before he turns around. I don't know whether this is right.

S.M.: I cannot tell unless I see it. Do you want a run-through or should I stop you?

NINA: Please stop us whenever it doesn't work. *(Scene)*

S.M. *(interrupting)*: When you say, "If this is the only star in the sky, you can make a wish," it is a way for you to start a conversation. But he does not have a monopoly over the stars, so why don't you make a wish yourself?

NINA: Oh, I like that idea. Then I don't have to wait until he turns around.

S.M.: Fine. Peter, do not worry about the book, just throw it down. She will see it anyway when the time comes. Nina, when you talk about the church, paint it more, give it more color because it tells a great deal about this girl. Before I forget, Peter, your standing with your foot on the bench at the end of the play does not help to project that you are in a hurry to leave. It is true that we do not have proper sets, but still I want you to find actions which will project that this is a ferryboat. Peter, why do you look at her when she asks, "I wonder how deep the river is?"

PETER: Because I think she has the same idea I do—about suicide.

S.M.: Good. Let us go on with the scene.

(Scene)

I still do not understand what is going on when you ask, "What are you doing here?" And I am not satisfied with the projection that you think she is a liar.

PETER: I know. It just doesn't come through.

S.M.: Did you try an improvisation on your action? What is the action?

PETER: "To disbelieve."

S.M.: Don't you think that is rather weak?

PETER: Would it be "to accuse of lying"?

S.M.: That might be better. Shall we try an improvisation on the action?

NINA: Oh, it is so difficult.

PETER: Could we do it later by ourselves?

S.M.: All right. Now about the ending. This girl, whom you did not trust, has finally made you trust her. And then she gives you another slap. What is your action, Peter?

PETER: "To cover up."

S.M.: No. Forget about that. Just give her a piece of your mind. She gave you the slap. What you do is not the right reaction to this. You must blame yourself because you think that you should have known better. What do you think would be your action? We must project the conflicts.

PETER: To give it to her, to ridicule her, to holler at her.

(Peter tries it.)

S.M.: Good. And then hurry to leave. Have your valise ready, put on your jacket, and go. Nothing will stop you now, and therefore you cannot sit there as you did. Oh, again, about the New York episode—you forget it too quickly. Do you really have a definite image of what happened in New York?

PETER: Yes.

S.M.: It may not be strong enough. I do hope that all of you work on your analogous emotions experienced in your life. I would like to suggest that Sally and Michael, who also do this play, exchange partners. I know you all hate this, but it forces you to be more aware of the other person. You like the security of knowing every move of the other person, but I think it is useful to have to readjust when you work with a different partner.

NINA: Jean and I have been working on a scene from *Twelfth Night*. May we show it now?

S.M.: Did you work on it in your Shakespeare class? You know that I insist on this.

JEAN: Yes, we did.

S.M.: Very well, then.

(Scene from Twelfth Night*)*

This will be a lovely scene. Nina, you must project that you as Olivia fall in love at once with Viola, whom you take for a man. And Viola, you are in love with Orsino; since he loves Olivia you want to find out whether she is really as beautiful as he thinks. If you read carefully what Olivia says after you leave, you will understand your behavior in this scene. Please, continue to work on it in your Shakespeare class.

MEG: Anne and I are working on *The*

Merchant of Venice, and after we work on it in the Shakespeare class we will show it to you. It's in prose, and there are fewer problems.

s.m.: Good, I am looking forward to seeing it. I like to see your Shakespeare scenes from time to time, but they are the responsibility of your Shakespeare teacher, who knows what I require.

I would like to see the *Mourning Becomes Electra* scene with Jean and Michael.

jack: May I try here the improvisation on "to defy"?

s.m.: Did you work on it at home?

jack: Yes.

s.m.: All right, then.

(Improvisation)

I would like you all to say what you think of it.

jeff: I think if he is defying, his posture is certainly wrong.

s.m.: I agree.

jack: It is very difficult.

s.m.: Yes, it is. But if you go through the whole scene with improvisations on actions, you will find the correct psychophysical behavior. The problem is that we don't have enough willpower to really do this work. I am happy, Jack, that you are working on improvisations. You know that you are learning the most perfect step of Stanislavski. When he started to introduce his technique, he didn't know a small percentage of what he knew later and we know now, thanks to his lifelong work. Stanislavski had great difficulty with those great actors in the Moscow Art Theatre. They did not want to start studying after having performed for many years. But a group of young actors who became excited about Stanislavski's teachings and began to study proved that they could act better than those giants. In our studio, too, I sometimes see the tendency to be satisfied with assimilating inner monologue and images alone, and I have to insist that you concentrate on psychophysical actions. I have always tried to make you understand that mastery of the choice of actions and their fulfillment will make you professionals. Then you will be capable of reincarnation, which is the highest step in theatre art.

Unfortunately, I have had bad experiences with some of my advanced students—I don't mean you, in this class. As soon as they have assimilated some of the steps, they feel that they know everything. And I am always thinking that I do not know enough. I continue to do research and am trying to pass my knowledge on to you. In the practice of any art, you can never be satisfied with what you have achieved. You cannot stop with it, or you regress. You must be in continuous training. After you have learned the basic technique, you are always free to come here and practice in order to grow. Now back to *Mourning Becomes Electra* with Michael and Jean as Orin and Lavinia.

(Scene)

Michael, do you know that Orin most of all is jealous of Avahanni?

MICHAEL: Yes, doesn't it come across?

S.M.: Frankly, not very well. But I must say that some of the moments in this scene are beautiful. Your physical expression is laconic and eloquent. Jean, when you say that you are suffocating from the heat, and so on, you must change your action because you must treat him more gently. Change your body before speaking.

JEAN: Yes, I know.

S.M.: Michael, it seems to me that you really see blood, knives, and hanging while you are speaking.

MICHAEL: Do I project the neighbors when I say, "What will the neighbors say?"

S.M.: What do the others think?

VOICES: Yes, yes.

S.M.: Were you thinking about the neighbors who believe your family is honorable, and wondering what would happen if they found out the truth?

MICHAEL: Right, right.

JACK: When Meg and I performed it, I also knew what I was saying.

S.M.: But it didn't come through. Your body does not help yet. Your images must be really painted. Michael, when she knocks at the door, what you do seems to be an indication.

MICHAEL: I am thinking, "Should I let her in or give her a piece of my mind?"

S.M.: Your physical reaction to the knocking is exaggerated because there is not enough inside. And all of a sudden, when she pushed you away, you didn't care. You should stop feeling sorry for yourself and attack her.

MICHAEL: I have always done it this way.

S.M.: No, you changed your action right there. You have no right to do this. Another actor on stage would have killed you for that. You must respect the play and not distort it with accidents. If you think that an action is wrong, by all means change it, but it must be done beforehand and coordinated with your partner. When you have worked on the play thoroughly, unexpected action may happen under inspiration, and then it will always be right. What you did was certainly wrong. But you must not be upset, you are doing very well. And we do not have to hurry; this is not summer stock where plays are prepared in a week. We are learning an important acting technique, and it takes time to do all the necessary work. Jean, you have made immense progress. . . .

Well, this scene from *Electra* is good, but I would like the atmosphere in it to be more tense. We should feel death in this room.

class 21

PETER: You have not seen *Desire Under the Elms* for a long time. Can we show it to you?

S.M.: Have you and Anne been working on it?

PETER: Yes.

S.M.: Come on, then.

(Scene)

I like it very much, except that you must stop that complaining, Peter. Stop it and fight her. Yes, fight, roar at her, especially when you talk about the farm. Stop being a little boy.

ANNE: Do you like what I do to project that it is hot?

S.M.: Yes, very much. As a matter of fact, Peter, you should wipe away the perspiration, too.

PETER: I was thinking of wiping my neck just before she says, "It's hot...."

S.M.: Why don't you do that? Let us see.

(Peter and Anne repeat part of the scene.)

Good, but I want you to put the handkerchief back into your pocket quickly because you hear something else in her voice when she is talking about the heat. She means something else, and you cannot possibly fail to understand it. That is why you do not want to admit that you are hot, too.

PETER: Oh, yes, I see.

S.M.: Good. The scene is very good. But Peter, I would appreciate a more interesting inner monologue during her speech.

PETER: I'll see what I can do about it.

S.M.: I want more aggression against her, though you are attracted to her. We must see more what the land means to Eban.

PETER: You know, many things have come out right now. I think I understand more.

S.M.: Wonderful. Yes, I think both of you know what has to be done.

PETER: To be honest, I think that my images were haphazard.

S.M.: The best thing about all of you is your honesty! I do appreciate the honesty, but I also appreciate work. I mean honest work!

Shall we see Tennessee Williams's *The Unsatisfactory Supper?*

(Scene)

It was very good. You have brought a great deal to it since last time. This is what we need, a serious creative attitude. If everyone will bring work, we can keep progressing. It is an especially happy event because last time I was not very pleased with it.

NINA: I wasn't either.

S.M.: Frankly, I was afraid you had picked up some terrible habits working in summer stock.

NINA: I was too.

S.M.: You were pushing. You know, today your face actually changes color.

NINA: Mrs. Moore, can you understand how difficult it is for all three of us to find a convenient time for rehearsals? Whenever one person can come, another cannot—it's just impossible. And when we finally get together to work in the Studio, all the rooms are occupied by other students rehearsing their scenes.

s.m.: Well, don't I know the problems! Talented young people need time to practice, and yet they have to make a living as well. There ought to be money available to people like you, to give you time to study and work at your art.

Now, what about *The Little Foxes?*

NINA: We have done a little work. I do not know what to do in the beginning.

s.m.: What is your action? Why do you enter this room?

NINA: Because I am disgusted with the talk my mother and my uncle are having in the other room when my father has just died.

s.m.: All right. Then is your action to get away from them?

NINA: Yes, but I want to talk to my mother.

s.m.: I thought that Alexandra had decided not to talk to her.

NINA: I am not sure whether she changes her mind in the other room or here.

s.m.: It is very possible that she changes her mind here. Otherwise, why didn't she go to her own room at once? Let us see. Come here because you do not want to hear their horrible conversation any more. Probably she still intends to talk to her mother. Come in and do anything that would project your objective.

(Nina performs the improvisation on the entrance.)

I am afraid there is not enough inner monologue in what you are doing. Or your body does not express it. It seems to me that you have chosen the right action, but please work on the inner monologue and images. Then your entrance will be very good. Liz and Evan, you should laugh louder, and then when you hear them coming, Alexandra, you sit down there. I like your going to the door to look at the staircase, but I thought the staircase was to the right because you came in from the dining room on the left. Let us see some more of it.

LIZ: Evan and I have never rehearsed together and would rather make another attempt at it before showing it to you.

S.M.: Well, there is nothing I can do but hope.

What about the beginning of *Mourning Becomes Electra*? We have real problems with the beginnings of our scenes. But the beginning is most important in a play or a scene.

(Michael and Jean perform.)

It is your best role, Michael. Now, when you sit down and do not hear her. . . .

MICHAEL: When is that?

S.M.: As soon as she enters, in the beginning, when you do not hear her. . . .

MICHAEL: Oh, I didn't look at her again?

S.M.: You did, but I have no idea why. And I do not know what is going through your mind when you see her looking at the closed drapes. What is your inner monologue then?

MICHAEL: I say in my mind, "I want it this way, and that's that."

S.M.: You might have thought it, but it is not projected because your body is dead. A slight movement will project what you think. And, Jean, what is your action here?

JEAN: I have an inner monologue, not an action.

S.M.: It is about time you knew that there are actions also when we are silent. The fact that you look at the drapes means that you want to know what is going on.

JEAN: Yes.

S.M.: This is an action. Now, why did you stop talking and listen to him?

JEAN: I think I know that he is writing down the crimes we've committed.

S.M.: Michael, I do not see any reaction to what she is saying. When she wants to open the drapes, stop her. This may help her. But why do you move so slowly?

MICHAEL: I am thinking. *(Laughter.)* Thinking is important.

S.M.: Certainly. But I do not understand why you move so slowly. It does not correspond to what is inside you. What is your action?

MICHAEL: To renounce the daylight.

S.M.: Oh? How about an improvisation on "renouncing the daylight"?... Any volunteers, because Michael does not seem very eager to do it? Can you really project this? No. I beg you, choose simple actions, easy to project. They are miraculously expressive. It is not enough to be satisfied with finding a name, a verb, for an action. Michael, when you say, "my work," do you have a good image for it?

It must project what this work is. You are much more convincing now when you are writing the confession.

MICHAEL *(pointing to his forehead)*: Something got in there somehow. *(Laughter.)*

S.M.: Good. I know what got in there—it is called inner monologue. And you can still improve on the way you sit while writing this horrible document.

(Scene from Edward Albee's The Zoo Story— *Ken as Jerry; Jeff as Peter)*

S.M.: Jeff, if we were working on the whole play, I would not like you to be so neurotic at the beginning. It should develop gradually that Peter is also neurotic. But since we have only a short scene, it may make sense.

KEN: You know, when I work I always try to find in Jeff something that I dislike.

S.M.: Now we are in the woods again. What you are saying may be responsible for the lack of communion between the two characters, the lack of interplay in your scene.

KEN: If I don't see in Jeff what I should see in Peter, I cannot play.

S.M.: You are talking nonsense. You must find actions and treat Jeff as Peter.

KEN: The relationship is very important.

S.M.: Yes, very. But that does not mean that you must dislike Jeff himself. You must dislike Jeff as Peter, not Jeff as Jeff.

KEN: But I found in Jeff something that I dislike, and it helps.

MEG: This is what I saw in a workshop when I

audited a class. One student almost killed another, and I decided it was not for me. And they think this is Stanislavski.

s.m.: Ken, if you don't stop this nonsense, you will drive yourself crazy. Your "theory" does not help you to communicate on stage. But if you worked on finding analogous experiences in your own life, you could remember someone for whom you have the same feeling that Jerry has for Peter. Then you must treat Jeff as this person in your life.

ken: When I worked on Tusenbach with Michael as Soliony, I discovered in Michael himself something I disliked.

s.m.: Well, obviously you think that you know more than Stanislavski.

ken: I think we must find a relationship.

s.m.: Yes, the relationship between the characters, not between Ken and Jeff.

class 22

ALBERT: May we show the Ruel and Oparre scene from *The Wingless Victory*?

s.m.: Of course.

(Scene)

It shows good progress. Albert, your tempo-rhythm is wrong when you swear at those people. Would you please start from this moment again?

ALBERT: Yes. I should move faster. But I'll have to change my inner monologue in the pauses.

s.m.: Of course. Now continue.

ALBERT: Can't we start from the beginning?

s.m.: I appreciate the difficulty of starting in the middle, but by now I hope you are able to start from any action. Do you know your action?

ALBERT: Yes.

s.m.: Do you have the images of those horrible people? Go on.... Do not touch her. She can take your hand as the older sister, or she can touch your arm. But you, who worship her, should not touch her.

ALBERT: I must work on this.

s.m.: Yes, please do. Shall we see *The Unsatisfactory Supper* now?

(Scene)

Meg, I still think that you should not move when you say, "I thought that you children were satisfied with the supper." First say it, and then, since they do not answer, go. What is your action?

MEG: To apologize for the meal.

S.M.: Yes, but your moving toward the garden does not help to project that. Nina and Jeff, your beginning is not yet expressive enough. As soon as both of you come out, having overeaten, hateful and blaming this poor woman for a bad supper, I want to see this. The man is able to spit in the garden which this poor woman adores. You as actors must know what you think of the character and express it. You must build two disgusting people, growing into symbols. Meg, though your task is easier because they have already established the situation, you still must contribute to it, avoiding talking about the supper and trying to be nice to these monsters.

MEG: So before apologizing, I should avoid talking about the supper? And then when I am sure they are dissatisfied, I apologize.

S.M.: Exactly. You speak about Sunday and the flowers in order to avoid mentioning the supper. You must try an improvisation on "to avoid" with Jeff and Nina, in the circumstances of the play. You know what it means for this woman to leave the house. If you remember all the circumstances, you will find the right psychological and physical behavior for her. In the beginning I was satisfied with the most primitive expression, primitive inner monologue, and simple but strong images. But now you must build a richer content; it must be truthful, and you must find an interesting form for it. Every thought and emotion must be brought to the audience in an artistic form. These two horrible characters of Tennessee Williams are interesting, and it is your duty as actors to build their inner world. This is what real theatre is. The whole Stanislavski System leads to building of a naturally functioning character. Building and projecting the unique inner world of a character is your contribution to the disclosing of the play. The Stanislavski System makes it possible for you to disclose the inner essence of the character and an author's way of seeing life.

Incidentally, I would appreciate it if you would settle your problems among yourselves. I should not be involved in your misunderstandings. Here we are all grown-up people, and if you cared about each other there wouldn't be such problems as not wanting to work with each other. You know, in the kind of theatre I am dreaming about, actors must have talent, technique, discipline, and ethics. You know how much I care that you learn the Stanislavski technique; that you be able to prepare a role and block a scene independently; that you work on speech, diction, voice, and your body——and of course your Shakespeare class. But it is simple truth that theatre cannot exist without discipline and ethics. There cannot be any artistic work where there are petty personal interests. And it is a simple truth that good theatre depends on a friendly atmosphere in a group and ensemble on stage. Incidentally, I want to repeat to those of you who still neglect your physical training that we do have excellent teachers, both energetic and stubborn.

ALBERT: So you think they can do anything?

s.m.: Not anything, but our speech teacher has certainly helped you. Speech is or rather was your most serious problem, Albert. Everyone has a different problem. For instance, you, Jeff, have difficulty in grasping the psychophysical action. Often you seem to be satisfied with the inner side of an action. No matter how interesting or how subtle your inner life, your psychology, it will be senseless if you do not find the form to express it.

And since I have started to talk about shortcomings, let me do the same thing with some of the others. I want to remind you, Jean, that Stanislavski does not permit on stage a finished result that is merely external. If you do all your inner work during every performance, your work will be fresh and your role will grow constantly. In life we do the same things every day, such as combing our hair or having coffee, but we do it differently every time, depending on the circumstances. We may be in a different mood, or be in a hurry, or have a headache. On stage, in addition, your behavior may also depend on the audience. Your imagination has developed immensely and you have good command over the choice of actions. Your work on scenes begins and progresses well. But as soon as you feel your work is ready, you sometimes stop working, and your role becomes dead. Then your performance is an accident. I never know what to expect, what will happen. Sometimes you sparkle, sometimes you are mechanical. Your performance may be better or worse, but it should be the best you can do today. Sometimes what seemed to be good suddenly becomes overdone because it is dead inside.

It is a question of discipline, or of willpower,

because you know very well what you must do. You have no right to demonstrate only the external form. If you do not fulfill actions every time, there is no hope for your emotions to be involved, and thus, no hope for subconscious creativity. Inspiration under these conditions would be a miracle. Inspiration does not come from heaven merely at your command. You must work for it—this is a law. You are learning the road to inspiration. You are learning to "harness" the phenomenon of inspiration on stage.

Now, Sally, your problem is still your speech, though you have improved a great deal. Your taking the Shakespeare class is not quite logical at this point. You must direct all your attention to the improvement of your speech and diction. But at least, now I don't hear from you anymore "It's just too bad," as you used to say when people complained that they did not understand you. There is no reason for an actor to be on stage if he is not understood. Last year, when you asked me whether you would ever be an actress, I said, "I do not know." Now I know, because you are becoming an actress. You are doing beautiful inner work. But actors must master the psychological *and* the physical techniques. The beginners often do not understand the importance of physical training, but you do know by now. And still, when I ask someone, "Why don't you take speech?" the answer is, "What is wrong with my speech?" Or if I ask about body movement, the answer is sometimes, "Why? I don't want to be a dancer." Will we ever really accept the fact that the acting technique is psychophysical? The inner work will never be adequate without a trained physical apparatus. Take this also for a law. If your voice, speech, and body are not trained, you will never be able to grasp the psychophysical process of human behavior in life.

Oh, Peter, I cannot stand your smoking on stage. Even before it was known that smoking was dangerous for your health, Stanislavski did not allow smoking on stage because it was disrespectful. I am trying to protect your health! You may smoke on stage if it is necessary for the character, but you do it in every improvisation. . . .

KEN: Mrs. Moore, what does an actor do if he hates the role?

S.M.: He should not touch it, but I think that you can make yourself become interested in a role.

KEN: And what if I don't agree with the director about the interpretation of a role?

S.M.: Quit the show. *(Laughter.)* I mean it. A good director is responsible for the whole, and he knows the play. You may tell him your views, but if he does not agree, you must follow his directions.

Albert, I am quite happy with the wonderful progress you have made with your speech. Try a little more with your *r*. . . . And Albert, you and Evan have this in common—you philosophize too much. *(Laughter.)* It is true. I do appreciate your theoretical work, and I do not intend to minimize its value. As I have told you, Stanislavski used to sit around the table talking with his actors for a long time, trying to find everything there at the table. But then he realized that sitting at the table was only impeding the grasp of the psychophysical process. I want you to learn to *do* it, not just discuss it. In practical fulfillment of actions, you are forced to analyze them and to find harmony between the psychological and the physical, or between content and form. I really appreciate such hard workers as you because I have met enough people who are afraid that Stanislavski is too scientific, and I have a hard time explaining to them that the technique is not the goal in itself but the means to the goal—the inspiration. And here you practically make the technique an end in itself. Stop talking and work in action, on stage.

ALBERT: I do work on improvisations.

EVAN: Don't we have to select the right actions first?

S.M.: Yes, but sitting and talking at the table will not tell you whether you have chosen the right action. Fulfillment of it will. The method of physical actions is analysis *in action*, an analysis with all your psychological and physical forces. And certainly you will not involve your emotions sitting at the table with pencil and paper. You are dividing the physical and the psychological. You know that you must try to unite them every time you are on stage, even in improvisations. I trust that you and Albert will someday help to spread the System because I think you really understand it. And Evan, never drop out of college again. Education will enrich your material for your work. You may sometimes be able to hide the lack of education on stage, but your superior cultural level will be always present with you there.

Jack, I told you before that you seem to be satisfied with the most elementary images and the simplest inner monologue. Now that you have no problem holding them in your mind because you have control over your body, they should have much more variety. They also should be more interesting.

Mary, I hope the day is not too far away when

you will overcome your reluctance to do improvisations. They are difficult and you have to use willpower, but this is the most efficient way to work on a play and on a role. And, Mary, I thought you wanted to become a director. There is no better way to find interesting staging. I also want to tell you not to insist on going on in class if you have not done the preparatory work. I do not quite understand why you do this. Sometimes I watch you, and I wait for you to admit that you have not worked at home on this, but you go on anyway. When your inner work is not ready, you go back to the old clichés you used before you came to this studio. I beg you to watch out for this. You are making very good progress, and I do not want anything to impede it.

Meg, your problem is still some of that inner tension, though it happens less and less. You must have more confidence. Your thoughts will show in your eyes because you have them, and a responsive body will make them move. Watch this.

Anne and Nina, you are doing wonderful work, and now you know that actions are most important. It used to be a long time before you began to merge with the character. But now you do, you really do. You are functioning as the character.

Oh, Evan, something else. You have a tendency to build every character as a positive character. But in this you are not alone. When Liz worked on Regina, she tried to build her as the sweetest person. Finally, I convinced her otherwise and she built Regina as she should be. It took quite a while to persuade you to change your attempt to build Nathaniel as a hero in *The Wingless Victory*. You are doing very good work, but if you do not project the character as he should be, you do not serve him, the play, or yourself—the actor.

There is something else I want to tell you all. Working on roles that are far from you may have pedagogical value and teach an actor that he cannot always play himself. But you will serve the play better if the role is close to you, because you will be able to open up your own personality. It is wrong for a young actor to play an old man if the company has an older actor capable of portraying the character, and vice versa.

On the whole, all of you have had a good taste of the Stanislavski System. You know what our laboratory work is. You have learned that one of the greatest contributions of Stanislavski is that he teaches an actor how to use his willpower. Never stop working, or your instrument will become stagnant. Again and again I tell you that it is the same as with musicians and dancers.

It is an acknowledged fact that our theatre today is not as good as it could be. It is often difficult to have good plays produced because artistic success does not necessarily mean financial success. Producers must be commercially astute. And unfortunately not all the plays that make money are good. Such plays as *King Lear* should be on stage all the time, but a good play must have good actors and a good director, and we have few actors who can perform *King Lear*. It is often said that the public is not interested in serious plays, but I am convinced that people *would* come to see a good play performed by good actors. You here know more about the Stanislavski technique than anyone else in the United States, and I count on you to spread it throughout the country. It is a duty to be proud of. *You* are the ones who know a great deal, not the people who say that they know Stanislavski "backward and forward." They know only a few of his early experimental steps. But you know his final deductions. I am also sure that now you realize that actors are the heart of the theatre, and a great deal is required from them. You understand now that your mere presence on stage is not interesting enough to the audience, even if you are a star. You must be able to stir the audience's imagination and emotions and achieve the participation of the spectators. This was Stanislavski's purpose.

Do you know how long Russian actors are required to study before they may have an audition to join a theatre? They must have four years of full-time study of the Stanislavski System, voice, diction, speech, dance, and body movement. Incidentally, Rudolf Nureyev has said that he considered Stanislavski one of his early teachers. Russian actors must be professionally trained actors before they audition. Directors must have *five* years of study, and the Stanislavski System is an essential part of their training. We also can have a theatre of great masters. If only we realized that it is a misunderstanding to think that actors can learn to act while they are performing. Of course, on stage you will acquire vital experience, and you will grow further, but you must be a skilled actor when you join a theatre. It seems to be such a simple truth. The number of theatres will depend on the number of trained actors and directors, not on how many theatre buildings we construct.

class 23

SONIA MOORE: Which scene from *Yerma* shall we work on today?

MEG: We have been working on the scene with the Old Woman from the first act.

S.M.: Let us see it.

(Scene)

Anne, it is beautiful, but when the Old Woman asks you whether you ever felt anything special with a man, you are still projecting that only now do you remember that you felt something like that with Victor.

ANNE: Because I feel that Yerma does not want to allow herself to think of Victor.

S.M.: You are right. But he is constantly in her mind nevertheless. Yerma longs for him.

ANNE: You are changing Lorca's play.

S.M.: I don't think so. There is enough proof in the play that Yerma is attracted to Victor. I want to bring out the conflicts in this play, the conflicts that will stir today's audience. And this is a great eternal conflict. The play, of course, is the source of the action, and there are limits to the director's interference with the play. But the director must transform the dramatic work into a theatrical performance. The play will not become alive through *mises en scène* which merely illustrate the author's text. A theatrical performance should not be a mere copy of the written play. If the director is able to "read" the play, he may give it new theatrical value. In this lies the director's primary importance. The time is past when a director simply told the actors how to move around the stage. The director must bring out the play's contemporary values. Every director sees the same life in a different way. And different actors create the same role in different ways; Hamlet and Othello are different in portrayals by Salvini, Scofield, Olivier, and Smoktunovsky, although they read the same lines. So may a director create a production of the same play in a different way, revealing contemporary conflicts.

I am trying to build Yerma in movement, in conflicts. Anne, you know that I am interested in this play and would like to stage it someday. The director has the right to include his own views without, of course, distorting the play. The director is responsible for bringing out the psychological content of a play. There are facts in a play, and as a director I must bring out the psychological process that accompanies the facts. I am searching for every detail that will help to disclose the play. Sometimes small details may be helpful in revealing the psychology of what happens. But as a director I am limited by what I can do—through my actors. It is you, the actors, who must make my thought alive. A director can be creative when he is able to have creative ideas and realize them through actors. It is the director's task to guide the fates of the characters on stage. He must go far beyond the literary content of the events. The director must bring out the meaning of the play and realize it in the movement of the performance toward the superobjective.

I do not think today's audience, seeing Yerma, will sympathize with a woman who never stops talking about having a child and finally kills her husband because he does not give her one. I want to bring out what is responsible for the catastrophe. There is no solution for the conflict, and that is what makes this play a tragedy. Everyone in the play must contribute to this tragedy. Yerma is in tremendous conflict because of Victor. She resents Juan even more because of her attraction to Victor, whom she cannot have. This, and the fact that she and Juan do not communicate with each other, are conflicts of today and of all times. My ideas, or any director's ideas, can be projected only through the real life of the human spirit on stage. No matter how interesting the director's inventions, he is helpless without skilled actors. After the production is ready it is entirely in your hands. It is not the same as the finished work of a sculptor, who is responsible for what he has done. The director's work is limited, because anything may happen to it during a performance. You may forget a line, or ruin a pause, or overplay. What can a director do then? The director's thought is dead if it does not acquire organic existence in the performers. But I repeat, I am fortunate that you know what I mean and are able to incarnate my ideas. I hope that all of you will bring enthusiasm to this project. I think your work is beautiful in this scene. But you must change your ideas, revise your objectives, and find different actions.

ANNE: Well, I will revise my actions.

S.M.: That is good, and now I may surprise you with something else. This is mostly for you, Meg. I think that the Old Woman may know a great deal about Yerma. She goes from one place to another visiting her sons, taking food to her husband, even visiting that hermitage ritual. How on earth could she possibly not know about Yerma?

ANNE: Then why doesn't Yerma know her?

S.M.: Yerma hardly steps out of her house, and it may be possible. But the Old Woman knew Yerma's family; she probably knew Yerma when she was a child, and there is little doubt that she heard a great deal of gossip about her. Moreover, I think that the Old Woman might already have thought of Yerma for her son.

MEG: Really? Well, that is interesting and seems quite logical.

S.M.: Maybe when Yerma asks, "Why do you tell me that?" it is because she senses that the Old Woman has something in mind. I would appreciate it if you would think about this.

And Anne, I do not want you to be continuously pessimistic. In the first scene, after the dream, Yerma is excited because she thinks that her dream is the annunciation of conception. Only after her disappointments does she become gloomy. After each setback she becomes more and more frantic. And everyone must contribute to the tragedy. The laundresses, all of you with your sneering and gossiping, are driving Yerma to catastrophe. Even her girl friend Maria innocently contributes to it.

I think we shall be able to project many facets of this play. It is human drama and can therefore help to bring about a better understanding of the world and of man. That is why I never stop studying the events and the actions of the characters. Everyone plays an important part in building the tragedy. Everyone is needed to sharpen it. The atmosphere should be impregnated with the tragedy of a human being for whom there is no future.

JEAN: Mrs. Moore, you cannot imagine how much the Stanislavski System I have learned from you has helped me with the writing of my play. I think that I know now what a playwright should do, because I know what actors must do with the play.

S.M.: I have purposely delayed telling you how Stanislavski helps playwrights. I wanted you first to assimilate enough of the technique because I knew that you would understand it better than if I had spoken about it before; it would have been only theoretical. Now you understand it organically. And I am certain that it is clear to you why Stanislavski was often critical of playwrights and said that they do not give the actor enough nourishment. He said, "Authors often fail to find the deep inner action which crosses the character's psychology, and so they substitute an external schematic line. . . . I often do not feel that there is a vast world behind the stage, and that what happens on stage is only a part of it. . . . The characters often do not have their biographies, and so we do not know how their life was built, and that is very important for an actor."

Great achievement is rare in any art; only rarely is there a playwright who is able to give us a full idea of the biography of his characters. It should be the playwright's responsibility to trace their destiny clearly. Otherwise even good actors may have difficulty in building major characters. A bad play will hurt an actor's and a director's art and push them into clichés.

A good play must have an important idea; sharp conflicts, and concrete, clearly delineated characters. A play will never be valid without these elements, which must be disclosed through events and the behavior of the characters.

JEAN: How familiar it sounds, now. I think I understand it so well.

ALBERT: Maybe I could become a playwright, too.

S.M.: Maybe you could. But I have not yet told you everything Stanislavski demands from a dramatist. Writers, he said, must know the organic laws of nature and the way they are used on stage. Stanislavski believed in Pushkin's demand from dramatists: "Truth of passions, truth of experience in given circumstances," for both dramatists and actors. You also know that events are the stimuli for actions. Therefore a good playwright builds events and establishes their influence on the characters and their actions. And you also know that the behavior of a character is expressed through psychophysical and verbal actions.

And Stanislavski advises the playwright to build his play through significant, intense events because the actions of the characters depend on them. A good playwright himself goes through all the thinking of his character while he establishes his individuality. Maxim Gorki said, "If you have the characters you have the material for unavoidable drama. Put these characters in front of each other and they will act at once." If a playwright has an important idea, his theme will be a natural interweaving of the events and conflicts that result from it. Conflicts are built from the struggle of ideas, and it should be expressed through the characters' actions. The more significance a dramatist gives to the events and to the actions of the characters, the sharper the play is.

The dramatist should take his characters from real life. The spectators want to see on stage people like themselves, with ambitions, thoughts, passions—all the behavior of real life in the process of either growth or retrogression.

The playwright should foresee psychological pauses. You know a great deal now about the inner monologue. A talented dramatist can imply intense inner monologue which would sometimes replace the text. Even a well-filled pause can disclose the subtext. And then, as in Chekhov's plays, the characters will *answer each other's thoughts*. A good playwright does not have one superfluous word. This is why I stressed the importance to you, the actors, of projecting everything you say.

The superobjective and the through line of actions are most important for a playwright. You know well that the through line of actions, the undercurrent of the life of the play, moves the inner world of the characters. A playwright should avoid any detail that does not help the through line of actions to disclose the superobjective. And if a playwright knows the Stanislavski System as you do, he will know that the through line of actions can continue its movement also in the thoughts in the character's mind.

Every action must have a counteraction that will strengthen its sharpness. There should be clashes between contradictory forces. The deep emotional response of the spectators depends on the depth of the conflict.

And now, Jean, in addition to what I have said, your *language* in the play must be active and poetic and must also reflect your own individuality. It will be active and poetic if you, the dramatist, are able to move the through line of actions as the undercurrent of your play in such a way that it will stir the images of an actor and of the spectator. You must also write in strong and picturesque language. And if you want the speech in your play to be musical, the tempo-rhythm must be taken into consideration.

All the events on stage must be important, but you must give special emphasis to: (1) the central event, which is the stimulus to the through line of actions; (2) the first event, which begins the through line of actions and explains the beginning of relationships in a play, and must be energetic; and (3) the final event, which either brings about the solution of the conflict or shows the impossibility of solution. A dramatist or director should not be afraid of a strong and dramatic finale. Well, I hope that Stanislavski's suggestions for playwrights will be useful to you. And Jean, when you write a play and it is staged, though you as the author will be most important, give the director independence in his field. Sometimes he and the actors bring out depths that the author himself has not suspected. The director is extremely important to the playwright—along with the actors, who will realize his idea.

You have learned how much the Stanislavski technique depends on a friendly and harmonious atmosphere in the group, and why his system is inseparable from his ethical principles. You must remember that theatre's aim is not merely simplicity but the creation of profoundly *alive* characters who help to make the idea of the play clear. It is not enough that your technique be organic; the objective of the Stanislavski System is the building of the unique individuality of a character. Remember that your goal is reincarnation—that intangible stage in an actor's work when he creates subconsciously, when his attitude toward the world around him has changed and his rhythm becomes that of a new man.

class 24

SONIA MOORE: Several among you have repeatedly expressed your interest in directing. I can well understand it. Directing is a fascinating profession, though perhaps at times unappreciated and a source of torment and anxiety. A director has many moments of frustration and doubt.

Every new production is an experiment because the artist strives for the new, for the unique, for the never-said-before. To find the harmonious relationship of content and form is a gigantic problem with each new production. Not every experiment succeeds. Geniuses have erred and failed; there are many examples in theatre history. Wagner's and Mussorgski's innovations were not recognized immediately, and yet they influenced opera throughout the world. Only those who do not strive for the new, those who are content to repeat their clichés over and over, do not make mistakes and do not fail. They do not make discoveries either. These are tradesmen, not artists. Goethe said, "Every artist has in him the potentiality for daring; without it, talent is inconceivable."

The road toward creation of an original

production is difficult for the director who is striving to express the idea of the work in the best possible way, perhaps better than the playwright did. The director is really competing with the author in his search for the most expressive form for the content. Although the director has no right to distort the play, he is not obligated to express himself only for the author. He must express himself *through* the playwright. After listening to Chaliapin reading Alexander Pushkin's *Mozart and Salieri*, Stanislavski said, "A talent like Chaliapin takes Pushkin into his service, and the one without such talent goes into Pushkin's service."*

The professional acting technique which you have been mastering will be of great assistance to you as directors, because it enables you to help the actor. You will be able to live every moment of the actor's role and will be capable of offering suggestions that matter. As important as the technique is for the directors, it alone is not sufficient. The level of your culture is also important in your work. Goethe said, "Watch out for two things: when you limit yourself to your specialty you become a corpse; when you step out of it you are a dilettante." And Leo Tolstoy said, "Without ceasing to be a live human being, one must also be an expert; expertise excludes dilettantism, and to be a dilettante means to be helpless."

You know what Stanislavski thought of this. Let me give you an idea of what Meyerhold, the rebel, who fought everything that was dead in the theatre, thought of the significance of culture for directors. When Meyerhold was asked to write a guide for

*Stanislavski's Notebook, 1915–1916, XVI, No. 674.

directing, he refused, saying, "It won't pay! It will be only a tiny booklet." Meyerhold believed that there were only a few rules for directing, that they could be described very briefly, and that not everyone was capable of understanding them. He thought that only a person of superior erudition and musicality would be able to use these laws in practice. Meyerhold demanded from his student directors a knowledge of every facet of the theatre. He saw the art of the director as a strict and precise mastership, spiritualized by poetry and fantasy. He detested those who knew how to patch up a performance. Meyerhold believed that in addition to poetry in art, there must be calculation—"arithmetic," intellect, and boldness. His motto in directing was: "The revelation of human destiny with brilliant theatrical effect." When he succeeded in both, the result was overwhelming.

Meyerhold insisted that his students frequent libraries, concerts, art galleries, and museums. "You will not develop your taste by window shopping," said the Master. "Think of Michelangelo, who was a painter, sculptor, and poet; he wrote sonnets, and when he had to, he could be a soldier."

Some young future directors, among them the now celebrated Georgi Tovstonogov, who were leaving for regional theatres to stage productions required for their degree by the State Institute of Theatre Art, came to Meyerhold for advice. He told them: "You must go to museums continually, not only when you are staging a production. And don't read any reviews of a previous production while your idea about the play is still maturing. Read them when you are ready to begin staging the play. When your intent has matured, then read the reviews and go again to the museums. This will strengthen your intent.... Use every opportunity to see paintings, even if only reproductions. Listen to symphonies as often as you can.... Imitation of others is an almost obligatory stage in the formation of the artist. Beethoven began by imitating Mozart, Stanislavski by imitating Meiningen, I by imitating Stanislavski. The more original the Master, the more difficult it is to free yourself from his influence." Meyerhold was a man of great culture. His education included architecture, painting, and literature. He was capable of detecting the slightest error in music.

And let me tell you what Meyerhold thought about the relationship between the director and actors—a problem that arises frequently. Meyerhold demanded that the actor follow the director's score. A slight deviation from this precisely calculated score leads to a violation of the composition as a whole. Meyerhold thought that artists must subordinate their individual interests in art to the interest of the whole as the director sees it. I personally think that Meyerhold did not mean that actors have no right to say what they think. The director should listen to the actor's suggestions. Unfortunately, the freedom given to actors often verges on dilettantism and leads to chaos. The director must surmount this chaos through artistic discipline, determined by his understanding of the objective and by his degree of aesthetic sensitivity.

One's capacity for feeling, for understanding and analyzing the times, depends on the progress of one's personal culture. As the director, you will organize the creative process and define the relationships among the actors.

When choosing the repertory, the director should be able to understand life's social and psychological phenomena. The director must be capable of perception and sharp analysis. He must have sound logic. The director must foresee all the factors that influence the aesthetic perception of the spectators. The audience should not be treated lightly. The director is responsible for the ideals of his theatre; he must have a stand. Theatre that has no ideals will please people who have no taste. The lack of an ideological and artistic stand will result in a chaotic and worthless repertory. You must not allow this. In the theatre we can reach the spectators with the most profound thoughts in the form of entertainment and can help the actor to transform the spectators into his friends and make them think in unison with him. We must have our spectators leaving the theatre spiritually nourished. We cannot allow trivialities on stage.

Unfortunately, truth and oversimplification have often been equated. Truth is not always simple. In pursuit of external truthfulness, one may be apprehensive about using daring and original forms, but the expression of truth will be undermined by both artificiality and inexpressive naturalism. It is a fact that, without sincerity, true simplicity, and truthfulness, theatre will not stir the audience. But neither will theatre achieve these goals without expressive form. Strong emotions and fierce inner conflicts must have external expression in space, in time, and in movement. The task of a mise-en-scène is the spatial expression of the character's inner and external behavior. Sergei Eisenstein called it "the director's gesture exploded in space." The search for the aesthetically generalized content of a mise-en-scène is, in fact, the director's effort to express individual psychology in space, time, and movement. Every separate fact must become an idea. The most complex ideas in the performance must be visualized through the actor's behavior in space. Actors who move on stage for such simple motivations as "I went to close the door," or "to greet someone," do not project true psychological reasoning. Space must be used for realization of the essence of the character.

The criteria for truly artistic creativity will never change. They include profound understanding of life, a high level of professionalism, and the super-super-objective of the artist—i.e., what he strives to contribute to his society.

Though we should not be tempted by what is "fashionable," unconventional means will not necessarily hurt the truthfulness of the action. Sometimes an unconventional approach may help to create an image in space and thus reveal an idea in a more expressive way. What is important is to reflect *man's* unique destiny, his relationships with his environment, his conflicts, sufferings, and joys.

Mastery of the Stanislavski acting technique enables the director to immerse himself in the experiences of an individual actor-character.

Make certain that you don't let anything else on stage escape your attention. The creation of the composition of the performance is the director's basic task. He must be capable of finding the relation between the parts and the whole and of subordinating the parts to the whole.

The director must excite his actors with his ideas. Precision and verbal imagery are helpful in this. But to be able to verbalize in a picturesque way does not mean that you know how to realize your ideas. Even if you know what you want to build, it is no guarantee that you know how to incarnate it. And yet the most important thing in the director's profession is to know how to realize what lives within him and stirs him. The vision and its realization are essential in the director's work. It often happens that the director has the intent but is unable to realize it. And sometimes there is a realization of a performance but no intent. This is not always the fault of the director. It may occur when the director is hindered by actors who are not ready to fulfill his suggestions. The director then wastes his time helping the student actors. This, of course, lowers the standard for the pattern of the performance. In such cases, the director is transformed into a teacher watching that everything should be organic, rather than incarnating the principal conflicts of the play. Transforming a rehearsal into a class does not help the director or the performance.

Performance is the visual incarnation of the action in space and in time. When the director searches for the solution of the whole and for the movements of the actors, he must have a feeling for the plastic in space. The play becomes visual when space dictates to the director and when actors are not indifferent to how they move in relation to their partners and to objects on stage. The form flows from the intent, and the director must "see" it before the set designer "sees" it. The director must excite the set designer with his ideas. Otherwise a conflict may arise which will destroy the integrity of the performance. Sets are the active force in the performance. Stanislavski said: "Designers are very sensitive people; we must tear out their ideas in the way we pull out a bad tooth—not with a single pull, but by shaking it little by little, and then, without their noticing, removing it."*

Another important and active element in the performance is music. As in ancient times, music in twentieth-century theatre becomes a contributing part of the action. From merely being illustrative, music has become a means capable of condensing the drama and of bringing a level of generalization that is hardly possible through other means. One of the most important tasks of a director is the creation of an atmosphere on stage. Music creates a special theatre atmosphere. It is capable of influencing the course of an action; it can make the action continuous. If the director is capable of inner vision and sees his intent in images, he will be aware of the utility of this inner "hearing" of music. If he has a feeling for contemporary times, he will know what music can do for his production and how to incorporate its specific composition into the mise-en-scène.

Music has an exceptional ability to reflect the life of the human spirit and transmit it in a beautiful and artistic form. Music increases the emotional

*From E. Y. Gremislavski, *Ivan Yakovlevich Gremislavski*, Moscow, 1967.

effect of the actor's performance on the audience without allowing itself to merge completely with the action on stage. Music may become the most important emotional factor in a production. Such use of music as an active participant in the movement of the action serves the superobjective.

CONFLICTS AND STRUGGLES ARE THE DIRECTOR'S MATERIAL

Aristotle said that conflict is the basis and the soul of drama. Another philosopher, Hegel, said: "Dramatic action does not consist in simply walking toward your aim without encountering any obstacles on the way. On the contrary, it is rooted in obstacles, in the colliding passions of the characters."

Although Stanislavski did not formulate rules for directing, his approach in practice is quite clear. Directorial work by Nemirovich-Danchenko and Stanislavski should be the springboard for directors. Stanislavski said: "Make sure that the idea of the play is firmly on the ground. The idea of the play must struggle with the environment, with people of different dispositions, with the events. Let them fight it. The idea will be born, it will triumph through the fierce struggle." Moreover, Stanislavski said that when an actor steps onto the stage, he has only one objective: to struggle.

When there is no conflict, there is no drama. The director's material is struggle. And his art will depend on his ability to unite everyone in the struggle that he is creating. One directs only if one has created the struggle for the expression of the given content.

Conflicts and contradictions are the motivating force and the kernel of the dramatic work. The director must be capable of revealing the knot of dramatic contradictions and the psychological states of the characters. He must find the inner logic of the contradictions and trace ways to overcome them. Every play presents a chain of changing human relationships, and the director must bring out the essence of these relationships in a theatrical image.

In every play there is a collision of the through-line-of-action with the counter-through-line-of-action. The outcome of the struggle must be revealed through subordinate struggles—each for a concrete object, thus revealing the most important element in the given conflict. The most significant theme will be lost if it is not revealed in struggles for concrete objects. The object of a struggle is what takes place on stage in the given episode; it is the center of attention of all who take part in the struggle, although their strivings and motivations may differ.

The analysis of a play should first focus on ideas concerning the basic conflict, on the ways of incarnating it and the determination of the subordinate conflicts. Analysis through events and actions, which you have been learning, is obligatory during rehearsals.

Expressiveness does not depend merely on the aims of the characters, but on the importance of these aims. Every objective must be completely fulfilled before one proceeds to the next one. Small details should not be fixed; the concentration must be on objectives. Details must be thoroughly selected and expressed in a sculpturelike way. Such detail will help the harmony of the whole, which is subordinated to a certain rhythm. Even a fully lifelike detail may carry meaningful weight and become a metaphor. Accidents cannot be allowed on stage; they interfere with the selection which differentiates art from trade.

The director must be capable of mercilessly eliminating anything that is superfluous, even if it is the most original idea he has ever had. A. D. Diky, an important Soviet director, said that the performance is like a watch mechanism. "Even if you place a diamond into the mechanism, the watch will stop. The stage does not bear anything superfluous, anything that does not serve the intent, anything that does not work for the superobjective. The stage demands absolute precision: every second in time and each half-inch of space must be strictly considered. Even if only one role is outside the unity, it will uproot the whole edifice of the performance, violate its symphonic process."* And the great Chaliapin said, "Emotions, intonations, and gestures must be expressed according to exact measurements corresponding to the given character and the given situation. . . ." The director is responsible for the clear pattern, which includes everything that may characterize its every moment, everything that expresses the idea in this pattern—generalization, thought, atmosphere—everything that influences its expressiveness.

The mise-en-scène is the visual plastic

*Konstantin S. Stanislavski, *Articles, Speeches, Talks, Letters*, Moscow, 1953.

expression of the states, conflicts, interactions of the characters. It should not be invented; it is born when the struggle is vividly clear. The mise-en-scène arises as a concrete form of the solution for the given episode.

The director's art depends on the extent of his ability to understand life's general conflicts and on his ability to build the struggle through interactions of the characters in the play. In art there must be both the universal and the subjective. To achieve his goal, the director must reveal the new and make the spectators understand what has not been understood before. They must understand the universal meaning of the play and the director's own way of seeing it. The struggle must project events that stir the inner world of those who take part in it.

The director will have found the solution of the performance when he has understood what is most important in the whole play, in every scene and in every role. This means that he has found the meaningful content of the new contradiction that is being revealed for the first time and will impress the spectators.

P. M. Ershov, the eminent Russian scholar of the theatre and of Stanislavski, makes invaluable suggestions for realizing a struggle on stage: In every given conflict there is one character who leads the struggle. The director must know who leads it at every moment and must distribute the "initiative." To have the initiative means to have the field of activity in obtaining from others what is needed. The process of determining who must have the initiative at a given moment clarifies the object of struggle and its theme; it leads to the concretization of the developing events and of the behavior of those who participate in them.

The action is led by the one who has the initiative in the given conflict of the episode. The other, or others, adjust to the one who leads the action. Everything the first actor does should be the springboard for the others in this particular episode. At any time it may be determined that the initiative is reversed. Actors, by not thinking of themselves only, and by not being indifferent on stage, may contribute to the play by bringing out during rehearsal unexpected and extraordinary mise-en-scènes, details and adaptations of which the director might not have thought of.

To use the initiative efficiently, the actor must be involved with the objective. Tempo-rhythm has great importance in reflecting the significance of the struggle. In fact, without changes of tempo-rhythm, struggle is impossible. Rhythm is indivisible from sincerity and belief in the given circumstances. Sincerity carries the actor away and reveals itself in emotions. . . . This is how rhythm unites with the dramatic temperament through involvement with the objective. When actors bypass this link, the acuity of rhythm is replaced by explosions of temperament. But demonstrative emotionality leads to clichés. Only when there is true involvement with the objective can there be an authentic emotional reaction. *Involvement with the objective is everything for the actor*. The distribution of initiative changes the content, while the text remains unchanged. Mr. Ershov advises us to begin rehearsals with the distribution of the initiative, with precise determination of who leads the struggle, because only one can lead and others must adjust to him. The distribution of initiative becomes a sort of foundation on which the complex construction of the performance will be built. The distribution of initiative is the way to concretize the theme because you have to ask yourself: If such an event is to take place, who should have the initiative? What are the functions of others?

The concretization of the theme is at the same time the motivation of its events. The clarity of the principal object of struggle depends on motivation. The struggle in process points to the main theme and its significance. While leading the struggle, the character moves to his objective. The obstacles that he encounters stall him, and this reveals his essence. Ershov says: "The struggle is a spectacle of experiences. The most meaningful are the experiences that are visual." The struggle, he says, is the "polyphony of actions," and the director resembles the conductor if the conductor is also the composer who writes music for the libretto.

I wish to remind you of Stanislavski's words: "The inner technique which is essential for the correct creative state is based on the person's willpower. This is why so many actors are deaf to my appeals. I had hundreds of students but only a few could be called my followers, and only few understand the goal to which I dedicated my life." I think that you understand Stanislavski's goal—at least some of you.

If you are an innovator, you may be isolated, since recognition may come only in the future.

Though the director has no right to have

"moods," you do not have to be afraid of your actors. One young Russian director confessed that his first rehearsal frightened him more than the war. Nemirovich-Danchenko, the great director, said, "Though the director, at times, may be the actor's servant, may have to adjust to the personality of the set designer and take into account the demands from the management, in the end the director is the master of the performance."

Appendices

I. scenes from chekhov's The Three Sisters

(Translated by Sonia Moore)

FROM ACT I

Opening scene

OLGA: Father died exactly a year ago, on this very day, the fifth of May—your saint's day, Irina. It was so cold, and snow was falling. It seemed to me that I would never live through it, and you were lying unconscious as if you were dead. And now a year later we can talk of it easily, you are already wearing a white dress, your face glows. (*A clock strikes twelve.*) And the clock was striking then, too. (*Pause.*) It comes back to me that when father was carried away, music was playing and at the cemetery they fired a salute. He was a general, in command of a brigade, and yet there were only a few people. But it was raining then. Heavy rain, and snowing.

IRINA: Why remember?

OLGA: Today it is warm. The windows can stay wide open, but the birches have no leaves yet. Father took command of the brigade and left Moscow with us eleven years ago, and I remember clearly that at the beginning of May in Moscow everything is already in bloom, everything is immersed in sunshine. Eleven years have passed, but

I remember it all there as if we'd left yesterday. My God, this morning I woke up and saw a flood of sunshine, saw the spring, and joy stirred in my soul, and I wanted passionately to go home.

TCHEBUTIKIN (*offstage*): Oh, sure!

TUSENBACH (*offstage*): Of course, nonsense.

(*Masha, pensive over her book, whistles softly.*)

OLGA: Don't whistle, Masha—how can you! (*Pause.*) It is because I'm at the high school every day, and giving lessons till evening, that my head aches continually, and my thoughts are those of an old woman. Really, these four years I've been teaching, I have felt my strength and youth leaving me every day, drop by drop. And only one dream grows and strengthens....

IRINA: To leave for Moscow. Sell the house, to finish with everything here, and to Moscow.

OLGA: Yes! To Moscow as soon as possible!

IRINA: Brother will probably be a professor, and all the same he won't live here. Yet, the obstacle is poor Masha.

OLGA: Masha will be coming to Moscow for the whole summer, every year.

(*Masha is softly whistling.*)

IRINA: God willing, it all will work out. (*Looking out of the window.*) The weather is good today. I don't know why my soul is so bright! This morning I remembered it was my saint's day and suddenly felt joy, and I remembered my childhood when mother was still alive. And such marvelous thoughts stirred me, such thoughts.

OLGA: Today you are radiant, you seem exceptionally beautiful. And Masha is beautiful too. Andrei would be good-looking, but he's gotten heavy, it's not becoming to him. And I've grown older and much thinner, probably because I get angry with the girls in school. I'm free today and am at home and my head's not aching, I feel younger than yesterday. I'm only twenty-eight, only...it is all good, it all comes from God, but I feel that if I had married and stayed home all day, it would have been better. *(Pause.)* I'd have loved my husband.

TUSENBACH *(offstage)*: You talk such nonsense, I became bored listening to you. *(Enters.)* I forgot to say that our new battery commander Vershinin is going to call on you today.

OLGA: Well, I'll be very glad.

IRINA: Is he old?

TUSENBACH: No, at most forty or forty-five. Obviously a nice man. Not stupid, certainly. But he talks a great deal.

IRINA: Is he interesting?

TUSENBACH: Yes, not bad, but he has a wife, a mother-in-law, and two daughters. Moreover, he is married for the second time. He pays visits and tells everyone that he has a wife and two girls. And he'll say it here. The wife is somewhat crazy, with long girlish braids, and she uses pompous language, philosophizes, and often attempts to commit suicide, obviously to upset her husband. I'd have left her long ago, but he bears it and just complains.

Irina and Tusenbach

IRINA: Masha is in a bad mood today. She married when she was eighteen, and he seemed to her the most intelligent man in the world. But now it's different. He is the kindest man, but not the most intelligent.

TUSENBACH: What are you thinking about?

IRINA: Well, I dislike and fear that Soliony of yours. He says only stupid things.

TUSENBACH: He is a strange man. I feel sorry for him and annoyed, but mostly sorry. It seems to me that he's shy. . . . When there are only the two of us, he's sometimes very clever and kind, but in company he's rude, a rabid duelist. Don't go. Let them sit down at the table. Let me be near you a while. What are you thinking about? *(Pause.)* You're twenty years old and I'm not yet thirty. How many years we have ahead, a long, long row of days, filled with my love for you. . . .

IRINA: Nikolai Lvovitch, don't talk to me about love.

TUSENBACH *(not listening)*: I have a passionate thirst for life, struggle, hard work, and this thirst in my soul has merged with my love for you Irina, and it is as if you are beautiful by some design, and life seems to me so beautiful! What are you thinking about?

IRINA: You say life is beautiful. But what if it only seems to be? With us, the three sisters, life is not yet beautiful, it stifles us as grass is by weeds. I'm crying—I shouldn't. We must work, work. We are bored and have such gloomy outlook on life because we don't know labor. We were born of people who despised work. . . .

FROM ACT II

Soliony and Tusenbach

TUSENBACH: You always sit by yourself, thinking about something—no one could tell what it was. Well, let's make peace. Let's drink some cognac. I'll probably have to play the piano all night long, play all kinds of nonsense.... Come what may!

SOLIONY: Why make peace? We haven't quarreled.

TUSENBACH: You always make me feel that something has gone wrong between us. You have a strange disposition, I must say.

SOLIONY *(declamatory)*: I am strange, and who is not strange? Don't be angry, Aleko!

TUSENBACH: And what has Aleko to do. ...*(Pause.)*

SOLIONY: When I'm alone with someone, it's all right, I'm like everyone else, but in company I'm despondent, shy, and...talk all sorts of nonsense. And yet I am more honest and noble than many, many others. I can prove it.

TUSENBACH: I'm often angry with you, you never stop nagging at me when we're in company, and still for some reason I like you. Come what may, I shall get drunk today. Let's drink!

SOLIONY: Let's drink. I've never had anything against you, Baron. But I have the disposition of Lermontov. I even resemble Lermontov somewhat, they say.... *(Takes a bottle of perfume from his pocket and pours some over his hands.)*

TUSENBACH: I'm going to resign. *Basta!* For five years I couldn't make up my mind, and now I've decided. I shall go to work.

SOLIONY *(declamatory)*: Don't be angry, Aleko.... Forget, forget your dreams.

TUSENBACH: I shall go to work.

———

Irina and Soliony
(Irina is walking around the room nervously
as Soliony enters.)

SOLIONY *(puzzled)*: No one here. . . . Where are they all?

IRINA: Gone home.

SOLIONY: That's strange. You're alone here?

IRINA: Alone. *(Pause.)* Good-by.

SOLIONY: I behaved tactlessly just now. But you are not like the others, you are superior and pure, you see the truth. . . . Only you can understand me. I love you deeply, endlessly. . . .

IRINA: Good-by! Go away.

SOLIONY: I can't live without you. Oh, my heaven! Oh, happiness! Such magnificent, wonderful, marvelous eyes as I have never seen in any other woman. . . .

IRINA: Stop it, Vassili Vassilievitch!

SOLIONY: It is the first time that I've spoken of love to you, and it is as if I were not on earth but on another planet. *(Rubbing his forehead.)* Well, it is all the same. You can't force anyone to love you, of course. . . . But I can't have lucky rivals, there must not be. . . . I swear to you by all that's holy, I'll kill any rival. . . . Oh, wonderful one!

Andrei and Ferapont

ANDREI: Good evening, my good soul. . . . What do you have to say?

FERAPONT: The chairman has sent you a book and some kind of paper. Here. . . .

ANDREI: Thank you. Good. Why didn't you come earlier? It's already after eight.

FERAPONT: Heh?

ANDREI *(louder)*: I say, you came late. It's after eight already.

FERAPONT: Yes, sir. I came here, it was still light, but they wouldn't let me in. The master, they say, is busy. So what. Busy is busy, I have nowhere to hurry. Heh?

ANDREI: Nothing. Tomorrow is Friday, I don't have to attend, but I'll go anyway...to occupy myself. It's boring at home.... *(Pause.)* Dear Grandpa! How strangely life changes and deceives us! Today out of boredom, because I had nothing else to do, I picked up this book—old university lectures—and I wanted to laugh.... My God, I'm a secretary of the District Board, the board where Protopopov is the chairman, I'm the secretary, and the most I can expect is—to be a member of the District Board! I, the member of the District Board, I who dream every night that I am a professor at Moscow University, a famous scholar whom all of Russia is proud of!

FERAPONT: I wouldn't know....I don't hear well....

ANDREI: If you could I probably wouldn't talk to you. I need to talk to somebody, but my wife doesn't understand me, I'm afraid of my sisters for some reason, I'm afraid they'll laugh at me, embarrass me.... I don't drink, I don't like saloons, but with what pleasure I would be sitting now at Testov's in Moscow, or in the Bolshoi Moscovsky, my dear fellow.

FERAPONT: And in Moscow, the contractor at the District Board said some merchants were eating bliny; one, who ate forty bliny, it seems, died. It was forty, or fifty. I don't remember.

ANDREI: You sit in Moscow, in a huge salon at

a restaurant, and no one knows you, and at the same time you don't feel like a stranger. And here you know everyone and you are known to everyone, but you are a stranger, a stranger and lonely.

FERAPONT: Heh? *(Pause.)* And the same contractor said—maybe he was lying—that a rope has been stretched across the whole of Moscow.

ANDREI: What for?

FERAPONT: I don't know. The contractor was saying.

ANDREI: Rubbish. *(He reads.)* Have you ever been in Moscow?

FERAPONT *(after a pause)*: Never been. God did not grant me that. *(Pause.)* Shall I go?

ANDREI: You may go. Keep well. *(Ferapont leaves.)* Keep well. *(Reading.)* Tomorrow when you come, you will take some papers there.... Go. ...*(Pause.)* He's left. *(Bell.)* Yes, some business.

FROM ACT III

Natasha and Olga

NATASHA *(enters)*: They are saying that we must form a relief committee as soon as possible to help the people who suffered from the fire. Why not? It is a wonderful idea. As a rule one must hurry to help poor people—that's the duty of the rich. Bobik and Sofotchka are sleeping, sleeping as if nothing had happened. We have so many people everywhere here; anywhere you go the house is full. There's influenza in town now. I'm afraid the children will catch it.

OLGA *(not listening to Natasha)*: In this room you don't see the fire, it's quiet here....

NATASHA: Yes ... I must be disheveled *(in front of the mirror)*. They say I have gained weight. ...And it is not true! Not at all! And Masha is sleeping, tired...poor thing.... *(To Anfissa)* Don't you dare to sit in my presence! Get up! Get out of here! *(Anfissa goes out.)* I can't understand why you keep that old woman.

OLGA *(stunned)*: Excuse me, I don't understand either....

NATASHA: There's no reason for her to be here. She is a peasant and she should live in the country.... What pampering! I like to have order in the house. There shouldn't be useless people here. Poor darling, you are tired! Our headmistress is tired. And when my Sofotchka grows up and enters high school, I shall be afraid of you.

OLGA: I won't be the headmistress.

NATASHA: You will be elected, Olitchka, that's decided.

OLGA: I'll decline it. I can't—I don't have the strength for it. You treated Nurse in such a rude way.... Forgive me, I can't bear.... Everything's gone black in my eyes....

NATASHA: Forgive me, Olya, forgive me...I didn't mean to upset you.

OLGA: Try to understand, my dear ... perhaps we were brought up in a strange way, but I can't bear it. That kind of behavior depresses me, I get sick.... I lose my strength!

NATASHA: Forgive me, forgive me...*(kissing her)*.

OLGA: And even the slightest rudeness, even a carelessly spoken word upsets me.

NATASHA: I often say more than I should, it's true, but you must agree, dear, she might just as well live in the country.

OLGA: She's been with us for thirty years.

NATASHA: Now, though, she can't work. Either I don't understand or you don't want to understand me. She can't do any hard work. She just either sleeps or sits.

OLGA: Well, let her sit.

NATASHA: Let her sit? But she's a servant. I don't understand you, Olya. I have a nurse, I have a wet nurse, we have a maid, a cook.... Why do we have that old woman too? Why?

(Offstage the fire alarm rings.)

OLGA: I've aged ten years tonight!

NATASHA: We must have an understanding, Olya. You are at school, I'm at home: You have the teaching, I have the housekeeping. And if I say anything about the servants, I know what I am saying. I know what I am saying.... And by tomorrow we won't have that old thief here, that old hag. That witch.... Don't you dare irritate me! Don't you dare! Really, if you don't move downstairs, we'll always be quarreling. It's terrible.

Irina, Olga, and Masha

IRINA: Really, how petty our Andrei has become, how empty and aged he has become beside this woman! Some time ago he was preparing to be a professor, and yesterday he was boasting that he has finally gotten to be a member of the District Board. He a member of the board, while Protopopov is the president.... The whole town is gossiping, laughing, and he alone does not know a thing, and does not see a thing. And now everyone has run to the fire, but he sits in his room and pays no attention to anything—only plays the violin. *(Nervously)* Oh, it is horrible, horrible, horrible! *(Crying)* I cannot, I cannot bear it anymore! ... I can't, I can't!

(Olga enters, straightens up her little table.)

IRINA *(sobbing loudly)*: Throw me out, throw me out, I can't bear it any more! ...

OLGA *(frightened)*: What is the matter with you, what is the matter, darling?

IRINA *(sobbing)*: Where? Where did it all go? Where is it? Oh, my God, my God. I have forgotten everything, forgotten.... Everything is confused in my mind.... I don't remember how to say "window" in Italian, or "ceiling".... I forget everything, every day I forget, and life moves on and will never come back, never, and we will never go to Moscow ... I see that we will not go.

OLGA: Darling, darling....

IRINA *(trying to control herself)*: Oh, I am desolate.... I can't work, I will not work. Enough, enough! I was a telegraph operator, now I am working at the town board, and I hate and despise everything they give me to do ... I'm nearly twenty-four, I've been working for a long time, and my brain is dried out, I've become thin, my looks are gone, I've aged, and I have nothing, nothing, not a bit of satisfaction, and time goes on and it seems as if one moves away from the real, beautiful life, moves further and further, into some abyss. I am in despair, and how I am still alive, how it is that I have not killed myself before this, I don't understand....

OLGA: Don't cry, my little girl, don't cry.... I suffer too.

IRINA: I am not crying. I am not crying.... Enough.... Here, I am not crying anymore. Enough...Enough!

OLGA: My dear, I tell you, as a sister, as a friend, if you want my advice, marry the baron!

(Irina cries quietly.)
You do respect him, value him highly.... It is true, he is not good looking, but he is such a decent man, so clean.... And one marries not for love, but to do one's duty. I, at least, think so, and I would marry without love. Whoever would propose I would marry, anyway, so long as he was a decent man. I would marry even an old man....

IRINA: I kept on hoping to move to Moscow. There I would meet my true one, I dreamed of him, loved him.... But it turned out all nonsense, all nonsense....

OLGA *(embracing her sister)*: My dear, my beautiful sister, I understand everything: When Baron Nikolai Lvovich left the military service and came to us in his civilian jacket, he seemed to me so homely that I even started to cry. He asks, "Why are you crying?" How do I tell him? But if God wills that he should marry you, I would be happy. This is different, quite different.

(Natasha, with a candle, silently crosses through the stage from door right to door left.)

MASHA *(sitting up)*: She walks as if she were the one who started the fire.

OLGA: You, Masha, are silly. The silliest in our family is you. Forgive me, please. *(Pause.)*

MASHA: I feel like confessing, my dear sisters. My soul is in anguish. I shall confess before you and then to no one else, never.... I shall say it this very minute. *(Softly)* It is my great secret, but you should know everything.... I can't be silent.... *(Pause.)* I am in love, in love.... I love this man.... You just saw him.... Well, here it is. In one word, I love Vershinin....

OLGA *(goes behind her screen)*: Stop it. I am not listening, anyhow.

MASHA: What is there to do! *(Holding her head.)* He seemed to me at first strange, then I felt sorry for him...then I fell in love...in love with him, with his voice, his words, his misfortunes, his two little girls....

OLGA *(behind the screen)*: I am not listening, anyhow. No matter what silly things you say, I am not listening anyhow....

MASHA: Ah, you are silly, Olga. I love—that means, such is my fate. It means, such is my lot.... And he loves me.... It is all frightening. Yes? It is not right? *(Draws Irina by her hand toward herself.)* Oh, my darling...how shall we live through our life, what will become of us?... When you read a novel, it seems that everything is old and all so understandable, but when you fall in love yourself, then you see that no one knows anything, and everyone must decide for himself.... My dears, my sisters...I have confessed to you; now I shall be silent.... Now I shall be like Gogol's madman...silence...silence....

2. notes on some scenes used in the classes

A Month in the Country by Ivan Turgenev. Dialogue in Act One, Scene Two, between Natalia Petrovna and her young ward, Vera. The former discovers that Vera, like herself, is in love with the young tutor Beliaev. Beginning with Natalia Petrovna's saying, "Well, then, darling, just whisper quietly in my ear—you don't want to marry Bolshintsov because he's too old and far from an Adonis—but is that your only reason?" and continuing to the end of the scene.

Another Part of the Forest by Lillian Hellman. Dialogue near the end of Act Three. Ben has forced his father to sign over his entire fortune; as he waits for his father to sign the papers in the adjoining room, Regina comes in and gradually learns that Ben now has the upper hand.

Desire Under the Elms by Eugene O'Neill. Beginning of Part Two, Scene One. Setting: outside the farmhouse. Dialogue between Eban and his new young stepmother Abie. She tries to attract him, and he accuses her of selling herself to his father to get the farm.

Ferryboat by Anna Marie Barlow. The entire one-act play. On the deck of a New Orleans ferryboat a boy and a girl, strangers to each other, strike up a conversation. Unable to understand each other, they part at the play's end.

Mourning Becomes Electra by Eugene O'Neill. Act Two of "The Haunted," the final part of the trilogy. Lavinia enters the study as Orin is secretly writing an account of the family's gruesome history, which he intends to use as a threat to control her.

Separate Tables by Terence Rattigan. From "Table by the Window," the first of the two plays. Setting: an English resort hotel. Dialogue between Anne and her estranged husband, John, beginning with John's "You married me because you were frightened" and ending with his tacitly agreeing to go to her room later.

The Children's Hour by Lillian Hellman. Dialogue near the end of Act Three, between Martha and Karen, who has just parted with Joe. Martha admits that she has been attracted to Karen. The episode ends with the offstage shot that signals Martha's suicide.

The Crucible by Arthur Miller. Beginning of Act One, Scene Two. Dialogue between Proctor and his wife, Elizabeth. She urges him to go to Salem and

speak out against the witchcraft trials at which
Abigail and their servant, Mary, and other girls are
making wild accusations.

Act Two, Scene One of the acting version.
Proctor and Abigail meet in a forest at night. He tells
her that if she does not stop her accusations of
witchcraft, he will denounce her even if it means
revealing their love affair.

The Little Foxes by Lillian Hellman. The
final dialogue in Act Three, in which Alexandra tells
her mother, Regina, that she is going to leave home.

The Wingless Victory by Maxwell Anderson.
From Act Three, Scene Two. The time is 1880. Scene:
a cabin of a ship. Oparre, the Malay princess whom
Nathaniel has brought back to Massachusetts as his
wife, has met with the scorn of the Salem townspeo-
ple. Nathaniel, who had sent her away, says he wants
to sail with her; she tells him that she has already
given poison to their two children and has taken it
herself.

Yerma by Garcia Lorca. Dialogue in Act One,
Scene Two, between Yerma and the First Old
Woman, from the beginning of the scene until the
Old Woman's exit.

3. notes for a "biography"

(Andrei in The Three Sisters)

I, Andrei, am the son of General Prosorov, who left Moscow because he was given a brigade to command in a small provincial town. I am twenty-three years old and have two sisters who are older than I and one who is younger. My family has showered too much affection on me. Of course, I am the only son and the only brother. This may be only a justification, but I am a weak character because of all the pampering I got from my sisters.

My life's wish is to be a professor in Moscow University. Though I love music and enjoy playing the violin and also adore manual work (for instance, carving wood), I want to be famous as a professor.

I love my family and especially my sister Masha—I do not know why. She seems to be strong, courageous, and great fun. I lived with my sisters before my marriage and after. The house we live in is spacious; the dining room and the living room are downstairs and the bedrooms are upstairs. The furniture is old-fashioned, but it is cozy. I feel that the whole atmosphere was too cozy before the trouble in our family started.

Before I married, I spent most of my time

studying, playing the violin, and doing a little manual work, which gives me pleasure. We have many friends coming to the house, but I am really not very close to anyone. People in this provincial town are not interesting. And, though the officers are educated people, I do not have much in common with them.

Soon after my marriage I began wondering whether I really was in love with Natasha. But I did not allow myself to think of it much. I keep hoping that in time everything will straighten out and that Natasha will change and my sisters will be more tolerant. I sense that I am gradually being destroyed, but I do not have the strength or courage to fight it.

I can see that I am following the destiny of Tchebutikin, who says continuously, "It's all the same," because he doesn't care anymore about anything. Even worse, sometimes I think I am no better than Ferapont. I sometimes look into the mirror and it seems to me that I begin to look like Ferapont. But I do not know what to do. How can I stop this process of decay that is taking place in me? I am unable to make any decisions and I do not even know whether I hate Natasha. I am only trying not to think, to block her out of my thoughts.

4. a brief chronology
of Stanislavski

1863   Born Konstantin Sergeevich Alexeev, in Moscow, January 5 (January 17 by the new calendar).

1877   Made his debut on his family's stage in an amateur show, September 5.

1885   Adopted the pseudonym Stanislavski.

1888   With the director A. F. Fedotov, the singer and teacher F. P. Kommisaryevski, and the painter F. L. Sologub, Stanislvaski founded the Society of Art and Literature and created a drama company of amateur actors associated with it.

1891   His first important independent directing work: Leo Tolstoi's *The Fruits of Enlightenment*.

1897   He had his famous encounter with Vladimir Nemirovich-Danchenko, during which they decided to found a theatre company of the most talented members of the Society of Art and Literature and Nemirovich-Danchenko's students in the Drama School of the Moscow Philharmonic Society. The company was to become the Moscow Art Theatre.

1898   The Moscow Art Theatre opened with

a historical tragedy, Alexei Tolstoi's *Czar Feodor Ivanovich,* on October 14.

The Moscow Art Theatre gave a production of Chekhov's *The Seagull,* directed by Stanislavski and Nemirovich-Danchenko, on December 5 (17). The play, a triumphant success, heralded the true birth of the theatre and of a great playwright.

1900s   Stanislavski began to formulate his teachings on an actor's creativity, known as the Stanislavski System.

1918   Became head of the Bolshoi Theatre's Opera Studio, which later developed into the independent Opera Theatre of K. S. Stanislavski.

1928   During his performance as Vershinin in *The Three Sisters* on October 29, Stanislavski suffered a heart attack. After this he abandoned acting and concentrated on directing and on educating young actors and directors while continuing his search for the best acting techniques.

1930s   Stanislavski made new discoveries in the method of creating a performance and a role; it later became known as the method of physical actions.

1935   Founded the Opera-Drama Studio.

1938   Died in Moscow on August 7.

5. suggested exercises

RELAXATION OF MUSCLES AND WARMING UP

Lie down. Relax all muscles. Solve a mathematical problem or remember a poem. Watch that not a muscle is tense.

Sit or stand. Check the tension of your body from head to toes. First check the muscles of your face. Watch that eyebrows are not raised, eyes not narrowed. There should be no artificial smile or widening of the lips, shoulders should not be raised. Let the arms hang loosely and flex the wrists. The spine must be relaxed, neither stiff nor limp. If necessary, use a mirror.

Expand the movement of the arms by imagining that the muscular energy is flowing through the arm from the shoulder to the fingertips. Shrink the movement by imagining that the flow is reversed. Justify the movements with saying, for instance, "Look here!" or "Come here!"

Imagine that you have a metal band around the chest. Stretch it with a vigorous expansion of the torso.

Rotate the torso vigorously.

Jump on a chair, keeping your legs together.

Lie down on your back. Roll the whole body to the left and then to the right.

An imaginary rope is stretched in front of you to help you advance. The arms and hands don't pull your body; the torso moves toward the hands. Lunge forward until the leg behind touches ground with the knee. The movement of the body must be sharp and strong.

Jump forward on your toes, bending the knees on landing. Return to the standing position with elastic and energetic movement and repeat the same jump forward on toes followed by bending of the knees. The impulse comes from the thighs. Arms are stretched to the side. There must be a feeling of being very light, soft, and elastic, like foam rubber.

"In a Magic Garden": Apples are growing at the level of your head. On "one," thrust with the right leg; an apple must be torn off with the left hand. On "two," thrust with the left leg, and the apple is torn off with the right hand. The apple must be thrown on the floor by sharply lowering the arm. There must be no pauses between the thrusts of the legs. After the exercise, have a run.

Stand, hands on the waist. On "one," rise on toes, heels together, toes slightly separated. On "two," "three," "four," slowly squat; the torso and the neck must be vertical. On "one," "two," "three," slowly unbending the knees, rise, and on "four" go down at once. The movement must be smooth, the torso vertical, toes separated.

Run as fast as possible. At the teacher's signal,

stop. Do not change the pose in which you stopped. Justify the pose.

CONCENTRATION OF ATTENTION

On "one," listen to all noises.
On "two," listen to the noises outside.
On "three," listen to the noises in the hall.
On "four," listen to the noises in the classroom.

Stand in a semicircle. One student stands in the center with his eyes covered and his back to the others. The others ask him questions. He must answer and also guess who is asking.

Improvising a song without words: The first student begins a song, the next continues it, etc. The objective is not to use any familiar melody but to compose one's own, even if a primitive one, inspired by attentive listening to the others.

Throw an imaginary ball and say a noun. The student who catches the "ball" says a verb, the third a noun, the fourth a verb, etc. Have an image of what you are saying. Students must be standing.

Concentrate your attention on the table and various objects on it. You are in the center of this "Small Circle of Attention" and are isolated from others. This concentration leads to what Stanislavski called "Public Solitude." The actor acts in view of everyone, and at the same time he is alone.

"A Medium Circle of Attention": The student takes in a larger space with more objects in it. It is difficult to embrace it at once, and he must look it over in parts. Gradually he absorbs separate parts of the space and then the whole. The vanished feeling of "Public Solitude" returns.

"A Large Circle of Attention": Again the student loses the natural creative state and he gradually conquers it, mobilizing his will, directing his attention from one object to another. Stanislavski speaks of attention that really grips the object.

Sit in a circle. At the teacher's signal, in half a minute change the shape to a triangle, then a square. The teacher accelerates and slows down the time—i.e., he directs the tempo-rhythm. Music is helpful in this exercise.

Students are divided into two groups. Each group is given a reproduction of a painting. They examine it and answer the teacher's questions about the composition, colors, etc.

Examine objects on the table and at the same time listen to voices in the street.

A student executes a series of actions in imagined circumstances. He must act logically and not exaggerate the sounds. Another student, behind a screen, must guess what the first is doing. To make the guessing more difficult, several students may execute the actions.

Look at a pencil, a wall, a view from a window, a book. No slightest detail should be overlooked. Make a strict analysis with nothing invented in it.

"Typewriter": Each student is assigned a letter of the alphabet. The teacher dictates a sentence, and it is "typed" as each student claps hands as his letter comes up. Feet are stamped for punctuation, and all clap hands together at the end of every word.

The student concentrates on memorizing a

poem or a piece of prose. At the teacher's signal other
students ask him questions. They may be on various
topics but should be simple to allow for short
answers. After having answered a question, the
student returns to the memorizing. He should not be
worried about interrupting the process of memorizing. In life our thoughts are often not on what we are
doing at a given moment.

A student must memorize a poem or an
excerpt of prose, while he has a toothache, he is cold,
hot, etc.

SENSE-MEMORY EXERCISES

Remember the taste of a strawberry, herring,
lemon. Remember a thunderstorm, a sunset, a
wedding.

With covered eyes, feel an object with your
fingers. Describe it in the minutest detail.

Handle a key, make a bed, pack a suitcase,
sew, make a salad.

SUGGESTIONS FOR IMPROVISATIONS
*Every improvisation must have a beginning,
development, and end.*

Tie your tie, put on a coat, comb your hair in
three different tempo-rhythms. Build the circumstances and justify each tempo-rhythm.

Approach another student and greet him,
coloring your greeting with an adaptation (irony,
mocking, reproach, despair, threat, warning, etc.).
The other must guess what is wanted from him. Do
not "show" your feelings.

Stand in pairs. Make a "sculpture" of your partner. Arrange his head, torso, hands. The "sculpture" submits to the "sculptor" and must justify the pose.

Rest in your own room. Rest in a waiting room.

Read at home. Read in a library.

Rent an apartment.

Come home to work. Come home to rest.

Discover that you are on the wrong train.

Awake and see that your room has been robbed.

Watch over a sick person. Persuade others to be quiet.

Two persons are playing cards; one of them is interested in a conversation taking place on the couch in the same room.

Treat a shawl as a cat, a chair as a vicious dog, as an electric chair.

Approach a friend to tell him bad news, to ask for money.

Improvisations on actions such as "to accuse," "to blackmail," "to persuade," etc.

Decide on a name for an event and reveal it through actions.

Index

index

George N. Fenin and William K. Everson

THE WESTERN
From Silents to the Seventies

Here are Tom Mix, Roy Rogers, Hopalong Cassidy, and Gene Autry—along with the other heroes of the celluloid ranch and range. Whether it's your first meeting or your fiftieth, you'll be happy to find all of them in this fully illustrated book, the only complete history of the Western. Discover (or rediscover) those wonderful movies (from the "B" pictures that were cranked out by the hundreds to the "adult" Westerns of today) and their great directors—Edwin S. Porter, Thomas H. Ince, James Cruze, John Ford, William Wellman, and many others. The costumes are also here, as well as the staging of fist fights and shoot-outs and the filming of the spectacular landscapes that are so often the backdrops for saloons and stagecoaches. First published in 1962, this acclaimed book has now been revised to include chapters on Japanese and Italian Westerns and to survey more recent American examples of the genre. The Western today is more relevant than ever before, say the authors, because it warns against a return to frontier violence—although it still provides "the vehicle for our dreams." "*The Western* traces the evolution of an art on its own terms and for its own sake...an eminently enjoyable book"—Andrew Sarris.

Sonia Moore

Preface by Sir John Gielgud
Foreword by Joshua Logan

THE STANISLAVSKI SYSTEM
The Professional Training of an Actor

This handbook, the first simplified guide to Konstantin S. Stanislavski's teachings, has long been a favorite among students and teachers of acting. Now, to bring it up to date in the light of recent books and articles published in the Soviet Union, Sonia Moore has made revisions that include a new section on emotional memory. She stresses the method of physical actions as the key to emotional memory and to organic behavior on the stage. She also places more emphasis on the actor's use of his body in the immediate expression of inner processes and urges her readers to study the system as a whole, without isolating its elements.

Edited by Eric Bentley

THE THEORY OF THE MODERN STAGE
An Introduction to Modern Theater and Drama

In this anthology, newly revised and edited by one of America's leading drama critics, Antonin Artaud, Bertolt Brecht, Gordon Craig, Konstantin Stanislavski, William Butler Yeats, and many other great theatrical theorists reveal the ideas underlying their productions and point to the possibilities of the modern theater.

Henrik Ibsen

Anton Chekhov

August Strindberg

Oscar Wilde

Bernard Shaw

Bernard Shaw was born in Dublin, of Protestant stock, in 1856 and died in Ayot St. Lawrence, England, in 1950. After a false start in nineteenth-century fashion as a novelist, he made a reputation as a journalist-critic of books, pictures, music, and drama. Meanwhile he had plunged into the Socialist revival of the 1880s and come out as one of the leaders who made the Fabian Society famous, figuring prominently not only as a pamphleteer and platform orator, but as a serious economist and philosopher, publishing major essays on Henrik Ibsen and Richard Wagner. He broke out in a new direction in 1892 as a playwright, although it was not until some twelve years later that the opposition he had always to face at first was overcome sufficiently to establish him as an irresistible force in the theater. His plays published in Penguin Books are:

Peter Ustinov

DEAR ME

"Dear me!" says Peter Ustinov as he traces the history of his ancestry, a mad tale of revolutions, dangerous border crossings, suitcases stuffed with money, and wild coincidences; recalls his ambivalent relations with his father, a journalist and spy; relives the vicissitudes of his career in the theater; and, indeed, recreates all the ups and downs of a life story so rich in droll and colorful anecdotes that even Ustinov could not have invented it. Primarily known as an actor, having made his debut as a pig in a school play, he has in his fifty-odd years also been a film and opera director, playwright, novelist, producer, and short-story writer, as well as one of the world's most brilliant conversationalists. This last talent is shown to perfection in these scintillating memoirs, which, incidentally, include delightfully witty verbal portraits of Laurence Olivier, Edith Evans, John Gielgud, Ralph Richardson, Charles Laughton, and David Niven, among many others. Said William Cole in the *Saturday Review:* "The trick has always been to write as easily as you talk. Peter Ustinov does just that, and he's the grandest monopolistic talker I've ever stood in a circle around, spellbound. Now here's his autobiography, *Dear Me*, and it's one of those books you hate to get up from and can't wait to get back to."